# City of

## An Elliot For

Elliot and partner Rivka Goldstein are hired to find the murderer of a teenage boy. The ensuing investigation leads them into the center of a Montréal drug distribution ring that goes deeper than they could have ever imagined. Before Elliot can crack the case, he is framed for the murder of his prime suspect and is forced to go underground. When he reaches out to Rivka and friend Rayce Nolan for help, he finds they are already engaged in struggles of their own. It takes all of Elliot's intellect to deduce that events tormenting all three of them are not what they seem.

During Elliot's efforts to solve the murder and clear his name, he is forced to make choices that will change his life forever.

The Elliot Forsman Book Series
- Ogrodnik
- City of Saints
- Passage into Darkness (Fall of 2018)

Current version (1.0b)

Cover Art by Grok Consulting Inc.

Many thanks out to Diane Young for the substantive edit on an earlier version of the book and for the advice and insight she provided.

A special thank you to my beta review team who went above and beyond:
- My lovely wife Kristina, who gets to read everything, including the stuff that ends up on the cutting room floor.
- Shaun, Ray, Carla, Rick and Paul, who, in their silence after reading the first draft, told me all I needed to know.
- Sisters Deb and Bev, who steered me in the right direction.

For queries of any type, please use email gary.raymond.coffin@gmail.com or visit my website: www.GaryRaymondCoffin.com

*Like adulterous lovers who know their fling will be short lived, Montréalers make frantic love to the seasonal warmth. They flee their winter confines at the first sign of the budding spring and cram an entire years' worth of living into a six-month window. Not willing to squander even a few hours of the precious summer, they cast aside their inhibitions and seek companionship wherever they can find it. The streets, still alive at 3:00 am, the patios still serving wine, and the sounds of nightlife still trumpeting from open-air bars even as the dawn creeps up on the eastern sky. For those who come here, who live here, who work here, this is life in the City of Saints.*

# Chapter 1

The boy was pinned down on the ground while the injection took hold of his nervous system. He felt the numbness spread through his body like a drop of food-color blooming in a glass of water. The drug administered was created to relax muscles in preparation for surgery, but the massive dosage used this night brought on paralysis without impairing awareness. Which was the intent.

The boy, now fully paralyzed, was pulled to his feet and held in place. His eyes were drawn to the glint of moonlight as it played along the cutting edge of the knife held before him. The only sign of panic was the fear in his eyes as they darted between the knife and the wielder's face.

The blade was carefully inserted from beneath, and pushed up slowly through his ribcage. He tried to spit out the gag and scream, but his muscles would not obey. The effects of the drug deadened all pain but still allowed the boy to feel the razor edge as it gradually made its way towards its destination. He felt the point of sensation touch his heart and he sensed the interruption in the heartbeat that followed. It was only then that he came to the realization that he was about to die.

As the light faded, he looked up from the knife into the face of his murderer. He saw the blaze of wild elation in his killer's eyes as his vision narrowed and collapsed into darkness.

The boy was lowered gently to the ground as if laying a young child down to sleep. "Don't forget the packets," said the killer while walking away.

# Chapter 2

*Two weeks later, Tuesday, August 22nd*

The afternoon sun had moved far enough west so that it now shone directly through the tall windows in the psychiatrist's office and directly onto her patients lap. Rivka Goldstein repositioned herself on the chair to circulate air between her bare legs and the soft leather of the chair.

The doctor was at her desk, gathering notes and files, on the opposite side of the room. She sensed, rather than observed, her patients' constant repositioning and wondered if it was nerves, or just the heat of the sun causing her to squirm. She put those thoughts aside for the time being, she'd know the answer soon enough.

"I'm Dr. Margie Maller, how are you today Rivka?" the psychiatrist asked as she sat down. Her chair faced in the general direction of her patient, but angled slightly so that both chairs faced a small table between them rather than directly at each other. Dr. Maller understood that a direct path between doctor and patient could be intimidating.

"Well, I'm here, so I guess I'm not totally fine."

"Yes, you are here," the psychiatrist nodded as she spoke as if already assessing the woman before her, which of course, she was. "You seem like someone who likes to get to the point; in that respect we're very much alike."

Rivka nodded without saying anything and waited for the doctor to continue. She understood that the first meeting was a feeling out exercise for both patient and doctor. The psychiatrist trying to ascertain how aggressively she was able to safely probe into the patients problems, and the patient deciding if she trusted the doctor enough to truly open up.

"Let's start with an obvious question then Rivka, why are you here?"

Rivka took a deep breath before answering. She already knew how she would answer that question. It was a question that she's asked herself many times since she decided to seek counsel.

"I'm having trouble sleeping," she replied, not wanting to spew out a stream of self-doubt and rambling that Dr. Maller didn't need to hear.

"Why do you think you're having trouble sleeping?" probed the psychiatrist.

"I don't know. I can't turn off my brain at night. I have too many thoughts running through it. I fall asleep, and two hours later I wake up, and I can't get back to sleep."

"What do you think of while you're lying in bed trying not to think?"

"All kinds of things. My leg, my training, my job, my personal life," she paused for a moment and then added, "the shit that happened earlier this year."

The psychiatrist nodded and scribbled a few notes on her tablet. "I've read your file," she said as she looked directly at her patient as if to say, '*I know your secrets*'. "Why don't we start with '*the shit that happened to you*', as you put it?"

Rivka went on to tell the psychiatrist about her ordeal the previous spring and her encounter with the serial killer known as Ogrodnik. She talked at length about her kidnapping, her rescue, and finally about how her leg was shattered by a bullet.

Chapter 3

*Wednesday, August 23rd*

Elliot freed the top two buttons of his shirt and rolled his sleeves up to the elbow. Whatever relief the cool of the night brought in had burned away hours ago, leaving behind a thick August heat. It was a heavy, clammy, heat that stuck to his skin like a wet shirt. The kind of heat that wanted to push him down and steal his breath.

His route took him down the south side of St. Catherine Street so he could walk in the shade as much as possible. He came to a pair of legs splayed at haphazard angles across the sidewalk in his path. The owner of the legs was a homeless man who, even in his impaired state, was still able to hold a sign soliciting for donations in both English and French. *'Even the destitute in Montréal know its good business to market in two languages,'* Elliot thought as he bypassed the man.

He walked past a neighborhood produce market that spilled out onto the sidewalk; the old man standing in front offered kind words for everyone who passed in a language that was neither French, nor English, but something in between. Elliot had seen and waved to the man for as long as he could remember. He didn't know his name, but nonetheless, the old man was part of his life.

The squeal of tires and blare of a horn interrupted his thoughts as a bike courier took liberties in lane definition. The courier saluted the irate cabbie, Québec style, and darted through a traffic snarl towards his delivery goal.

These were the bits of everyday life not written about in brochures or travel magazines, but they were intrinsic to the life he loved in the 514.

He slowed down to a saunter when l'Oiseau café was two blocks away. He'd never met Dr. Maller and didn't know what to expect, but showing up wearing a frothy sweat and a stained shirt didn't seem like a good idea.

Before he entered the café, he paused in front of the glass door and checked out his reflection. From the front, he thought he looked presentable. He didn't see any shaving omissions and the bags under his eyes were hardly noticeable, at least that's what he told himself. He turned his head slightly to the side for a semi profile view and smoothed out a tuft of grey temple hair that didn't want to play nice. 'Good enough' he thought as he continued through the door.

A blast of cool air punched him in the face when he entered the café. It felt good and caused his skin to shrink a bit so that it felt like it fit his body just a bit better than it had in the heat. He'd given himself plenty of time to make the walk from his Oak Avenue house eastward along St. Catherine to l'Oiseau Café. He didn't like being behind schedule, and liked it even less when the people he was meeting were late. For a man who deduced much from small details, showing up late spoke volumes about a person's character.

He picked up a strong Columbian brew at the trough and took a seat by the window to wait. As the morning commuters funneled by his window, he played a game trying to guess who Dr. Maller was before she entered the café. Although he had no idea what the psychiatrist looked like, he had already formed a mental image of her. He immediately discounted anyone who wore the vacant gaze of drudgery. A psychiatrist wouldn't be resigned to another day of work, toiling and waiting for the weekend. No, he watched for someone with alert eyes, someone who saw the world around her, not just stared blankly at it. He also discounted many based on their clothing. He would be looking for someone with high quality, but boring, business-like attire. He watched for a person who intentionally did not stand out in the crowd, but still sought to impress in a subtle way.

An agreeable looking woman of the right age came in and surveyed the café as if looking for someone. He quickly dismissed her as a possible Dr. Maller. Her clothing was colorful and loose fitting, not the type of clothing someone in a position of authority would wear. She looked more like a grownup child of the 70's, someone who marched in protests as a young woman and still wrote letters to the editor expounding the injustices of society. He was not waiting for this woman.

"Elliot Forsman I presume."

"Dr. Maller?" he said as he stood to greet her. He regarded the woman before him with a new perspective. Her hair, kept short with no attempt to hide the evident grey indicated that she was confident and comfortable in her own skin. He found it refreshing that she didn't fit in his pre-formed image and that, in the first minute of their meeting, she was already unpredictable. While he was in the midst of his hasty re-evaluation, he realized that he too, was the object of scrutiny. The psychiatrist was engaged in an appraisal of her own as she observed him coolly. He now understood what a psychiatric patient would feel like while under observation.

"That would be me," she said as she finished sizing him up. "You're taller than I expected."

"You were expecting Hercule Poirot?"

"Something like that."

"Sorry to disappoint."

"Not at all," she laughed as she sat down. "I try not to employ stereotypes, but I'm as guilty as the next person."

"Don't we all. I have to admit you're not what I expected either."

The doctor wasn't sure if she should pursue that statement and in the end decided to move the conversation ahead. "You don't know me so I'll tell you right off that I like to get to the point. I'm looking for your help Mr. Forsman"

"Rivka told me you were a straight talker."

"She used the term 'straight talker'?"

"No, that was my interpretation. She said you talked like a longshoreman, but without the filters."

"I don't believe in insinuations and inferences, if I have something to say I'll say it in a manner that will be understood."

"I can see why Rivka likes working with you, so let's get to it."

"I met with your partner yesterday and she tells me she's ready to get back to work, and I agree with her. "

"That's great news. We have a client coming in later this morning and I'd love to have her there with me."

"There is one condition I'd like to put on her return. I'll endorse her desire to go back to work immediately on the condition that you play a part in her recovery."

"How would that work?"

"You've worked together for a few years and you know her well. I'm just looking for you to keep an eye on her," the psychiatrist paused while choosing her next words. "Rivka is an interesting patient in many ways. I don't often see personality types like her sit on my couch until it's too late. She is the embodiment of confident extroversion, but she's in a fragile state right now. She doubts herself for the first time in her life and she doesn't know how to deal with it. She's been sitting on her couch for the past four months, rehabbing her leg, and it's allowed her to delve much too deeply into inner reflection. The best therapy for Rivka at this time is to occupy her brain with something other than her situation. That said, the way she will respond is difficult to predict. I wonder if you can keep an eye on her over the next little while and if you see any behaviors that cause you concern, give me a call."

"So you want me to spy on my partner?"

"Not at all. Obviously I wouldn't be talking to you about a patient if she had not already agreed to it."

"I'll do whatever it takes but I have to say, it seems like an unusual way to treat a patient."

"It is unusual in North America but in many parts of the Eastern world, families play an integral part in treatments like Rivka's."

"Then consider me part of your treatment plan Dr. Maller."

"Margie."

Elliot looked at her without saying anything.

"Margie. My name is Margie."

"Yes, of course. Margie."

"Mr. Forsman, as much as I'd like to have a coffee and chat, I have patients waiting, so I'll have to excuse myself. Thank you for helping out with your partner. Here's my number in the event you want to bring something to my attention," she said as she handed Elliot a business card.

Elliot nodded and watched as she exited the café thinking that he just met an interesting woman.

# Chapter 4

"Riv, get out of bed. We have a case."

"Bed? Really, it's 10 in the morning."

"The client will be here in 30 minutes. I need you."

"I have to shower and eat."

"You have 29 minutes."

"Feh!" she said and the phone slammed down.

* * * * * * * * *

Elliot watched from his desk as Marie Bernard got out of her car and crossed the street toward the JFK office. This type of unnoticed observation provided him a wealth of information. The manner in which she crossed the street without hurrying told him she was a person who didn't bow to pressure, someone who was in control of her life, not being controlled by it. His keen eye noted that even though she carried an expensive Coach purse and wore designer clothes, she was not who she was pretending to be. From the way she carried herself he could tell she was not born into money, she came from humble beginnings. Her clothes could not hide that.

"So tell me Madame Bernard, what brings you to JFK Investigations?"

"I want something investigated."

"Yes. Well, perhaps you can be a bit more specific."

"My nephew was murdered a couple of weeks ago. Stabbed to death in the street. "

"Here in Montréal?"

"Yes, that's why I'm here in Montréal, trying to find a competent investigator. Do you know any?"

Elliot rolled his eyes involuntarily, but stayed the course. "There's no need for sarcasm Madame Bernard. I'm just trying to establish facts. Tell us more, please."

The woman took a deep breath and pulled the fabric of her blouse tight down from the waist.

"My nephew was stabbed to death in a back alley just north of Murray Street about two weeks ago. It was drug related, just as the police said, no doubt about that. I won't say that he got what he deserved—no child deserves to be killed—but he got exactly what his lifestyle demands. You live by the sword and you'll die by the same type of sword that you use."

Elliot cringed at the butchered aphorism and moved on. "This wouldn't be the young lad who was found in Griffintown was it? Alphonse something?"

"That was him. Alphonse Leduc. My nephew Alphie. 16 going on 30. Too goddam smart by half for anyone around him."

"I'll assume there was a police investigation. What did they uncover?

"Oh sure, there was a police investigation all right. They came up with a theory that Alphie was involved in drugs and got himself into an 'insalubrious' situation. Duh," she said providing air quotes around 'insalubrious'.

"So you agree with their assessment?"

"Yes. He was a bad seed that one. In and out of trouble since he was old enough to walk and talk. His mother, my sister Lisa, didn't have an answer for that one."

"Where is the mother today?"

"She died a few years ago. Took her own life while he was in juvie. She lost a long fight with the black dog. Depression is a nasty way to live one's life. That said, there's a part of me that's glad she's out of her misery. Her torment is over. "

"I'm sorry to hear it. And the father?"

"He was never part of their lives. He bugged out as soon as the going started to get tough. I have no idea where he is now."

"So your nephew was murdered and you want us to find the killer?"

"I think it's the least I can do. I wasn't there for Lisa, or Alphie, when they needed me. If I can help put the killer behind bars then I'll have done something. "

Elliot looked over at his partner and locked eyes with her as he processed Marie Bernard's story. He knew Rivka was doing the same. After a moment, she gave him a slight nod. Almost imperceptible but it told him everything he needed to know.

"We'll take the case Madame Bernard. Can you stick around for a bit? Rivka needs you to answer some background questions on the crime and victim, and to discuss terms."

\* \* \* \* \* \* \* \* \* \*

"What did you think of Madame Bernard's story?" Elliot asked Rivka after their client left the office.

"It was interesting. You already knew about the boy?"

"I read about it in the paper. They didn't say much, just that a 16-year-old boy had been found dead in a back alley in Griffintown, stabbed to death. And drugs were involved."

"That was what, two weeks ago?"

"About that. Let's divide and conquer. I'll go to his work place and you to his neighborhood and check out his group home. Let's establish how credible the police theory is on his drug involvement. Was it a deal gone bad? Did he owe money to the wrong people? Maybe it was just a robbery?"

"Okay chief," she winced as she got up.

"How's the leg? It looks like it hurts."

"It aches like a bad tooth, but not just where the surgery was. My back and butt are killing me. "

"Are you still keeping up your Ironman training?"

"I'm trying. I might have to quit and join titanium-man training with all this hardware in my leg. I'll play it by ear. The doc says I may never be able to run without pain. That bullet did some serious damage and it could take years for the bone to fuse onto my metal knee. For now, I swim as much as I can."

"I thought your physio therapist wanted you to use a cane?"

"That`s not happening, I might as well carry a big sign that says *'pity me'*."

"Well, I think you already know you'll get no pity from me. "

As Rivka made her way slowly to the door Elliot asked, "remember when we got a copy of the case file for my dad's murder? Can you ask your police contact if she can get a copy of Alphie's case file? "

"You mean Stella? I'll ask her."

"Okay. Let's hookup later this aft."

## Chapter 5

Elliot pulled up to the Lav as they called it, short
for lave-auto, French for carwash. It was a big
operation, three wash bays and a smaller
administration building at the back of the lot. The Lav
took up a long corner lot on the corner Descartes and
St. Catherine East streets. He maneuvered his way
through a line of waiting cars to a parking spot on the
north side of the lot, not far from the administration
building. The smell of soapy water greeted him as he
stood by the car and watched the operation for a
while.

The first half of each bay was an enclosed wash
area where automated sprayers did their work. He
could just make out the top of the car through the
worn plexi-glass windows as it was pulled ahead by
some unseen locomotion. The second half of the wash
bay was where the manual detailing took place. A
half a dozen kids scurried around each car as they
exited the auto-wash armed with buckets, hoses, and
washcloths. Some of them concentrated on putting a
shine on the areas that the automatic sprayer could
not clean. Others had legs sticking out of the open car
doors vacuuming and polishing chrome and plastic.
It looked like the kids were having fun. A water fight
broke out as the kids waited for the next car. Elliot

didn't blame them. A little water to cool off in this heat would be a welcome distraction.

Satisfied he had a good feel for the carwash, he made his way across the lot to the administration office, if the manager was on site, he'd likely be in there.

He knocked once as a courtesy and entered. The office was one long room with the business end of the operation at the far end. There was a low table surrounded by a couple of chairs and a magazine rack to his left. The chrome on the chair legs was mostly worn off exposing a dull grey metal beneath, and a thin layer of foam could still be seen poking through the ripped vinyl. He didn't pause long enough to check the magazines but assumed they were out of date.

The two windows on the right wall looked out over the parking lot toward the carwash bays. A single window on the left wall faced a chain link fence that marked the back boundary of the carwash property. A sticker advertised an OPUS II alarm system and Elliot noticed the intrusion detection hardware on the windows.

The man at the other end of the office saw Elliot enter but was engaged in a phone conversation. He motioned for Elliot to come in and sit by his desk to wait.

Elliot squeezed past a coat rack where a carwash owner's trade tools hung, a raincoat and a pair of rubber boots beneath. He took the opportunity to survey his surroundings as the man, now facing the window with his back to Elliot, continued his conversation. He instinctively looked at the man's right arm, searching for the trace of a tattoo of tumbling dice that he knew was on the arm of his mother's murderer. The long sleeved shirt offered no glimpse of what might exist underneath. It wasn't that he thought the man in front of him was the man he had sought for so many years; he looked for a tattoo on the arm of every middle aged black man he met. After 32 years, it was force of habit.

Elliot guessed the man was in his late forties, although he looked older. His face, with skin like worn leather, had a pronounced mouth; deep creases extending from the sides of his nose and around the edges of his mouth, Elliot wondered if he was a smoker. His hair was short and greying and a wispy white beard covered the bottom of his chin. The beard, closely trimmed, except for a few rogue strands that twisted out at odd angles, like a well-used Brillo pad.

He turned his attention to the office. He knew that the manner in which a person furnishes his surroundings usually says a lot about his character.

The entire open area of the building served as the office, and he presumed a couple of doors on the left hand wall likely fronted a bathroom and a storage room. Just past the doors along the same wall was a sink area with coffee making accessories on the counter. The back quarter of the office, where the desk sat, was where business was conducted.

The desktop was neat with only a computer screen and keyboard on the left side. This type of organized behavior told Elliot that the carwash manager probably had an ordered, methodical mind. He knew that this type of personality made for good managers but often lacked the ability to think strategically.

Elliot turned his observation to an enormous marlin on the wall behind the desk, frozen in time, as if mounted while in the throes of being caught. He wondered if the owner knew that no part of the original fish was used to make this mount. Even the most honest taxidermists would only use the original fish to cast a mold, less honest shops would just pull a right-sized blank out of inventory and present it as the real thing.

Below the over-sized marine effigy was a large photo of the proud anglers. The photo showed two men squatting down in front of the landed fish, and the apparent skipper of the fishing charter standing a few yards behind them. Palms trees in the background told Elliot it was probably somewhere in the Caribbean and the two squatting fishermen would be tourists. The photo also caught part of the outfitter signage, a weathered wooden sign with the picture of a fishing boat underneath the name of the outfitter. Most of the name was cut off in the photo so that only the words "Fishing Expeditions," were visible.

He noticed the shadow of the photographer on the ground at the bottom of the picture. The shaded silhouette of a thin arm extended out from the photographers body as if to tell the posing fishermen to focus on the hand, not the camera. Whoever had taken the photo had caught the anglers in mid laugh; it was the perfect union of a spontaneous moment within a posed picture. The skipper behind them was also enjoying the moment but unlike the tourists was looking directly at the photographer, not at the extended hand. He had a peculiar smile on his face that made Elliot wonder what he was thinking at the time.

At first glance, he didn't recognize anyone in the picture, he certainly didn't recognize any of the fisherman. It took him a second look to determine that the black man standing back from the tourists, the man who looked like he was the skipper of the charter, was a younger version of the man who stood before him. Yes, if he imagined the man without his baseball hat, the gaudy island scene shirt, and erased a dozen years from his face, they were the same man.

Elliot snapped back to the present, as the man on the phone seemed to have gotten his point across and turned his attention toward his visitor.

"How can I help you?" said the man on the far side of the desk as he hung up his phone.

"I'm looking for the manager."

"You've found him."

"My name is Elliot Forsman," said Elliot as he stretched his hand forward.

"Chalwell, Jack Chalwell."

"I'm a private investigator looking into the death of one of your former employees."

"Jesus," the man muttered in disgust. "You guys haven't asked enough bloody questions yet?"

"Do you have a few minutes to talk about Alphie Leduc? It won't take long."

"I've already told the police, numerous times, what I know about the kid. If you want to know what I said, go ask them."

Elliot ignored the man's crustiness and plowed forward.

"I'm just asking for a few minutes of your time. A boy was murdered."

Chalwell looked at Elliot, clearly frustrated, bordering on anger, "You want to know what I know? Here's what I told the police, He was a good kid. I didn't know, or care, that he used drugs. I didn't know he was dealing. I don't know who his friends are or whom he hung out with, and I don't know who killed him. This is a rough neighborhood. Why do people get stabbed in back alleys in the middle of the night? I don't know. Was he there for a purpose, or was he in the wrong place at the wrong time? I guess those are the questions you're going to need to answer. Now please, I'm trying to get some work done," he said as he pointed to the door.

Elliot readied to leave but continued to press, "I get it, you're busy, but surely you feel compassion for the kids in this neighborhood? The cops have closed the books on this case. To them he's just another druggie who doesn't score high enough on their status chart to warrant a real investigation. He's not a statistic, he was a real live boy, part of someone's family, and he deserves better than this," Elliot shook fist as he made his point.

Chalwell countered with a raised voice, "Compassion! You want to talk about compassion. This is not just a carwash. I hire dozens of kids, not cuz I have to, because I want to. There's no shortage of adults who'd take a job here, even at minimum wage, but my policy is to give the jobs to the kids. It keeps them off the streets and gives a little bit of structure in their life, structure that many of them don't get at home. I'm like a goddamn father to some of these kids. You think I don't care that one of them is killed? You're damn right I care, but if I start asking questions and butting into their personal lives, they stop coming here. That defeats the purpose so I give them what I can and let them sort out their lives. That's all I can do," he said as he emphasized each word in the last sentence.

"Now get the fuck off of my property before I call the police and have you removed," he said, now yelling.

Elliot pulled out of the lot and parked on the street in an empty spot in front of the carwash. He stood on the roadside and watched for a while as kids drifted in for the next shift. After some time, a small knot of teens left together so he made his move and approached them.

"Excuse me, my name is Elliot Forsman. Your boss said it's okay if I asked you a few questions about Alphie Leduc. Did any of you know him?"

The circle of kids looked at the investigator silently.

"I'm trying to find out what happened. Do you think you can answer a few questions?"

The small kid on the end spoke, "Yeah, we knew him."

"Why do you think he was killed?"

Again, silence until the same kid spoke up again, "Dunno. Maybe he was in the wrong place at the wrong time."

"Was he dealing drugs?"

"Not that we knew about."

"Did the police already ask you these questions?"

"Yeah, a few times."

"Who did he hang out with when he wasn't at work?"

They answered the question with feet shuffling and shoulder shrugging.

"You do want to help find his killer don't you? Is there anything you can tell me?"

Again, no verbal response, but their body language told Elliot everything he needed to know.

He took a handful of JFK business cards from his pocket and tried to hand the cards out, "If you think of anything give me a call."

Elliot noticed a red haired girl at the back of the group who didn't have the slack faced look of indifference the others were displaying. Her eyes were wide and her head canted slightly to the side in an effort hear every word of the conversation. Despite her interest in the proceedings, she offered no answers and stayed at the rear of the departing group. Elliot pushed past one of the teens to get close to her and she looked up at him, eyes wide and locked on his. He thrust one of his cards into her hand, "Call me, please."

Elliot watched the kids as they drifted away looking for non-verbal clues. He already knew that kids were often more difficult to read than adults. One thing he did notice was that a couple of the kids looked toward the administration building as they left. He followed their gaze and saw the shaded form of the manager watching from the window.

## Chapter 6

Elliot drove east on Ontario Street and then north on Pie-IX to Parc Etienne-Desmarteaux. Alphie's group home was across the street from the park.

The low-income row houses he cruised past looked to be forty to fifty years old but were more likely no more than twenty. Residents tend to take less pride and care in their homes when they do not own them. These dwellings checked off the boxes that drove design for most low-income housing. The design and build specifications were approved as long as they had doors, windows and a roof. Less essential qualities like curb appeal and workmanship were never considered. He slowed as the house numbers increased and wondered which of the dirty brown row houses had been Alphie's. He pulled up behind a familiar Kia Soul and waited.

"Fancy meeting you here," he said as his partner walked out of one of the brown structures.

"It's a small town. What brings you up this way? I thought you were investigating the carwash."

"I finished and thought I'd come over and see if you've made any progress."

"I just interviewed the people at his group home. They didn't tell me anything we didn't already know.

The resident leader said she always suspected he was still into drugs but didn't see any evidence of it. He didn't always come home at night but she couldn't say where he was staying. He told them he was at a friends but he never offered a name. I got the feeling that they weren't all that sad to see him go. They described him as un-cooperative, uninterested, and disengaged. He didn't want to be there and they didn't want him there."

"What about the other teens in the home?

"Their story wasn't much different. He didn't socialize with the other teens. When he was home he'd stay in his room and keep to himself. They didn't know who he hung out with. He was the only teen in the home who wasn't still in school so he didn't really fit in with them."

"Did they let you into his room?"

"Yeah. I poked around a bit but most of his stuff was already boxed up. They're getting ready for the next tenant. They told me they didn't come across anything unusual while they were packing up, there were no drugs. I did take this off his mirror though. I'm not sure what it means, if anything," she said showing Elliot a scrap of paper with the name '*Anderson*' on it and the date '*Aug 7, 3:00pm*'.

"August 7. That was the day before he was killed."

"That's right. Nobody at the house knew of an 'Anderson'. It's something we'll have to keep in our back pocket. How'd it go at the carwash?"

"More of the same. The carwash manager talked a bit but was clearly not interested in sharing information. I got the feeling he was holding back. When I talked to some of Alphie's co-workers, they were intentionally unhelpful. We'll need to dig deeper into the carwash."

"What now?" asked Rivka.

"Let's go talk to those kids over at that skateboard park." Elliot had his eye set on a small park area diagonally across the street.

Passing from the sweltering heat of the day into the shade of trees was a relief. Elliot felt the breeze blow through his shirt and pull it away from the sweaty skin on his back. It felt good as he walked under the shade of the large oak trees bordering the trail that bisected the park. It reminded him of good times from his past, when he and Sarah would take Jake to the swings. Elliot would push Jake for hours, both of them enjoying the peace that it brought, and Sarah would find a cool spot beneath trees much like these and watch the two favorite men in her life. He didn't dwell long on those thoughts, they depressed him. Sarah was gone now, and Jake might as well be.

Elliot and Rivka slowed down to watch as a child, squealing with delight, was chased by her older sibling with a water gun. They were captivated by the reckless abandon of sheer delight that only a child could experience. Elliot envied the child and he wondered if Rivka felt the same.

They made their way up to the edge of the cemented skateboard area and watched as a half a dozen youths took turns showing off their latest boarding maneuvers. Having an audience seemed to spur them on to try increasingly difficult moves with mixed success until one of the youths took a hard fall and was unable to bounce back up. As the queue of waiting boarders went to their fallen comrade, Elliot and Rivka took the opportunity to engage them.

"Are you all right?" Rivka said.

The teen was now on his knees and the question turned the focus of the boarders to Rivka.

"Be alright," said the teen as he rotated his injured shoulder. Elliot let Rivka take the lead on the questions for a number of reasons. Not only was she a trained interrogator, courtesy of the Montréal Police, but she also had an ability that made people want to talk to her. Young or old, male or female, it didn't matter. Maybe it was the infectious, unconstrained smile she flashed, or the overt confidence she displayed in her every movement. It certainly didn't hurt that she was attractive in a fascinating way. At first glance you might think her eyes were too far apart or her nose hooked too much but as you looked at her, you realize that when taken together, it all worked. Elliot often found himself looking at her when she was otherwise occupied in an attempt to unlock the mystery of her fascinating look. In short, she was someone other people wanted to connect with.

"Glad to hear it, you took quite a spill. Hey, did you guys know Alphie Leduc?"

The teens shrunk back from the question as if she had an infectious disease.

"We're not cops; we're just trying to find out why he was killed," she added.

The bony kid with wild hair answered, "He lived across the street."

"We're looking for info about what might have happened that night. "

"Just like the newspaper said. He was knifed."

"Was he your buddy?"

"No," he said as if slapped, "He was a druggie. A loser."

"Do you know who he hung with?"

"Dunno. Nobody we know. He hung with the gangs uptown."

"Which gangs?"

"Dunno. We don't hang with gangs."

"Do you know of any reason someone would want to kill him?"

"Like I said, we didn't hang with him."

By now, a few mothers and young children had approached to get a closer look and were listening to the conversation, including a toddler of 4 or 5 who had inserted himself in amongst the teens.

"S'alright," said the injured boarder as he waved them away.

"Mamelon a tué le garcon," the toddler said looking toward Rivka.

"Excusez moi," she replied.

"C'était Mamelon. Il a tué le garçon."

"Mamelon? Qui est-ce?"

A woman pulled the toddler out from between the teens and marched him away.

Rivka followed behind as the mother scurried away.

"Madame, qui est Mamelon?"

She stopped and faced the following investigator, her lips tight and face flushed.

"Stay away from us!" she said pronouncing every word very deliberately with a heavy French accent.

They watched as she stuffed the child in a stroller and hurried away.

When Rivka turned back to the teens, she saw they too were dispersing, away from the cemented board park.

"Wait," she called out to the teen who had been doing most of the talking.

The teen looked back and without replying jogged out to the street and jumped on his board.

"What did you make of that?" Rivka asked. "The teens were fine saying that they didn't hang with Alphie but when the toddler mentioned Mamelon it was like someone opened a door that shouldn't have been opened. I was watching body language. It was loose and easy and then ..."

"Mamelon. Isn't that a tit?"

"More precisely it's a nipple, or teat," she replied. "But why would the kid say that a nipple killed Alphie? And why was the mother freaked out when the kid mentioned that name?" Rivka mused.

"I don't know. Let's head back to the office and compare notes. I'll pick up a late lunch on the way."

"I have an appointment with my physio guy. It shouldn't take long, but take your time. I'll be there in an hour and a half."

# Chapter 7

Elliot entered the office carrying their lunches and saw Rivka, already at her desk. She didn't look up when he entered; she was like that, as if she considered herself on display for all to see.

"Here ya go Riv," he said sliding the poutine over to his partner, "and Sammy wants you to know he made this one special for you."

"Thanks Elliot. I'll have to stop in later to say hi."

"How'd the physio appointment go?"

"Same as usual. I'm making progress, don't overdo it, use a cane when you walk, be patient. Yadda Yadda Yadda."

"Did you tell him about your sore back?"

"Yeah. He said I've probably changed my natural gait trying to compensate for the bad leg and that it's putting undo stress on my healthy body parts. He gave me the number for a massage therapy clinic. I called them and they'll send someone over tomorrow. Imagine that, a house call in this day and age."

Elliot changed the subject to the case, "I've been going through the case file Stella sent. I'm not finished yet but I can tell you that there's a bad smell around this investigation," Elliot said.

"What makes you say that?"

"The interview process was light. They talked to a few of the kids at the carwash, the carwash manager, and they took statements from his juvie officer, as well as his aunt, Marie Bernard. There was nothing of note in those interviews. Alphie had a small roll in one pocket, less than $200, and few packets of cocaine in the other pocket, so it wasn't a robbery. It's as if they decided not to waste resources on the investigation when they found out he was already in the system."

"So why do you think it stinks?"

"The report said he was carrying a small roll of bills in his left front pocket and, in his right front pocket were 3 foil packets of coke, along with a couple of dollars in change and a folding pen knife."

"Yeah, so?"

"Riv, no experienced druggie would mix hardware like a knife, or small change, in the same pocket as his stash. He would never risk the foil being damaged by rubbing alongside of the other items. The cops should have known that."

"Who were the investigating officers?"

Elliot scrolled through the electronic copy of the report on his computer. "Bernard Pelletier was the primary. Do you know him?"

"Pelletier, yeah, I know him. He's a tight ass with ambitions. We didn't get along very well."

"That's a recurring theme for you. Do you think he's crooked?"

"Pelletier? No way. As I said, he's ambitious. He wouldn't waste time on a loser like Alphie. There's no upside in it for him. If the case doesn't have the possibility of advancing his career he'd want to close it and move on as soon as possible."

"Okay. It doesn't sound like we could accomplish much by talking to him. If we work on the premise that Alphie wouldn't have kept his stash in that pocket, and the cops didn't plant the drugs, then a more likely possibility is that the killer planted the drugs."

"Sounds logical," Rivka pondered as she tasted her poutine. "If we run with that theory then we can rule out a drug deal gone bad or a robbery. This murder was premeditated, planned out with the intent of misleading the investigation. They wanted to make sure that the police knew the victim was an active drug dealer so that the investigation would be nominal."

"Exactly what I was thinking. Do you know Jacques Bessette? He was the coroner," Elliot asked as he scrolled through the case file.

"Jacques the Ripper. I've worked with him a few times. He's a good guy but usually plays it by the book."

"Do you know him well enough that he'd talk to us about an open case?"

"There's only one way to find out. I'll see if I can get us in to talk to him," Rivka replied. She thought for a moment and then added, "I get the feeling that nobody cares if this murder goes unsolved, and the only reason we're looking into it is because of Marie Bernard's guilt."

"You're probably right Riv. That's why we're going to solve it. Maybe nobody cared about Alphie when he was alive but that doesn't change the fact that someone took his life. He was only 16. He had his whole life still in front of him and more than a good chance to turn things around. Someone took that chance away from him, and someone will answer for it."

Rivka busied herself trying to get the coroner on the line and Elliot moved over to his most prized possession, a vintage barber chair. When he needed to think through weighty issues, or when a major decision was needed, he sought the solace of his thinking chair. He didn't try to rationalize why sitting in the barber chair enabled him to think more clearly, he just knew it worked. He sunk back into the comfort of the worn, vintage leather and looked at the board in front of him. As usual, it was full of reminders and notes, but the one note that held his attention was a yellow sticky on the upper right. He knew what was on the yellow note; it had been on his mind for weeks.

He wiped a sweaty palm on his pant leg and pulled the note down. He'd found the name of the headmistress of the Westmount Boys school a few weeks previous but wanted to prepare himself before he called the number. After 32 years of thinking about the death of his mother and the killers that were never caught, this note represented the first and only clue he'd ever found. If it didn't pan out, he'd likely never solve the case and his mother's murder would not see justice. He stared at the note in his hand and the number scrawled across it. He had purposely waited for Rivka to get back to work before phoning the number. At least that was how he rationalized his reluctance to act. Now that Rivka was back he realized he still wasn't prepared to deal with it. As much as he wanted to pull his mother's cold case from the Police vault to find closure on her murder, he realized he still wasn't ready. He tacked the yellow sticky back up on the wall where it came from with a tenderness that he didn't try to explain.

## Chapter 8

*Thursday, August 24*[th]

"Good morning Rivka."

"Morning Doc."

"You look well. How have you slept since we last met?"

"Generally much better, the pills you prescribed are helping. I fell asleep early last night but woke up around three, stiff and sore. I couldn't get back to sleep. My back was talking to me like a hangnail from hell and my butt was singing the blues."

"Is that because you're training for the Ironman?"

"Was," she stressed, "I was an Ironman competitor. Now I'm just a gimpy wanna-be," she snorted as her lip curled into a half smile and her foot started tapping. My physio therapist says it'll likely always hurt when I run."

"But you still train as if you'll be competitive."

"I do what I can."

"Why do you train so hard?"

Rivka shrugged off the question without really thinking about it, "I like the way it makes me feel."

"Yet, you just said it hurts like a hangnail from hell."

"It does," she nodded quietly.

"Why do you feel you need to punish yourself? Why do you feel you have to push yourself past your limits when you know what awaits you afterwards? "

Rivka said nothing.

"I can't answer that question for you, you must answer it yourself. In order for you to move ahead you need to ask yourself why you train so hard when you know it's going to hurt, and you can't be afraid to answer it honestly."

The psychiatrist noticed the look of indifference on her patients face.

"Rivka, you've been through a lot over the past months. We talked about your kidnapping ordeal, your wounded leg, and the impact it's had on your life and aspirations. These are life altering events, but I don't believe they're at the root of your issues. You are still harboring strong emotions about leaving the Police Force, about your former boss, Serge Amyot, and your failure to catch Ogrodnik."

Rivka looked at the psychiatrist and replied, "If you say so. What can I do about it?"

"Let's talk about your failure to catch Ogrodnik. I understand that one of Ogrodnik's victims was your niece," the psychiatrist said. Her intent was to lob an emotional grenade and gauge her patient's reaction.

Rivka straightened in her chair, "that's right," she answered as she raised her head and set her jaw.

Rivka's body language did not go unnoticed by the psychiatrist. "Why do think you feel so strongly about not catching Ogrodnik when you had the chance?

"I don't know. Maybe it's guilt?"

"Guilt? About what? Did you do something wrong."

"I didn't do anything wrong."

"And yet you feel guilt."

Rivka stared at the floor while trying to make sense of her feelings.

"Maybe it's not guilt. Is it possible you feel you let some people down? "

"That's a given."

"Do you think those people feel you let them down?"

"Some do. The families of Ogrodnik's victims. They need closure."

"What does closure mean to you?"

"Something that will put an end to their grief. Knowing that the person who murdered their loved one is no longer out there. Being able to put it all behind them and move on in their lives."

"Do you really think that knowing Ogrodnik was in custody would put an end to their grief? Do you think they'd stop thinking about the loss of their loved ones just because the murderer had been brought to justice?"

Rivka reflected on the question before answering. "No. I guess not."

"No. You're right. They'll always think about their daughter, their mother, the sister or the friend that is no longer with us. The fact that the murderer has not yet been brought to justice plays a part in their recovery, but it's a small part. Rivka, closure is an illusion. Don't count on it."

The psychiatrist let the silence work before zeroing in on the root of her patients problem. "So if your issues do not stem from your ordeal with Ogrodnik, or the fact that you didn't catch him when you had a chance to, what is causing you to lie awake at night? You told me you let someone down Rivka. Who was it? Who did you disappoint?"

The psychiatrist heard a sniffle and knew that her patient was on the edge of self-discovery. She also knew that if her patient refused to open the door, she would never entirely heal. From the discussion they had in their first meeting the doctor knew that Rivka's issues were related to her leaving the Police Force. She needed to steer her patient toward that subject.

"Rivka, you left the Police Force of your own volition, do you regret that decision?

"Not at all," she said without hesitation.

"Yet you are still hanging onto emotions related to leaving the Police Force?"

Rivka, trying to interpret her feelings, said nothing.

The doctor pushed ahead, "Rivka, do you feel that you let your mother down? You told me she was supportive of your decision to leave the Police Force. You said she never uttered a word about your decision to leave. You told me she never blamed you for not finding her granddaughter's killer, but you never believed her, did you? You didn't find the killer when you were with the Force. You allowed yourself to be pushed out of your career, a career that you loved, and when you had another chance to make it right, to apprehend Ogrodnik, you failed again. Is that the way you feel Rivka?"

She replied with a nod.

The psychiatrist waited while that admission sunk and in and let the moment pass.

"Do you know that I know your mother?"

"No," she said quietly as she shook her head.

"Yes, in fact, I know her quite well, and have known her for years. We go to the same synagogue and have been in the same Sisterhood group for many years. Don't worry, I never talk business, I'm not even sure she knows I'm a psychiatrist. "

"You never told me."

"No. It's had no bearing on your case. Your business is yours alone. I wouldn't disclose that without asking you first."

"So what are you going to say? Are you going to tell me that she forgives me? That she doesn't care that her granddaughter's killer is still roaming free and that she's okay that her daughter threw away her career."

"No. Your mother never said anything to you because she never blamed you," the psychiatrist paused a moment before continuing.

"I remember the day when your mother talked about her daughter, the police woman, and how her daughter was no longer with the Force. She told us about the way your captain had belittled you in front of the unit and how you reacted. She told us that you walked out on your job. A job you loved. Rivka, I have never seen a person more proud than your mother was that day. She was proud because you stood up for what you believed in, that you refused to let it slide. You could have gone back to the job the next day. You could have pretended it never happened, but you did not. You did what all of us would want to do, but most of us would not. You have principles and you respected them. A mother could ask no more of her child."

Rivka said nothing as she blinked away the well of tears.

"We've made progress today Rivka. You still have my prescription for something to help you sleep, use it when you think you need it. In the meantime, let's schedule our next meeting," she said looking at her calendar.

"I understand you met with Elliot yesterday?" Rivka inquired.

"Yes. As we discussed last meeting, he's agreed to be part of your support system. I think this arrangement will work out well."

Dr. Maller checked her schedule online and then asked offhandedly, "Rivka, what is the nature of your relationship with Elliot?"

"We work together."

"There's no chance there's something more than that simmering?"

"No chance," she said decisively.

"Okay. We're making progress and I don't want to lose momentum. Let's meet again tomorrow morning. 8:30am, here at the office."

"Whatever, I'll see you in the morning," Rivka said flippantly.

The psychiatrist could not ignore her patient's agitation.

"Rivka, visualize your life as a stream. When your life is good, your stream flows down through a mountain pass. The water is swift and cold and as it hits rocks on the streambed, it flows around and over them without being impeded. The rocks in this allegory are obstacles in your life. Sometimes your obstacles seem so large that the water no longer flows freely. What we're trying to do is make sure your stream flows freely again. This is accomplished by understanding the root cause of your obstacles. Eventually they'll be understood and your stream will flow unconstrained again. It'll happen gradually, but it will happen," said the psychiatrist as a signal to Rivka that the session was over.

## Chapter 9

"JFK Investigations," Rivka answered, now back at the office.

"Mr. Forsman please."

"Mr. Forsman isn't here at the moment, can I help you? I'm Mr. Forsman's partner."

"My name is Rebecca Boyle. Mr. Forsman came to the carwash yesterday asking about Alphie Leduc and gave me his card."

"You're the girl with the red hair?"

"That's right."

"You have information about Alphie?"

"I'm not sure what you're looking for. I was his girl…, his friend."

"Can we meet?"

"Yes. I'm at the Langlois seniors home on St. Hubert and Duplessis; we can meet here if that works for you."

"I know it. I'll be there later this morning."

\* \* \* \* \* \* \* \* \*

Rivka pulled into the Langlois senior's home parking lot on rue St. Hubert.

It looked like an old school house from the turn of the century and, understanding how municipal building regulations worked, it probably was. There were strict regulations preventing the destruction of any buildings that could be deemed historically or architecturally significant. The interpretation of those regulations were broad and not well defined but, as a matter of course, any buildings older than 100 years were generally off limits for redevelopment. What often happened was that the interior of the old buildings were gutted and restored to code while the exterior was restored to period. Rivka thought that was probably how this old school house came to be a nursing home.

It was a grand looking building, the original brick frontage was still in place, but the windows, small by today's standards, looked to be new, high efficiency coated glass. The five-step walkup to a set of massive front doors looked period, although Rivka doubted that the stonework was original. It looked too unblemished to be 100 years old. Off to the side, there was a long ramp for wheelchair access leading up to the front door landing. That definitely didn't exist in the original building. She walked up to the doors and pushed the handicap sign to open them.

A swell of stale heat hit her as she entered the building. She stood on the threshold of an expansive living area and surveyed the room. It was obvious this was the common room where the seniors would spend a good part of their days. The overhead whir of ceiling fans did little to cool the room; it was as hot inside as it was outside. She noticed most of the tenants were wearing pants and long sleeved tops. That told Rivka that the circulatory systems of the elderly tenants were not what they used to be.

A passing attendant pointed out Rebecca across the main room sitting with an elderly woman. Rivka kept her distance while watching the young woman feed the senior. After each spoonful, the senior labored with the effort to dab the corners of her mouth. Even in her advanced age and limited capacity, the senior refused to abandon her sense of decorum.

Rebecca patiently helped the elderly woman through her meal, all the while keeping up a steady stream of inconsequential banter that seemed to dampen the indignity of being nursed. She brushed back a long lock of her hair, now matted against her forehead in the sweltering heat, and looked up to see Rivka. When she mouthed her name as a question, Rivka nodded affirmatively and was given the 'in a minute' signal. Rebecca finished up and led Rivka into the staff break room.

"Tea or coffee?"

"No thanks," Rivka said as she took a seat.

"So you work here?"

"Volunteer. I've been here a few years now. I'd like to go into social work one day."

"I saw by the way you interacted with the elderly woman that you're already very good at it. You've got a gift."

"Thanks," she managed.

"You called."

"Yeah, I'm not sure if I can help but if there's something I can do to help catch Alphie's killer, I'll do it."

"So Alphie was your boyfriend."

"Sort of. We used to hang out."

"How long were you seeing him?"

"Almost a year."

"Tell me about him."

"He was a nice guy, a quiet guy. He didn't have many friends; most of the people he knew were part of his old life, the life he left. I know he'd had many troubles in the past, but he was making a real effort to move on. He was dealing drugs when we first met, but he hadn't been involved in that for, at least six months. He was planning on going back and finishing high school. For the first time in a long time, maybe in his life, he had hope."

---

"The police say he was carrying when they found him."

"I don't know about that. It's hard for me to believe he fell back into his old habits without me knowing about it."

"Why do you think he was killed?"

"I don't know but there were a couple of events recently that I should tell you about."

"Go ahead."

"He was in a fight last month. I was there with him but it didn't seem at the time to be anything that would blow back on him."

"Tell me about it."

"We were walking downtown, up Atwater towards St. Catherine and we passed a couple of guys hanging out under the overpass. One of them called out to Alphie, so he went over, and I could tell it was someone he used to hang with. They talked for a few minutes and Alphie put his hands up as if saying no way and started walking back to me. As he was leaving them, I heard him exclaim, quite loudly, '*It's wrong. People are dying.*' So one of them charges over to Alphie and pulls him around, as if he's going to confront him, and Alphie slugs him in the face. We took off and left them there, and that was the end of it."

"What did he mean when he said 'people are dying'?"

"They were selling crack and were pissed that Alphie got out of the business. Apparently dealers don't like it when one of their own leaves, they feel betrayed. Alphie told me later that the stuff they've been selling lately is cut with fentanyl and people are dying because of it."

"Yeah. That's been in the news a lot lately. Did he ever mention them again?"

"Not about those dealers specifically but he told me he was going to do something about it and that he was meeting with a lawyer."

"Did he say who the lawyer was?"

"No. He said it was one of the regular customers at the Lav that he knew was a lawyer, and they arranged to meet."

"Did he mention the law firm?"

"No. That's all he said about it. He didn't want me involved, he said it could be dangerous."

"Do you know a customer named 'Anderson'?" she asked thinking about the note on Alphie's mirror.

"No. not that I've ever heard of," she replied.

"Hello Rebecca," said a voice from behind.

Rivka turned to see a tall, statuesque black woman approach. Her clothing was utilitarian and functional, exactly what you'd expect to see worn by someone in the service industry. But on this woman, the clothes looked fashionable and smart, similar to the way they would look on the window front mannequins. Her steel hair was pulled back tight on the front and allowed to fall freely in the back giving the impression that she was both neat and orderly, as well as free and fun loving. She glided more than walked, as if she was afraid to upset an unseen object balanced on her head.

"Theresa Chalwell, I try to manage this place," she said in a smoky voice that rolled like morning fog.

Rivka shook her outstretched hand, "Rivka Goldstein, pleased to meet you."

"Rivka is a PI," Rebecca piped in, "she's looking into Alphie's murder."

"I'm glad to see he's not being forgotten, such a tragedy. Have you made any progress?"

"Not really, we're just getting started. I'm hoping that with help from people like Rebecca we'll be able to make headway," she said as she looked at the woman with interest. She had a kind face with a broad, unrestrained smile, like the face you thought your grandmother might have had when she was young.

"I wish you well then. I'll leave you two alone to continue your chat. Good luck, and nice to meet you."

"Likewise," answered Rivka.

"Chalwell? Is she related to the carwash Chalwell?" Rivka asked when Theresa had exited the room.

"She's his wife."

"So you work for both husband and wife?"

"Technically I volunteer here. I've been here for 3 years now, and when I started looking for a part time job last year, Theresa got me in at the Lav."

"She seems nice."

"She's incredible. She calls herself the manager but she's much more than that. Without her, this home wouldn't exist. This home caters to seniors who are not able to fend for themselves but can't afford a nursing home. The money that the government allots her helps but it's not enough to run this operation. She organizes fundraisers, solicits for government help, and works with local businesses to keep this place afloat. She's an amazing woman."

"I could tell by the way she looks at you that you have a special bond with her."

"I hope to be like her one day. She calls me her prodigy."

"I think she's found the right person for the job," Rebecca's face flushed.

"Is there anything else you can tell me about Alphie?"

"Nothing I can think of."

"Tell me, why didn't you take the information about Alphie to the police? Or did you?"

"No, I never did. I thought about it, and eventually decided that when they interviewed me, I'd tell them. They never requested an interview and I never reached out to them. It wasn't until your partner gave me his card that I knew I was obligated to tell someone."

"Rebecca, my partner talked to your boss at the carwash, Jack Chalwell. He described him as evasive and uncooperative. Do you ever see anything unusual happening there?"

"Not that I can think of, but I haven't been looking. To tell the truth, Mr. Chalwell doesn't get involved with us kids much. He hires us and signs our pay cheques. Other than that, he stays in the office and lets his supervisors handle the day to day. You don't suspect Mr. Chalwell in Alphie's murder do you?"

"No, we have no suspects, only questions," a thought struck Rivka as she was winding down.

"Rebecca, have you ever heard of Mamelon?"

"Of course, everyone in this part of town knows about Mamelon."

"Do you think he killed Alphie?

"I dunno. That's what some people say."

"What do you know about this Mamelon?"

"Not much. He's more of a legend, or a folktale, than anything."

"So you don't believe he's is real?"

"There've been many reports about him killing people. Mamelon gets credit for the death of every loser murdered in this part of town. I sometimes think it's just a story that parents tell their kids to scare them straight."

"Do you know anyone else who was supposed to be killed by Mamelon?"

"Not personally. I've heard of many but don't know them. Five or six years ago, two brothers were murdered and the story was that Mamelon did it to shut them up. I was only 10 at the time but I remember it well, everyone in this part of town remembers it. The older brother worked at the Lav at the time."

"Really? That seems coincidental," said Rivka with raised eyebrows.

"Not really. Given how many kids the Lav employs. At any one time there's probably 50-60 kids working part time, and the turnaround is constant. Most kids living in this end of town would have worked at the Lav at some point."

"Interesting. So what did he want them to shut up about?"

"Drugs."

"So Mamelon is a drug dealer too?"

"That's what people say."

"What else can you tell me about the mysterious Mamelon?"

"That's about it. Nobody knows who he is or even if he's real. Anything good or bad happens that can't be explained, it was Mamelon who did it."

"Thanks Rebecca, you have my number, call me anytime and, if you do see anything unusual at the Lav, let me know."

"Thanks Rivka, I will."

## Chapter 10

"What's up Riv?" Elliot said as he answered his phone.

"Just thought I'd give you an update on the conversation I just had with Rebecca Boyle."

"And who might she be?"

"She's the redhead you gave your card to at the Lav. You were right, she did know Alphie."

"What did she have to say?"

"She was Alphie's girl, or whatever passes for that with kids these days." Rivka went on to tell him about Alphie's encounter with his old drug dealer buddies, his planned meeting with a lawyer, and Rebecca's thoughts on Mamelon.

"Interesting. So we can assume that the name 'Anderson' we found on the note and this lawyer are one and the same. Can you work your magic and find all the lawyers named Anderson in and around Montréal?"

"Not a problem, I'm going home to meet with my masseuse and I'll try to stop in at Alphie's interment afterwards, but I'll get on it later today."

"Good. What's your take on this Mamelon character?"

"As our red headed friend said, she doesn't even know if he exists but apparently there are many people in her part of town that believe he does. I'll err on the safe side and assume there is someone enforcing their law in the drug trade."

"I'm with you on that. Where there's smoke, there's fire, and sometimes it's a forest fire. Thanks for the heads up Riv."

# Chapter 11

Rivka sipped her tea while waiting for her masseuse's house call. She tried to calm the feeling of anxiety that she brought with her from Alphie's interment without success. She flinched when the doorbell chimed.

Rivka answered the door to a smile and a hand, "You must be Rivka."

"And you are?" she questioned.

"Lydia Morgan? Your massage therapist."

"Yes. Yes, of course," she replied while nodding her head.

"Were you expecting someone else?"

"No. I just thought… I was expecting someone short and hairy. I don't know why," she shrugged her shoulders.

"I can have them send someone who better fits your expectations if that's what you prefer."

"Not at all," she chuckled. "It's a welcome surprise, come on in."

Lydia hefted a massive rectangular case through the door when she entered.

"You planning on moving in?"

"Ha. No, this is my massage table. Where can I setup?"

"I've cleared a place in the spare bedroom in the back," she said as she showed Lydia the way.

"Nice place. I like the woodsy view out the back."

"I'm with you there. I sometimes get an errant golfer in my back yard but that I can deal with. It's better than living amongst strangers and having no privacy at all."

Rivka watched as Lydia deftly unfolded her package into a sturdy massage table. She thought it looked like doing reverse origami. Lydia then moved a potted plant off to the side and looked over to Rivka with a dubious smirk. Rivka glanced down at a pair of barren stalks rising from the dirt like broken straws.

"What can I say, I was born with a black thumb," she said as she shrugged her shoulders.

"Before we get started why don't you tell me a bit about why you need a massage therapist and what areas I should focus on."

Rivka's quick summary of her gunshot wound, broken leg, and metal rods morphed into a lively conversation about everything except Rivka`s medical challenges. After an hour, Lydia broke into their dialog "Look at the time! We need to get some work done."

"I've never worked with a massage therapist before, what do you want me to do?"

"It would be best if you warmed up a bit. Can you do 5 minutes on the bike before we start," she said pointing to the stationary bike against the far wall.

"I'd like to observe your range of motion while you're pedaling."

"I never heard a request quite like that but it's your dime," Rivka said as she mounted the bike and started into a stress-free but vigorous pace.

"You've got a very athletic style; you must be a serious rider," Lydia asked after a few minutes of observation.

"I'm an Ironman competitor. At least I was. This leg injury is putting a kink into my training."

Lydia watched for a few more minutes before motioning Rivka to shut it down. "Okay, that's enough of the bike. Can I get you to walk down the hall in your normal gait?"

Lydia watched as Rivka walked back and forth down the hallway, "very nice," she said talking to no one in particular.

"Now, up on the table face down. It looks to me like you have a cluster in your left glute. Before we can fix your back pain, we need to identify the source. But, before we start, I wonder if you have a phone I can use? I left mine at home and I've got to leave a message for another client."

"No problem, my cell is on the kitchen table."

"Thanks, you stay where you are, let you muscles settle down. I won't be a minute."

Rivka felt her heart rate slow as she lay on the table thinking about nothing in particular.

"I'm back," Lydia said as she entered the room. "Sorry for the delay, let's get started."

"No problem," Rivka said as she laid face down on the massage table. "You know, I blame my physio guy for all this. He's a sadistic bastard. The more pain he gives me the happier he is."

"That's his job. He needs to work the muscles and joints in ways that the patient is afraid to. That usually involves some discomfort," said Lydia.

"Discomfort," she snorted. "Do all you therapists go to the same school? The school of understatement. Discomfort is what my ass gets after I've been pedaling for a few hours. I'm talking about gut wrenching agony."

"I'm not going to criticize my physio colleagues. A lot of my business comes from their patients. It's a symbiotic relationship, they find'em, and I grind'em. Now, for our first session I'm going to focus on getting rid of some of the knots you have. I'll use a method called petrissage, basically it's a kneading motion deep into the large muscles, and it may hurt a bit."

"You mean discomfort?"

"Ha. Yes, I mean discomfort," Lydia said as she started working the muscles. "You've got beautiful muscle tone. For most of my customers I have to find the muscle first, yours are just sitting there just begging to be worked."

Rivka replied to the masseuses' banter with a soft groan.

"Am I hurting you?"

"Yeah, but it's a good hurt. Keep going."

Lydia continued in silence as her thumbs and palms methodically worked the knots.

"You've got strong hands."

"The better to give discomfort with," she said as she continued working the muscles hard, the silence broken only by the occasional moan.

"How was that?" asked Lydia as she finished.

"Magnificent," replied Rivka as she got up slowly rolled off the table.

"What's next?" asked Rivka as Lydia packed up her table.

"That's up to you. It's going to take a few sessions to fix you up. Your medical coverage is good for two massages a week but you may be in luck. This is a new gig for me and I don't have a full plate yet so we can probably squeeze in some pro bono work if you need it. Besides, I love to hear the front end of your bullet story sometime."

"Tomorrow?" asked Rivka with a smile.

"I'm free most afternoons after 2:00; I could be here at 2:30."

"It's a date. I'll see you then."

## Chapter 12

It was 3:00pm when Elliot crossed the Champlain Bridge over to the South Shore. The bumper-to-bumper traffic leaving Montréal reminded him of what most of the working world contended with every day. He felt lucky to be in the position he was in.

Once over the bridge, the traffic cleared and he sped along Highway 10 out towards the Eastern Townships and the US border. By the time the low rounded profiles of Mont St. Hilaire and Mont Rougemont were on his left, he'd reached his exit. He drove through the small town of Chambly and it brought back memories of the last time he visited Rayce Nolan. Memories of a stalking assassin who ended up with a knife in his back for his efforts came flooding back. He often thought about the mercenaries killed during the Ogrodnik case. He felt no remorse, they had made their choices.

The gravel parking lot of Rayce's Bike Shop came up faster than he remembered and his tires chirped as he slowed down abruptly to make the turn into the graveled lot. He unfolded his lanky frame from the car and his face contorted in pain as he straightened out his back and stretched the muscles. Elliot knew that sore muscles and joints were the norm for anyone entering middle age but even more so for a 6' 3" man living in a 5' 10" world. He walked stiffly and worked the kinks out while making his way toward the service bays of Rayce's Bike Shop.

The glare of the afternoon sun prevented him from seeing inside until he passed into the shadows and entered the garage. The three bays doors along the front of the shop led into a single open area filled with motorcycles, parts, tools, and other hallmarks of a bike mechanic. At the far end he saw a man in grease stained overalls working on a Harley, and beside him was Rayce, sitting at an over-crowded desk that was clearly too small for a man of his size.

Rayce looked up when Elliot came in and stared at him for a moment trying, and failing, to hold back a look of irritation. Despite his irritation he relented and bobbed his head to the side in a gesture that said, *meet me in the back*.

Elliot nodded and walked out and around the shop to the grassy area behind the house, the same area where he first approached Rayce over four months ago. He remembered it well; it was where he first told Rayce the story of death and betrayal that had been his life at that time. Rayce listened but never said a word through the entire discourse. That was

Rayce, the few words that he spoke were well chosen. He had no need for run-on dialog.

Elliot sat in one of the chairs at the back of the house and listened to the roll of the river rapids that bordered the property until Rayce came out through the side door with two bottles of cold beer held easily in one hand. Rayce wasn't a huge man, a shade over six feet and maybe 220, but he had the frame of a much larger man. Elliot noted that he didn't have the over developed chest and neck of a bodybuilder, he had more of an arms and shoulders physique. His arms were long and hung loose like meat on a hook. They were attached to his body at a set of shoulders that stretched the seams tight in even the largest of shirts. He plunked a beer down on the table and tilted his own towards Elliot in a gesture that replaced a handshake.

Elliot couldn't help but notice the way Rayce's hand dwarfed the bottle in his hand, as if he was drinking from an infant's bottle.

"Forsman, what brings you out this way?" he said as he took a seat.

"I'd like to say I was out for a drive but I think you'd know that's BS."

"You're right, I would," Rayce didn't prod Elliot to answer the question again, nor would he.

Elliot finally broke the mini silence "I'm looking for some help."

Rayce paused before replying as if to choose his words carefully, "Forsman, what I did earlier this year was for your wife Sarah, not for you, or not for the greater good, so I don't want you to get the idea that every time some bully kicks sand in your face you can come running to me. I've got a life and it doesn't include JFK Investigations," having said what he wanted to say he leaned back in his chair to let his words sink in.

"I'm not here for your help. The hacker friend you know, Evan. I'd like to hire him. I need a guy who knows his way around electronic security, someone who doesn't mind stepping outside the lines if need be."

Rayce thought about it for a moment before replying, "I'll give him your number. If he decides to pursue it, he'll call you, otherwise you're on your own."

"That's all I can ask."

They sat in the back sipping on their beers in the shade of house listening to the rush of the water saying nothing. Elliot broke the silence first.

"Did you get my email explaining what happened when Rivka and I went to the airport after we left the Biovonix bunker?"

"I did. Well done Forsman. When we started out, I didn't think you were going to cut it. I didn't think you'd be able to pull the trigger."

"You're talking about taking another man's life?"

"I'm talking about doing whatever it takes."

"It's not something I'm proud of. I still think about it."

"You did what needed to be done Forsman. Move on."

Rayce hesitated a moment before changing the subject. "Did the cops ever track down Ogrodnik?"

"No. They think he probably caught a lift on a freighter out of the country. There's no way we'll ever know unless he decides to come back. There's a part of me that hopes he doesn't come back, that's the safe way, the easy way out. But I know I won't be able to rest until he's brought to justice. He killed my father, not to mention all those women. I can still see the fire burning in Rivka's eyes when we talk about him. She's in the same boat as I am. There will be no real peace until Ogrodnik is brought to justice."

Rayce said nothing and continued sipping on his beer and looking out towards the river.

Elliot, uncomfortable with the periods of silence, finished the rest of his beer in one long swig and put it on the table with a bump to signal that he was leaving. He reached into his pocket and handed Rayce a piece of paper.

"Give him this number," he said as he handed Rayce a the paper.

## Chapter 13

Rivka drove south on rue Cote de Neige up into the parks and open areas of Mount Royal. She turned left into the Mount Royal Cemetery and slowed down on the narrow, single lane trails that provided access to all corners of the Cemetery. She pulled over to the side of a feeder road that offered an unobstructed view of the small gathering she was looking for. She was initially surprised when she found that Alphie's interment would be at a cemetery so far from his social comfort zone. She concluded that it must have been paid for by the guilt of Alphie's aunt, her client, Marie Bernard. She stayed in the car and watched from a distance, not wanting to intrude where she didn't belong. From her vantage point she could see a small grouping of mourners, no more than a dozen, gathered around an open niche where the urn would be placed and sealed.

She observed none of the usual signs of mourning amongst the gathering. There were no heaving sobs, not even the flash of Kleenex to wipe away the tears of regret. She wondered if the attendees were there to mourn the tragic death of a young man, or to satisfy something within themselves. Rivka thought she recognized a couple of the kids from his group home, but at her distance, couldn't be sure. She saw a girl standing in the back, off to the side as if afraid to violate an unwritten rule for interment attendance. She watched as the girls red hair twisted and flickered in the wind, like a flame fighting to stay alive in the wind. It made her think of Alphies short life, and the gust of wind that finally ended it. She wasn't surprised to see Rebecca Boyle here, she might be the only person present who actually cared about the boy while he was alive.

She watched in silence and speculated that the priest was droning on about the inequalities of life, about how Alphie Leduc was freed from his mortal coil, and was now in a better place. A few readings later, the service ended with a minimum of fuss.

She kept a watch for others who might be also watching from a distance. The idea that the killer might show up seemed farfetched, but she also knew that it is not unheard of. For reasons that Rivka couldn't understand, the derangement in some killers compelled them to observe the fruits of their labor by coming to the interment. She wondered if observing the grief and sorrow filled some kind of void inside the killer.

She didn't see anyone who might fit that behavior; she also didn't see any police watching who might have the same idea as her. She didn't expect to see the police, it confirmed that Alphie's murder held no rank within the Montréal Police investigative unit.

As the sparse gathering dispersed she noticed the quality wear of Marie Bernard talking to the priest. This was her cue to leave the car and approach her client.

"Mrs. Bernard, my most sincere condolences. It looked like a lovely ceremony," she lied.

Marie Bernard excused herself from the priest and turned to the investigator. "Thank you Ms. Goldstein. I'm surprised to see you here."

"Leave no stone unturned, as they say. "

"I know it's only been a day but how is the investigation going? Do you have anything to report on? "

"Nothing concrete but we're starting to get a picture of your nephew's killer," said Rivka as she absent-mindedly let her gaze wash over a heap of flowers that surrounded a vase that obviously held Alphie's ashes.

"What have you found out?"

Marie Bernard waited for a response that didn't come.

"Ms. Goldstein? Are you alright?"

Rivka snapped out her reverie and feeling flustered and anxious.

"Sorry. Sorry Mrs. Bernard. Can we discuss this later? I need to be somewhere else," and without waiting for a response she hurried back toward the car.

# Chapter 14

*Friday, August 25th*

"Morning Dr. Maller, it's basket case Goldstein here for her morning head shrink."

"Morning Rivka, there's no need for self-deprecation. You've got a few issues and you need help to get through them. It's nothing to be ashamed of. You need to stay positive; it's part of the healing process."

"Okay, color me positive."

"How have you been sleeping?"

"If I said better, I'd be lying."

"I got the impression that, after our last meeting, you had come to an understanding about the root cause of your issues. Do you still have doubts?"

"No. It's different. I feel different. When I left your office, I felt relieved, as if I'd made a breakthrough. I didn't realize it at the time but there was a constant band squeezing my chest. The afternoon after our last meeting I felt it lift, like someone had loosened the straps of my straight jacket."

"And yet you're still not sleeping," the psychiatrist noticed that Rivka was wringing her hands but said nothing.

"No. I'm agitated, anxious. For whatever reason, I can't keep Ogrodnik out of my brain."

"In our previous meetings I didn't get the sense that you were still anxious about Ogrodnik and the kidnapping."

"And I'd agree with your diagnosis. I haven't thought much about Ogrodnik for months. I really believed I was over him, but for reasons I can't explain, he's all I can think of over the past couple of days."

"So you're still not able to sleep properly but for different reasons. When did that change?"

She thought about it for a moment before deciding on the time. "Elliot and I are investigating the death of a young boy. I first felt anxious at the boys interment. I was fine when I was sitting in the car and then, as I was talking to our client, Marie Bernard, I felt a wave of anxiety sweep over me and I had to leave."

"Talk me through it. Talk me through the conversation with your client."

"The service was over and most of the people had dispersed. I saw Marie talking to the priest I thought I'd check in with her before leaving. We started talking about nothing really, just making small talk. She asked me if we'd made any headway on the case and that's when I felt I needed to get out of there."

"Did she mention anything?"

"No, nothing that comes to mind."

"Perhaps you saw something, or someone."

"There was no one else there aside from us two and the priest. I was just standing there talking, looking at the flowers…" The hand wringing increased visibly and her toes started tapping the floor rapidly.

"Tell me about the flowers."

Rivka's hands were grinding, she was clearly agitated to the point where she looked down and realized what she was doing. She dropped her hands down to the chair arms. "There were a few small bouquets, nice flowers that lay surrounding a central bouquet, a magnificent arrangement of Cyclamens."

"What significance do Cyclamens have for you?"

"They're the national flower of Israel, my mother's favorite. They are, it was…"

She took a deep breath, "Ogrodnik called me *my petite Cyclamen*, "she said quietly. The psychiatrist could see the realization dawning on her.

"Rivka. What you're going through is completely normal. You've spent the last 4 months trying to forget about your ordeal, to get past it. It's inevitable that through the course of your day to day life, things will crop up out of nowhere that will remind you of the very things you're trying to forget."

Rivka could only nod as she processed her thoughts. "I feel so fragile," she said quietly.

"Take it easy on yourself. It's all part of the healing process. Rivka, this might seem like a setback but I think you're on the right track. It's Friday, let's take the weekend off and meet again Tuesday morning."

"Sounds good."

## Chapter 15

"Hello."

"Elliot, Evan Rodriguez here."

"Evan, thanks for your prompt reply."

"Rayce told me you were looking for some help."

"I am. I've been hired to find the murderer of a teenage boy. I have a couple of thin leads but in order to chase them down I need someone who understands electronic security and how to get around it."

"I might be able to help, shall we meet?"

"How about 6:00 tonight at La Cage aux Sports in Old Montréal?"

"The one on St. Paul?"

"Yes."

"I'll see you there."

## Chapter 16

Elliot and Rivka met at the JFK office and drove over to the coroner's office together.

"Did I tell you I went to Alphie's interment yesterday?"

"No. How'd that go?"

"Mostly uneventful. I saw Marie Bernard there, we chatted for a minute. "

Elliot noticed that Rivka had started squirming in her chair and nervously rubbing her hands together but didn't say anything about it. Her anxiety was interrupted when they reached their destination.

"Thanks for seeing us on short notice Jacques."

"Ms. Goldstein. I hope this doesn't take long, I've got a lineup of bodies to wade through by tomorrow," he said nodding toward the window at the back that lead to the refrigeration room.

"Goddam drugs, bad enough they're ruining people's lives but this bloody fentanyl problem is killing them by the boatload. Not a week goes by when I don't get 2 or 3 on my table," the coroner stopped when he realized he was ranting. He looked at the PI's and remembered why they were here.

"It's been a while Goldstein. I hear you are no longer on the Force," he said looking at Rivka.

"That's right, I'm a PI now, and this is my partner, Elliot Forsman."

The coroner nodded in Elliot's direction. "What can I do for you today?"

"We're looking into the murder of a teenager a few weeks back, Alphie Leduc, and I saw your name on the docket. I wonder if we can ask you a few questions."

"You know damn well I'm not allowed to discuss an open case with the public."

"And you know damn well that this case isn't even being worked. That file will never see the light of day again unless someone else opens it. That's what we're trying to do."

"I'm sorry, I can't jeopardize my position by discussing an open case with you."

"Look Jacques, a boy was murdered and nobody looked at it twice. He deserves better than that."

"My hands are tied," he said wanting to end the conversation quickly.

Rivka turned to Elliot with a look of resignation on her face and turned to leave the office.

The coroner had already dismissed them but was still looking at Elliot as if trying to squeeze out a memory. "You wouldn't be Hubert's boy, would you?"

"I am," replied Elliot as he halted his retreat.

"Hubert and I went to med school together, he was a good man. I apologize for not getting to his funeral."

"You're right, he was a good man," Elliot replied. He saw an opening and went for it, "one of the things I admired about him most was that he respected his Hippocratic Oath. He never lost sight of why he became a physician. He never let the system interfere with what his original mandate was, to help people. He wanted to make the world a better place for people to live in."

The investigators turned and advanced toward the exit.

"Perhaps I could answer a few questions," said the coroner before they reached the door. "Lock the door please; I wouldn't want anyone walking in on us."

"Thank you Dr. Bessette. I assure you that our conversation will remain confidential."

"What would you like to know?"

"The report states that Alphie died by a single knife wound to the chest."

"That's correct. As stated in the report, it would have been a heavy hunting blade, approximately 1.5 inches wide and eight inches long with the top of the blade serrated like a saw blade. Knives like this are common and can be found in any hunting or army surplus store."

"And the only other mark on the body was some bruising on the right hand side of the boy's neck."

"That is correct."

"To what do you attribute the bruising?"

"Also stated in the report, the bruising is consistent with the theory that the murderer held the boy's neck with his left hand and plunged the blade into the boy's lower chest with his right hand. It penetrated between the 5th and 6th rib, ran through the upper angle, running through the lower lingula and pierced the left ventricle."

"So death would have been immediate?"

"Not necessarily. I didn't write this into the report as it's conjecture and not fact, but I believe the knife was inserted slowly, with deliberation."

"And what makes you think that?"

"Remember the serration I mentioned on the top of the blade. If the knife was plunged in aggressively, the tissue and flesh would have been shredded, especially as the blade was pulled from the wound. In this case the flesh on the top of the blade was mostly intact, as if the blade had been inserted and retracted with care."

"Do you think that has any bearing on the case?"

"It might give you a bit of insight into the killer. This was not a violent, hostile act. It was done slowly, with precision."

"He enjoyed it," stated Elliot.

"Without a doubt," the coroner said nodding his head, "this was personal for him. Let me demonstrate how it appears to have been done," he said as he positioned Rivka in front of himself.

Elliot thought the coroner was relieved to be able to tell his story. He acted grateful that someone was taking an interest in the life of a boy nobody else cared about.

"The killer held the victim by the neck with his left hand like this," he said demonstrating the positions. "The boy was small and slight, so the killer's hand had a good hold on the neck, and the knife would have been inserted from below at an upward angle like so," as he mimicked the angle and direction of the knife. "The flow of blood on the boy's clothing tells us that the act was committed while they were both standing up and only after the knife had been withdrawn was he lowered to the ground, again, with care, as there were no abrasions on the boy's elbows or head that would indicate a collapsing body."

"So the killer was looking into the boy's face as his life slipped away. Looking into the face of death, as they say."

"Precisely."

Elliot was lost in thought for a moment while they digested the coroner's words.

"Have you seen this MO before?"

"No, not like this. We get stabbing victims all the time but none like this one. None that I remember that felt this personal."

"Would you say that the murderer acted alone?"

"Almost certainly not. The killer would have needed at least one other person to hold the boy. A slight as he was, the human body is capable of amazing feats of strength when in peril."

"You've been extremely helpful Dr. Bessette," said Elliot as they made their way to the exit.

"Many corpses pass through my lab," the coroner said to no one in particular. "Over time, they've lost their humanity with me. They're no longer people, they're just bodies," Rivka wasn't sure if he was talking to her and Elliot, or to himself.

\* \* \* \* \* \* \* \* \* \*

"Did I tell you I think I found our lawyer Anderson?" Rivka said as they drove back from the coroners.

"That didn't take long."

"No. There are only 2 lawyers named Anderson in the Montréal area. One of them has been in Europe for the past couple of months so I scratched him off the list. The only other lawyer, Joel Anderson, works at Smithson in the west end. By default he's our guy."

"Excellent. Send me his coordinates and I'll pay him a visit. What did you think of the coroner's theory?" he asked.

"It was interesting. It was interesting that his theory wasn't followed up on. It tells me how little effort the department actually wanted to put into the investigation."

"I agree. It also gets me wondering if this guy has killed before. If it did go down like Bessette said, I'd be surprised if this was his first."

"Bessette said he'd never seen this MO before."

"I don't mean the exact MO. I'm wondering how many unsolved murders there have been where the act was performed with the same care and precision. Where the murderer literally watched as the victim's life slipped away."

"I can ask Stella to help."

"Stella? I know she's sent us case files a couple of times in the past but why would she jeopardize her job for us?"

"For me, you mean. Stella and I have a history. We went to university together. That's where we both decided to go into Law Enforcement. When the police hired us, I started out as a constable. I wanted to

*'Serve and Protect'.* Stella didn't care to walk the beat or carry a gun, so she went directly into the research branch of detection. Her job is to do research for other detectives who need her specialized skills."

"What skills are they?"

"Police staff have access to many of their own databases that capture data on the criminal elements in society, they also have access to other Law Enforcement databases, the RCMP, Interpol, and FBI to name a few. Stella understands where information exists and more importantly, how to use it."

"I get that, but it still doesn't explain why she would risk her job by passing classified information out to a civilian."

"Firstly, she doesn't consider helping me much of a risk. The nature of her job dictates that her research is all over the map, so anyone looking at her research history wouldn't see anything unusual. Stella also knows that the process of solving crime in a big city is not perfect. The police have to focus on high profile cases, it's a perception thing. If the public perceives that the police are good at what they do, they are less inclined to break the law when the opportunity presents itself. It's a preventative measure that works well. Unfortunately, it also means that many lower profile cases, like Alphie Leduc's, aren't investigated fully. It's a numbers game, there simply aren't enough law enforcement professionals to investigate and solve every crime. Stella, being the idealist that she is, sees an opportunity to make a dent in the crimes that don't merit a full investigation by feeding me classified information. And she knows the info she sends me will be used for all the right reasons."

"Makes sense, so you think she can help us?"

"It'll take a bit of work but I think I can entice her to come over to my place with the promise of fermented juice of the grape. We can execute the searches from my computer using her remote access. What do you want me to use for search parameters?"

"Go back five years, Montréal area, looking for any unsolved murders where there were no witnesses, and no known motive, and a personal slant to the murder."

"Okay, should we narrow it down by age or sex?"

"No. We have no idea what his motivations are so keep it open. Any age, any sex."

"Ok. It might take a couple of days," she said as Elliot dropped her off at her west end home.

## Chapter 17

Rivka heard the doorbell chime and checked the time. She cursed under her breath as she quickly straightened her hair and grabbed the towel she had ready for the upcoming massage. She wondered how she could have lost track of time when she had been looking so forward to the next rub down. She noticed a jacket hanging in the vestibule as she went to answer the door and quickly concluded that Lydia left it there the day before.

"It's me again. I'm here to make your life miserable," said Lydia as she was let in.

"My partner tells me that if I'm not miserable, I'm not happy," answered Rivka.

"Partner?"

"Business partner."

"Oh. You live alone?"

"Yeah. I'm thinking about getting a dog, I just haven't pulled the trigger yet."

"I have a dog, it's a Shih Tzu so I can carry it around under my arm and it's easy to find a sitter," she said as she flipped open her wallet to show a photo of herself with her dog tucked under her arm.

"He's a cutie. I'd prefer to get something bigger, like a Lab, or a Shepherd," Rivka replied with a sudden feeling of anxiety she couldn't account for.

"Labs are nice; I wish I could get one, but a dog that size doesn't fit into my routine. So, no man in your life?" Rivka noticed that Lydia tried to sneak the question into the conversation casually.

"No."

"Bad experience?" Lydia probed.

"No. Just didn't work for me, you know."

"Yeah, I know what you mean," she said following Rivka into the back bedroom where the table could be set up. Lydia started unfolding the table and noticed a photo on the shelf of Rivka and another woman in full hiking gear. The photo was taken from the trail ahead and above them so that both women were looking up at the photographer. In the background was a panoramic view of the Mont Tremblant village at the bottom of the steep trail. They were laughing at something as if the photographer had just told a joke. Lydia noticed the look of pure and natural joy on their faces. The way they held on to each other in their fit of laughter looked like much more than friendship.

"What an awesome photo."

"Thanks. I love that picture. Tremblant is so beautiful in the fall."

"I agree. Is that your sister?"

"No," she laughed pretending to be offended. "That's my friend Angela."

"It looks like you two are close."

"Yeah. We are, or we were. I don't see her much these days," Rivka said. Her smile faded as if saying it aloud made it more true.

"What about you?" Rivka asked changing the subject. "Are you into training, it looks like you take good care of yourself," Rivka asked as Lydia was wrestling with the table.

"My training is mostly vanity. I like the way I look and feel when I work out. I don't compete in anything."

"Whatever you're doing you're doing a great job."

"Thanks for noticing," Lydia smiled.

"So, who massages you?" Rivka asked as she sat on the edge of the massage table and swung her legs up.

"Nobody. Masseuses are like the shoemaker's children. All give and no take."

"Maybe you can show me the basics and I'll return the favor," she said nonchalantly as she flipped over to lay face down.

Lydia folded back Rivka's towel to uncover the superb musculature of her backside. "Okay. What we're working on today will cover some of the basics so I'll talk you through it. I'll start with the big muscles in the lower body. Here we have the glutes that control pelvic stabilization," she said as she put her hands on Rivka's hips.

"These are part of your problem. On the outside of the hips are the gluteus minimus and medius," she said as she put her hands on the outside of Rivka's hips and pressed in firmly which elicited a muttered lament.

"The Gluteus Maximus are the large muscles here," she said as placed each hand near the bottom of her buttocks, pressed her thumbs down between her legs, and kept them in place for a moment longer than needed.

"The glutes, along with the hamstrings, are the engines of your lower body," she said as she ran her hands from the buttocks to the area just above Rivka's knee.

"All the muscles that run from the top of the knee up into the buttocks and hip area, are considered your hamstrings," she said as she ran her hands back up Rivka's thighs until her hands were once again gripping the buttocks. Lydia couldn't help notice that Rivka shuddered as goose bumps rose on her legs and back. "These are the muscle groups we'll be focusing on in today's session."

* * * * * * * * * *

"That was magnificent Lydia."

"Thanks. I'll let you in on a bit of a secret. A great massage is a wonderful thing, but giving a great massage is not without its rewards, especially on a body like yours."

"What are you doing the rest of afternoon? I had ambitious plans to sit in the shade of that maple tree in the back and empty a bottle of Pinot. Feel free to join me."

"I might take you up on that if you promise to finish the story about your leg."

"It's a deal, stow your gear and I'll meet you in the back."

## Chapter 18

Elliot checked the time and saw that his meeting with Dr. Maller would need to be brief if he wanted to get to his scheduled supper with Evan Hernandez. He rushed from the JFK office, east along Sherbrooke to l'Oiseau café. If asked, he would say that he hurried because he didn't want to be late. If he really thought about it, he might come to a different conclusion. He often thought about their first meeting three days ago. Margie Maller intrigued him.

When he entered the café she was already there waiting. Looking cool, calm and collected, not to mention attractive in an understated way.

"Thanks for setting up this meeting Elliot."

"My pleasure Margie."

"Well, how's our favorite PI doing?"

"You really do like to get to the point don't you? No small talk? No 'it's-a-beautiful-day-Elliot', or 'you're-looking-well-today-Elliot'. Just straight to the point."

"I'm sorry. I didn't realize you needed banal flattery or frivolous chitchat before we start."

"Okay, I guess I deserve that," he said with his hands raised in a surrender pose. "She seems to be doing well. It's good to have her back."

"Have you seen any signs of stress or anything that is unusual for her?"

"I have, hence my asking you to meet today. We were debriefing yesterday about our progress on the case and she told me about going to Alphie Leduc's interment. She was clearly agitated but I don't even think she realized she was anxious. She was wringing her hands and her foot was tapping like a Morse code operator.

"We covered that this morning. She's having trouble putting the Ogrodnik case behind her. She'll get through it."

The psychiatrist looked at Elliot without saying anything.

"Go ahead, say it," she finally said after a few moments of looking at Elliot as if she was reading something from his face.

"Say what?"

"Say whatever it is you're thinking about."

Elliot shrugged, "I noticed you're not wearing a wedding ring."

"Is that an example of the astute insight that Rivka talks about?"

"I also noted that you were holding your chin high and jutting out your chest. A sure sign that you are putting yourself on display."

She sat back in her chair with a wry smile, "Two can play that game. When I noticed you glance at my left hand, I knew you were interested. I also know who you are and that you'd be reading my body language, so I answered accordingly."

"Corpus Lingua, well done. Then I wouldn't be out of line asking you out to dinner."

"Not at all, but Elliot, we're both adults with busy lives. Can I suggest we forego the dating phase of this and cut to the chase?"

"What did you have in mind?"

"How about supper, my place, tomorrow night. And if you're inclined, we could also have breakfast."

"I like a gal who plays hard to get," he replied with a chuckle. He looked at her as her head whipped back and she let out a raucous snort of laughter that caused him to join in.

"Our second meeting and you're ready to jump in the sack with me?" he questioned playfully.

"I know how these things play out. Why waste time dancing around being awkward. Let's get it over with and take it from there. "

"Usually it happens the other way around. Two people get to know each other socially before getting physical."

"What can I say, they're all doing it wrong. The concept of courting before consensual sex is a throwback to ancient times when society was ruled by abstinent philosophies, which ultimately stem from religious philosophies. Being a psychiatrist, I understand that true commitment is achieved at an emotional level. The physical connection should not be viewed as a reward for being emotionally compatible, but to facilitate the decision to determine if your mate is an emotional and psychological match."

Elliot nodded at her sage wisdom, "I'm not one to rain on your parade. What type of wine should I bring?"

"Hmm," she thought as she looked at the man across the table. "I like my wine sophisticated but with a rough edge to it. Something pleasing on my palate that sticks to the back of my throat, and of course, with a long, smooth finish."

"Interesting," he laughed as he surveyed the woman across the table from him. "Personally, I like a full bodied, jammy wine. Something that'll leave a spicy taste in my mouth."

"You shrewdster. I'll look forward to jousting with you."

"And yet me, with the only sword among us. But enough on the unending innuendo. Are you going to give me your address?"

She scribbled something on the back of her business card and slid it across the table without actually letting it go.

Elliot reached for the card, took her hand in his and lifted it from the card. "You're not going to psychoanalyze me tomorrow are you?"

"Oh please. One person analyzing another is the foundation of all human interaction. It is done so instinctually that we don't even know we're doing it. Laymen know it by other names like judging someone, or first impressions, but it's all the same. Being a trained psychiatrist just means that I have a name for the behaviors that I observe. So the answer is yes, of course I'll be analyzing you, as you will me."

## Chapter 19

Elliot left the café and hopped on the #147 bus to the corner of St Catherine and St. Laurent. He remembered when, not many years ago, this corner was the domain of winos, hookers, and dealers. Since then the spread of corporate offices and high-end residentials had displaced the undesirables who once occupied this area. It didn't eliminate them, just pushed them farther out from the city core.

Elliot observed that growth and renewal in a large city moved like the ripples on a still pond, and that over the course of a generation, a ripple of renewal would spread outward from the downtown core. The cycle was consistent and predictable. The city infrastructure at the front edge of the ripple would fall into a state of neglect as investment in that area dried up. Developers and owners would not invest money when they knew the older buildings would be gutted, or torn down and replaced. As the housing on the leading edge of the ripple falls into disrepair, rents drop, vacancies climb, and winos, druggies and prostitutes take up occupation. These outcasts on the fringes of society are like surfers trying in vain to catch the next wave. Each ripple of rejuvenation would push them forward, away from the city center, to the next ripple frontage where the housing is neglected, and the cycle would begin again.

Elliot walked south on St. Laurent, past the sex shops, down the hill and through the ornate gate that guarded the boundary of Chinatown. The St. Laurent frontage in Chinatown was crammed with a mix of electronics shops, Asian grocers, and eateries. This was one of the few retail areas in Montréal where the struggle to respect the French language sign laws was non-existent. The signage displayed French verbiage prominently, as per the Québec language law, but the Chinese Hanzi characters beneath carried the real message. The language police never received complaints from slighted French consumers in this part of town.

He continued through Chinatown, past a two-block area that was clearly in the throes of municipal rebuilding, and down into the low-lying streets near the river to the part of the city known as Old Montréal. His route turned east on rue St. Paul and he walked along the narrow cobblestone streets that led into the touristy area frequented by locals and visitors alike looking for a taste of Europe in North America. Old-world architecture lined the streets in this area and provided an atmosphere normally only found in the narrow streets of Paris, London, or Rome. The smell of manure left behind by the many horse drawn calèches emphasized the feeling that one was walking back in time.

Elliot entered the restaurant, went upstairs, and a man sitting by the second floor rail overlooking rue St Paul flagged him to come over. He was surprised at the man's appearance. He wasn't the overfed, living-in-mother's-basement, hacker stereotype often portrayed in Hollywood. The man in front of him had the look and demeanor of a typical businessman. If one discounted the ponytail that spread out over the back of his jacket, this man would look at home in any high-end business luncheon or trade show. The neck of his Larsen button down collar was open and it matched his pair of Chinos and leather Sperry loafers. He hardly looked like a man someone would call upon to dredge up closely guarded secrets out of the corporate world.

Evan stood and offered his hand, "Elliot, good to meet you."

"Likewise, how did you know it was me?"

"Think about who I am and what I did for you earlier in the year. The nature of my business dictates that I be diligent in my research when taking on new clients. I think you can understand the situation I'm in."

"I guess I do."

Elliot flagged down a passing server and ordered a beer. He preferred to test the offerings from local microbreweries but didn't want to sidetrack the conversation to come, so he ordered a beer that every bar in the province would have in stock, Labatt 50, or, as the locals call it, '*Cinqante*'. While he was ordering, Evan had started a texting conversation on his phone and in classic Canadian style, apologized to Elliot stating that he needed to attend to another client and that he'd be finished shortly.

Elliot watched from his seat on the second floor balcony as a steady flow of people drifted along the cobblestone street like cattle in a livestock run. They didn't appear to care where they were going; they were just content to be members of a group, as if they actually belonged to something. Unable to escape from their programmed behaviors, they appeared to find contentment by queuing into a line and walking slowly. Activities that city dwellers have practiced for most of their lives. Occasionally the passage of a horse drawn calèche interrupted the monotony of their movement. The calèche moved through the crowd like an oversized bully in a crowded schoolyard. People in the crowd would re-form into a moving open area as it made its way up the street.

Elliot took a long sip of his icy Cinquante, the bottle already slick with perspiration. It was cold enough to burn the back of his throat when he swallowed and it threatened to give him a freeze headache. He enjoyed the crisp taste and the feeling of the razor-sharp carbonation bubbles scouring the inside of his mouth. Enjoying a cold beer on the patio was a pleasure that Canadians did not take for granted. The fact that it was only possible six months of the year made the times that it was possible, that much sweeter.

It was now about 6:30 and the sun was already low in the western sky. Late August was a bittersweet time of year for Montréalers. It was sweet because the heat of the day still lingered well into the evening but without the cloying humidity. It was bitter because the relative cool they now enjoyed was a harbinger of the season to come. Even though there was another month of nice weather before they donned the shackles of warmer clothing, the cold and dark were not far off. Winter was coming.

Evan, finished with his text-based conversation, put his phone on the table and nodded to his tablemate.

"You don't look like a hacker," Elliot said to break the ice.

"I'll take that as a back handed compliment. What do you know about me and what I do?"

"Rayce told me you're a hacker and that your services can be secured for a price."

"Rayce has a simplistic view of me and my world that isn't entirely accurate. It'd be more accurate to refer to me as an information broker. It's true, I do have knowledge and skill in electronic security and have, on occasion, hacked," he said as he put his hands above the table and indicated quotes using sign language.

"The hackers you watch on television and read about in crime novels are mostly fiction. Gone are the days when a smart guy who can type fast, is able to hack into corporate networks and steal information. Firewalls and security systems are much too secure and the companies operating them are too knowledgeable," he took another sip of wine before continuing.

"There's an entire network of people who have access to confidential data through their everyday jobs, and other people, like me, who make it their business to know those people."

Elliot tilted the beer to his mouth with a nod that said, 'please continue'.

"Let me explain it this way. I know a person who works for the phone company. She is a friend of mine and, in her day job, has access to phone logs. For a small fee, she'll look up information for me. I have a number of friends who have access to different pools of data, motor vehicles department, credit cards, and the like. I also know other information brokers, much like myself, who have their own resources with access to other confidential data. Between myself and the other information brokers in my network, we have access to much of the data that clients, like you, are willing to pay for. Actual hacking is not usually needed."

"Now that you've explained it, it doesn't sound so shady and mysterious."

"Why don't you tell me what you're looking for?"

"My firm has been hired to find the murderer of a teenage boy. We've discovered that the murdered boy met with a lawyer the day before he was killed. We think this meeting is related to his murder, and perhaps the reason he was killed. We also think the murder might be related to a drug trafficking ring, and this could be part of something much bigger than the death of one teenage boy. "

"Okay, I get it. How do you think I can help?"

"I'm going to meet with the lawyer and confront him about his meeting with the boy."

"He's a lawyer. You understand he's not going to give you anything."

"He won't give me anything intentionally," Elliot said making a point. "I have some skill in reading body language; I'll be watching his body movements and facial micro-expressions."

"So you'll know if he's lying, what then?"

"If I know he's lying then your work will mean something. I need you to find out whom he contacts after I meet with him. If my suspicion that the boy's murder is part of something bigger is correct, then I expect the lawyer will contact whomever it is he works for or with."

Elliot watched for some sort of confirmation from Evan that he would accept the job but Evan seemed to be processing as he looked out over the bar railing into the waning daylight.

"I'll need his name and law firm. If you have his cell number and email address I'll take those too."

"Shall we discuss compensation?"

"No need. When it comes from Rayce, I'll work pro bono, so consider this first one a freebie."

"You owe him a favor?"

"More than you know my friend. Do you have a pen? I'm going to give you a secure email address so we can exchange info."

## Chapter 20

*Saturday, August 26th*

Elliot sat in the law office foyer waiting for Joel Anderson to make his way to the front. The lawyer in question came into his view down the hall. The man he watched was on a mission, there was no dawdle in his step; he strode with a purpose towards Elliot wearing a wide smile. The lawyer introduced himself and acknowledged Elliot with enthusiasm as if Elliot had just saved his child's life. His practiced intensity and earnestness was wasted on Elliot.

The lawyer was a handsome man in the classic sense, hair oiled and slicked straight back, like you might see in an old Hollywood film star. His blunted features accentuated a pair of deep-set eyes that seemed to hold Elliot in their gaze.

"You must be Mr. Thompson," said the lawyer.

"That's me," Elliot lied not wanting the lawyer to know his real name.

"Come this way please," said the lawyer as he ushered Elliot into a briefing room that probably cost as much to furnish as Elliot's entire house cost. The oaken wainscoting was polished so deeply that the whorls and grain looked three-dimensional. He surveyed the art on the wall as he made his way to the first available chair and decided that they looked expensive and tasteful, which of course was the intent. The table they sat at was a single slab of wood, two inches thick with natural tree edging including the bark. It further emphasized the law firm's message, that Smithson's was so successful they could afford to spend indecent amounts of money on superficial indulgences. The lawyer took a seat directly across from Elliot and leaned forward in order to command all of his prospective client's attention.

"Your phone call has me intrigued Mr. Thompson. Murder cases always command a lot of attention here at Smithson, but I wonder why you said that *you'd feel a lot better if I was in the courtroom.* I'm quite flattered of course, but we don't know each other so I have to ask, was I recommended by a mutual acquaintance?"

Elliot did not intend to string this conversation out longer than he needed. He ignored the lawyers question and looked into his face, "The murder I'm referring to is that of a young teenager named Alphonse Leduc."

"I don't think I'm familiar with that case," the lawyer replied.

Most people would have said that the lawyer took the statement in stride and was whole-heartedly sincere in his claim about not knowing about the case. Elliot Forsman was not like *most people*. As soon as

Elliot mentioned the name Alphonse Leduc, the lawyers face flicked through two very brief displays of emotion. Elliot first saw the eyebrows lift straight up, a sign of surprise. Contrary to his spoken words, the lawyer recognized the name 'Alphonse Leduc'. The second emotion was more telling. The lawyer's upper eyelids raised, exposing the whites of his eyes, followed by a momentary grimace. All told, the micro expressions took less than a second to flash across his face but time was not an indicator of truth when reading body language. There was no doubt that Elliot had observed a flash of surprise across the lawyers face followed by fear. Elliot had what he came for, his mission now accomplished; he rose to full height and looked down at the lawyer in disgust.

"The reason I'd *feel a lot better if you were in the courtroom* is because I think you are involved in his murder. The only person you'll be defending in the courtroom is yourself, so strap yourself in Anderson, I'm coming for you."

Elliot marched out of the law office without looking back.

# Chapter 21

A couple of hours later Elliot was back in the office and called Evan for an update.

"Evan here."

"Did you see anything after my meeting with Anderson?"

"Not what I expected. I looked into his cell phone and his office phone and he didn't call anyone."

"What about email?"

"Nothing."

"You said you didn't find what you were expecting, what did you find?"

"I tracked his cell phone through my phone company contact using their HLR database that tracks cell phone movement. Shortly after your meeting he drove to an industrial area on St. Patrick street in Ville Émard.

"Do you know the destination?

"I have an approximation, precision on HLR tracking is about 50 yards. I took a look on Google maps and the only building that looks to have any activity is a warehouse business named Labrosse and Sons. I'll send you the address."

"Okay. How long was he there?"

"Less than 15 minutes."

"And then?"

"He drove back to his office downtown."

"Okay, send me the coordinates."

Elliot spent the rest of the morning researching Labrosse and Sons before calling the company. He pondered the latest developments in the case and what his next steps should be.

He could send the names of Anderson and Labrosse to the police and let them pursue it. There was certainly no guarantee that they would act. They'd already determined that this case did not warrant further investigation and he thought it unlikely they'd reconsider their position.

He could investigate them further, maybe with the help of Evan and Stella they could dredge up some incriminating evidence that could be used against them. That also seemed like a long shot. A lawyer would understand evidence and more importantly, how to avoid leaving any. He determined that his next best strategy would be to take the bull by the horns and go see Joseph Labrosse. At a minimum he should be able to determine if Labrosse is dirty.

"Joseph Labrosse please," he asked.

"One moment," answered a gruff voice on the other end of the connection. The fact that there was no receptionist and that he was passed directly to the owner without validation confirmed Elliot's research. Labrosse and Sons was a small industrial operation without need of a polished public presence.

"Joseph Labrosse speaking."

"Mr. Labrosse. Thanks for taking my call. We have never met but I see that you're in the business of buying and selling outmoded telecom equipment."

"I am," the voice on the line answered.

"I've come across a fairly significant supply of Cisco networking equipment. A firm I deal with is closing it's Canadian operations and has given me the opportunity to dispose of the equipment. Telecom is not an area that I usually deal in so I'm looking to get rid of the equipment quickly."

"I might be interested depending on price and product."

"I have the inventory sheet with me, can I drop by your office to have you take a look? I promise you, the prices will be attractive."

"I guess I can take a look. I'm at 4370 St. Patrick in Ville Emard. By the old canal."

"I'll be there shortly."

## Chapter 22

Rivka heard the doorbell and jumped to answer it. She hadn't realize she'd been waiting for Lydia until the door chimed. As she was about to open the door she saw Lydia's jacket still hanging on the hook in the vestibule. She paused for a moment and then, without thinking, reached up and stroked it.

"Come on in," Rivka said as she answered the door. They made their way to the back room chatting more like old school chums than the recent acquaintances that they were.

"I brought you something," Lydia said as she handed Rivka a loosely wrapped package about the size and shape of a large pop bottle.

"Is this the free set of Ginsu knives that comes with every massage?"

"No, it's something you'll appreciate more than that," she said with a chuckle.

Rivka tore off the paper with a minimum of caution to find a potted cactus inside.

"Even your black thumb won't be able to kill that."

"Thank you Lydia," she said as she gave Lydia a hug. Rivka carried the gift to the back room where the massage table would be setup and didn't understand why a feeling of unease had settled somewhere deep inside. She saw a home for the plant on an unused shelf near the floor. A wave of tension rolled through her as she bent down to place the cactus and almost caused her to drop it.

Lydia watched Rivka's spell of clumsiness but said nothing, letting the moment pass instead.

"How did you feel after yesterday's massage?" Lydia finally asked.

"Fine. Why do you ask?"

"Sometimes working those large muscles causes aggravation and they're sore for a couple of days."

"I gotta admit, they are a bit tender, or as you might say, *'they're giving me some discomfort'*."

"Are you okay to do another session today? We could put it off for a day if you want?"

"I'm fine. My shrink tells me I want the pain, and that I feel a need to be punished. That's all psycho-babble; it's not what she thinks. In the world of Ironman training, the motto is *'No pain, no gain'*. So let's get on with it."

"Okay. Yesterday we worked on the large muscles, your glutes, and hammies. We'll do a bit of work on those again today but I'd like to get up into your shoulder area. I notice when you walk, you're tilted slightly to the left. Think of your skeleton as your frame, like the frame of a house. The human

frame is designed to support weight that is stacked
vertically. If your frame isn't vertical, if the angles
aren't quite right, it introduces stress on other areas
of your body. That's what's happening in your case.
You've been favoring your bad leg for months and
that has introduced a misalignment in your frame.
The real issue is your glutes and hammies; we need to
pull those big core muscles back into a vertical stack.
We can also provide some relief for your shoulder
area. Because of the tilt, the muscles up high in your
frame are pulled in ways that aren't natural.

"Stop talking about it and start rubbing me the
right way."

The massage was similar to the previous session.
Rivka lay face down on the massage table, her towel
peeled away to give Lydia full access to her backside.
Lydia started with her gluteus minimus and medius,
massaging her hip area with a long deep kneading
motion. She applied oils, warmed to body
temperature, so that her hands slid smoothly across
Rivka's skin. She moved to Rivka's side so she could
deliver a long kneading motion starting at the
backside, all the way down the back of her
hamstrings.

Rivka let out a soft groan on every kneading
motion and shifted under Lydia's push to find
comfort beneath.

After each shift, Lydia noticed Rivka's legs parted slightly more, and she detected the faint odor female arousal. Subconsciously, Lydia's kneading motions became shorter and quicker.

Rivka moaned deeply in accordance with each stroke. Waves of shiver rolled up through her body, every follicle on her back now swollen and erect.

Lydia was no longer providing commentary on her method. Seeing Rivka in this state was stimulating, there was no place for dialog.

Lydia pulled up on Rivka's hip, "We'll work the thigh muscles now." Rivka was flipped over onto her back without resistance. Lydia took an involuntary intake of breath as she looked down at Rivka's body. Perfectly sculpted, nipples erect, eyes closed and mouth slightly parted. She started a slow massage, working the left thigh from knee to hip, letting her hands press deep into Rivka's muscle as they slid up her leg towards the juncture where Rivka's thighs joined.

Her legs parted further as Lydia's hands moved higher until her hand brushed against the tender spot. Her back arched, she shuddered, and she tried to press her hips down into Lydia's hand. All pretense was lost when she took Lydia's hand, placed it on her bared breast, and pulled her down into a long passionate kiss. Her hand still pressed Lydia's fingers into her breast, squeezing it hard so that Lydia's nails dug into her skin and threatened to draw blood.

"Hurt me," she whispered hoarsely, "please."

\* \* \* \* \* \* \* \* \*

"Do you want to stay the night?" asked Rivka as she repositioned her pillow so she could look into Lydia's face.

"I'd love to, but I can't. You know, the dog, no clothes, just not a good night for me."

"No problem," Rivka replied trying to hide her disappointment.

"There's no reason I can't stick around for supper though," Lydia replied.

"That works," Rivka looked back at her nightstand at the clock and couldn't help but notice her gun on the table unholstered. "It's only 4:00, we've got a couple of hours to kill."

"I could finish the massage we never completed."

"It might end up the same way as the last one."

"Maybe we should just forego the massage part and stay in bed."

"You're reading my mind," she said as she reached out for the masseuse.

# Chapter 23

"Hey boss, three bikers just pulled up in front wearing their colors."

"Who are they?" Rayce asked as he got up from behind the desk.

"Henchmen."

"I'll talk to them," he said as he wiped his hands and tossed the rag on the table. He stepped out into the noonday sun just as a short squat biker dismounted his Harley. Rayce could clearly see the emblem of Hades Henchmen stitched across the back of his leather jacket. The Henchmen logo was a flaming skull with a cobra coming out of its mouth. Above the skull was the gang name 'Hades Henchmen' in a semi-circle. Below was the crew motto *'Live the life or don't live at all'*. He'd seen it many times before but the Henchmen didn't often frequent the roadways away from Montréal. They were based on the Island and usually stayed close to their own turf unless they were on a road trip.

The squat leader removed his helmet to reveal an unblemished skull, still shiny from a recent shave and polish. Hanging beneath a heavily furrowed face was an unkempt beard, ragged and loose, like a growth of lichen clinging to a rock. His biker's garb was comprised of leather and denim, worn and shabby, much like his beard.

His bike was another matter, all chrome and fire, the tank painted in metallic red so deep you could fall into it. Every spoke buffed to a brilliant sheen and the tires, shining black as broken coal.

"You the owner?" said the squat biker as he turned to face Rayce.

"I am," Rayce replied without extending his hand. Rayce saw that the biker had a tattoo on the outside of his shoulder that said "Chunks" in a gothic print style.

"I've got a spotty fuel injector that needs some TLC. I've been misfiring for the last thirty clicks."

"We'd be happy to take a look if you want to leave the bike; we're pretty busy right now."

The biker was about to counter Rayce's argument but Rayce started before he could say anything, "and we don't serve customers with their colors showing. I think you can understand, it puts the business in a bad light."

"We don't take off our colors for anyone my friend," he said as he wiped his head with his right hand as if brushing his non-existent hair back into place.

"Well then you have yourself a good day," Rayce said and turned to go back inside.

"Friend, my tiny comrade will be disappointed if the bike doesn't get fixed today," said Chunks as he nodded to a fellow biker behind him who had already dismounted his bike. The advancing biker was anything but tiny. He was well over six feet tall and half as wide. An unbuttoned leather vest stretched tight across a massive chest. A pair of heavily muscled arms covered with tattooed scenes of skulls, death, and half-naked women hung from the cutoff sleeves.

Rayce stopped his retreat to the bike shop and approached Chunks until he was standing only a couple of feet in front of the squat leader.

"Look pal, I know your play," he said in his gravelly voice. "You're trying to intimidate me into ignoring my business rules and fix your bike ahead of my regular customers. You've already made three mistakes; I'm not your friend, I don't intimidate, and I'm not going to fix your bike, so get back on your hogs, and clear out before I call the police."

"You think the police will be able to protect you," replied Chunks as he brushed his hairless scalp back again.

"The police are for your protection."

"Tiny, we've got a tough guy," said the leader looking at Rayce but beckoning the big man behind him to advance.

Rayce didn't move a muscle and returned the leader's stare until Tiny reached out for him.

Rayce's movements were easy, nothing violent or hurried, as if he'd been practicing this move his entire life. He slapped Tiny's outreaching hand with his left and drove the heel of his right palm hard into the chest of the reaching biker. The strike into the chest of the reaching biker wasn't enough to hurt him, but was enough to knock him off balance. Rayce had timed the strike to perfection. The palm struck the chest exactly in mid stride so that all it took was a nudge from Rayce's foot to the side of the biker's raised ankle that prevented him from regaining his balance. He went down hard into an awkward heap.

As a follow-through to the striking motion, Rayce's hand whipped around and grabbed Chunks by the wrist. The squat biker's first instincts were to react, to stand up for his fallen comrade, but he found his lead arm locked in a hold that surprised him in its unyielding firmness. The leader looked down and saw a massive hand clamped around his lower forearm in a grip so rigid that his arm ached. The hand was connected to a wrist like framing lumber, corded with muscle that coiled up into Rayce's rolled up sleeve.

"You're outgunned here pal. Move on now while you can."

The leader had already decided to move on but was searching for a way not to lose face; Rayce gave it to him by releasing his grip. The leader gestured for Tiny to stand down and that it was time to move on, as if the choice was his.

"Let's go boys. We have what we came for," and once again brushed back his hairless scalp.

Rayce watched as the Harleys rumbled out of the parking lot back the way they came. Rayce had spent the past twenty years working on motorcycles and had reached the point where he could diagnose a misconfigured engine by sound alone. He heard nothing but sweet music coming from the departing Harley.

## Chapter 24

Elliot saw the building half a block away before actually getting there. It was an older warehouse building that was well past its best days. The original brick façade still stood, worn and defiant, but the wooden detailing around the windows and doors was weathered and broken. Between the first and second floor windows in white milk paint directly on the brick, was a barely legible sign that read 'Labrosse & Son.' Based on the age of the building Elliot concluded that Joseph Labrosse was the son, or perhaps the son of the son.

He entered the building through the main doors and proceeded to the service counter to his right.

"Joseph Labrosse?" he said as a question.

The counterperson pointed him to a set of stairs back the way he had come. He took the steps two at a time and was greeted by a sturdy metal door at the top. There was no door window, no buzzer, or instruction of any kind, so he knocked once and entered.

"Joseph Labrosse?" he questioned the man sitting at the only desk in the room.

"You must be the guy with the Telecom gear," he said standing up to greet Elliot with a practiced smile and extended hand.

"Elliot Forsman, pleased to meet you."

Elliot took the hand of the man while silently appraising him. Labrosse was a large man, over six feet tall with a thick, pear shaped body. He had the soft physique of someone who did not exercise and hadn't taken part in any form of physical labor for many years, if ever at all. His hair was receding and it gave one the impression that his face was jutting out in front of his head, as if put on display apart from the rest of his body. His wispy hair receded back and eyebrows were all but non-existent which put even more emphasis on a ruddy face, looking as if it went through regular bouts of sand blasting and was sensitive to the touch.

"Be seated, please. You'll have to excuse the office. I've never been one who indulges in excessive décor. I find I work better in surroundings that reflect my business. I run a working class organization here and, as you can see, my office mirrors that attitude," he said while pointing to a small sitting table near the back of the office.

The office was large, about 20 feet wide and 30 feet long, and had no exterior windows or other doors. The far wall to Elliot's left was lined with windows overlooking what he presumed to be the warehouse section. Aside from the desk that was in the middle of the near wall to his right, the rest of the walls were covered with shelving units filled with boxes, paper, and old electronic equipment. The office also served as a storage area.

"You have a big operation here Mr. Labrosse," he said as he sat down. Elliot really didn't care about the operation, or the size of it, but he knew that if he could get his interviewee talking about things he had a passion for; the verbal momentum would often carry on into the real interview.

"It's not as big as it once was but I manage to pay the bills."

"How is it that you deal in Telecom equipment, this looks more like a manufacturing facility?"

"It was a manufacturing facility but now I export Telecom equipment to developing countries. We've supplied the phone exchange infrastructure for many third world countries. You might say we helped open up many remote locations for growth. Over the past half dozen years, with the proliferation of cell phone technology, countries need less and less communications equipment. What little they do need comes from Asia. They make a better product at a quarter of the cost; we can't compete with that. For the past number of years the business has shrunk to a point where my only telecom business is servicing legacy infrastructure in the Caribbean. In order to make ends meet, I own and operate a number of arcades across the city. It's not really my bailiwick but it gives me the cash flow I need to support the business."

Labrosse looked across the table at Elliot and set his jaw forward, "My grandfather started this business sixty years ago. It was prosperous for many years, we employed seventy-five staff at one point, we were respected, we made a difference in the community," he said as his voice got louder. "Now, now we're just another dying company trying to hang on while the yellow tide comes in, takes our jobs, and robs us of what little self-respect we have left," he said as his lip curled up in a twisted half-smile.

"We can't stop the future Mr. Labrosse," Elliot replied knowing he needed to derail this line of conversation.

"Before we get started, how did you find out that Labrosse and Sons might be able to help you with your gear? We don't have a strong internet presence and we certainly don't market ourselves," Labrosse asked.

"I got your name from Joel Anderson."

Elliot could see Labrosse's wheels turning and then, for the first time saw a wave of comprehension cross his face, as if he just realized something significant.

"Joel Anderson, my lawyer?"

"Yes. He told me about your operation at a function last week," Elliot lied knowing full well that Labrosse would see right through it.

He watched Labrosse's face for tells. Elliot understood that movements like the twitch of an eyebrow or brush of a nose told a story on their own, regardless of the words that were spoken.

Labrosse looked at Elliot for a moment while trying to phrase his response. "Are you some kind of con artist?" he said as he stood, voice rising in intensity as he rose. "You've come to shake me down? Is that it? Who the fuck do you think you are? You come into my goddamn office and have the gall to run a scam on me. "

Labrosse was a big heavy man so when he grabbed Elliot by the back of his jacket and heaved him up, Elliot was launched out of his chair and onto the floor towards the door. Years of martial arts training had not been in vain. He rolled through the toss and up into the Karate ready stance.

The advancing owner did not hesitate, he grabbed for Elliot again with the intent of throwing him out of the office. Instinctively Elliot brushed aside the grabbing hand and landed a straight fist strike to the center of Labrosse's face.

Labrosse's nose exploded into a red mess and he went down to a knee. The motivation that ignited Labrosse was no longer there, the fight now gone from him. He pointed to the door while trying to stem the flow of blood from his nose.

Once in the car Elliot took the time to let his pulse slow down and the rush of adrenaline recede. He thought back to the encounter. On the surface, Labrosse had been taken aback by Elliot's deception, his integrity wounded, his morals offended. His involuntary actions though, told a different story. Immediately after Labrosse realized that Elliot was not who he pretended to be, he noticed Labrosse's head nod slightly. This action is almost always performed when a person comes to an epiphany or a realization has set in. That was immediately followed by a flicker of movement above his eyes, a momentary wrinkling of the forehead between the brows, a sure sign of fear. What did he fear? Did he fear that Elliot was here to expose him for the role he may have played in the murder of a young boy? Aside from the fear, he observed no outward signs of anger before Labrosse went into his tirade. One would normally expect to see tensing in the face along with quick jerky movements of the hands and arms. He saw none of those. He was convinced the entire episode was an act, his anger faked and his actions rehearsed. Labrosse knew that someone had confronted the lawyer regarding Alphie Leduc. When he made the connection between the lawyer's story and the man sitting in front of him, he feigned anger and rage and attacked Elliot.

*Does that make him guilty*? He thought. Not necessarily, but Joseph Labrosse will certainly need further scrutiny.

# Chapter 25

"Riv, what are you doing?" Elliot asked.

"I've had a busy day, including a great supper with a friend, and now I'm researching other possible murders that could have been attributed to Mamelon."

"How goes the research?" Elliot asked.

"Slow going but I'm getting there. What about you?"

"My story will be easier to relate in person. I'm not far from your place, can I stop in for a cup of tea?"

"I'll boil some water."

\* \* \* \* \* \* \* \* \* \* \* \*

Elliot recounted his meetings with Anderson and Labrosse while sipping a steaming cup of Oolong.

"Let me get this straight, you pretended to be someone you are not, lied your way in to see a local business owner, and when he found you out, you broke his nose?"

"Yes, not my finest moment, but he left me no choice," Elliot replied as he settled into his chair. "He acted offended when he realized I wasn't who I pretended to be. He launched into a tirade and tried throwing me out of his office. All that got him was a broken nose and messy floor. It was all a charade; he didn't exhibit any of the normal outward signs of anger. I'm positive it was staged."

"To what end? Doesn't he realize that this puts him at the top of our suspect list?"

"I don't know Riv. We have to assume that Labrosse and Anderson met to discuss my meeting, and the accusations I fired at Anderson, when we met."

"So you're convinced they're both guilty. But guilty of what? Let's review what we have. Alphie was murdered in a very personal manner. It's likely that whoever killed him also planted drugs on him. The word on the street is that the mysterious Mamelon killed him, but nobody even knows if he actually exists, let alone who he is. Alphie supposedly met with the Anderson the day before he was killed. Anderson has something to hide but we don't know if it's related to Alphie's murder. Anderson then contacted Labrosse immediately after you rattled his cage. He also acted as if he has something to hide, but we don't know what it is. Then there's Jack Chalwell. A shady carwash manager who also acts like he's hiding something. Is he connected to Alphie's murder? Does he know Labrosse and Anderson?" she asked.

"All questions and no answers Riv. Here's another one to add to our list. Rebecca Boyle told you that Alphie knew Anderson as a regular customer of the carwash. This begs the question, why would Anderson be a regular at that carwash? He works all the way downtown and he lives in the west end. Why go out to Hochelaga to get your car washed?" Elliot said. They pondered the outstanding questions for a few minutes and then Elliot said, "Let's inject a bit of analysis into those questions."

"Does Mamelon exist? The answer is yes. Someone has been killing people involved in the drug trade for years. Is it one man? Unknown. But for now we'll assume that Mamelon exists and that he killed Alphie."

"Are Anderson or Labrosse the mythical Mamelon? We know Mamelon is connected to the drug trade but have no evidence that either of those men are involved in drugs. The fact that I saw fear in them when they were confronted goes against everything we know about psychopathic killers. Serial killers did not experience fear in the same way as normal people. So I think the answer is probably no, neither Anderson nor Labrosse are Mamelon."

"If neither of them are Mamelon, then what are they afraid of and what are they hiding? Unknown," stated Elliot.

"Does Chalwell know Anderson or Labrosse? Unknown. Now that I've spooked them they'll be very cautious so we can expect that if there is a connection between them, they will not expose it."

"So what are our next steps?" asked Rivka.

"I think we should look into the carwash owner, Chalwell. He wasn't forthcoming when I met with him."

"Let me talk with Stella and see what she has on him. I'd also like to ask Rebecca about Anderson and Labrosse, I still have time to drop by at the senior's residence this evening and see if she's there," she said while drumming her fingers on the table.

Elliot noticed Rivka was more fidgety than usual and decided to ask her about it. "Riv, I noticed you wringing your hands the other day so I brought it up to Dr. Maller. She said you had already talked about it and determined it was because the flowers you saw at Alphies interment reminded you of Ogrodnik. I notice you're fidgety today, are you still stressed out? Is Ogrodnik still haunting you?"

Rivka took a deep breath that shuddered on the way in, and slumped back into her chair. "Elliot, I think I'm losing it, I can't sleep without pills, and every time I turn around something new sets me off again."

"What happened?" Elliot probed.

"Yesterday it was a picture of a Shih Tzu and today it was a goddam cactus. Lydia witnessed my ability to kill any plant known to man and brought me a gift cactus as a joke. The minute I saw it I felt my chest squeeze and I got light headed. It wasn't until later that I realized it reminded me of the huge cactus display Ogrodnik had in his lair. Fucking Ogrodnik is messing with my head and he's not even here," she lamented as she got up to pace the room.

Elliot was worried.

## Chapter 26

"Nice place," Elliot commented upon entering Margie's downtown condo.

"Thanks, I love living here in the center of chaos. The sirens, traffic, busy streets, walking to the corner market to pick up fresh dinner every night. I don't think I'd be able to live in the burbs. I'm a committed city dweller."

"I'm the same. I've lived my entire life in the city and wouldn't dream of living anywhere else."

Margie watched Elliot as he gazed out over the city from her 20th floor condo and seemed to be avoiding direct eye contact with her.

She moved closer so she could share his view. He looked down at her, smiled, but made no attempt to sidle closer.

"My knowledge of the corpus lingua may not be as finely tuned as yours, but I can clearly see that you're on edge."

"It's probably just the case wearing me down."

"You sure it's not something else?"

"Pretty sure."

She looked at him as he returned to gaze out the window and across the city and understood. Expectations were sometimes debilitating. She turned him away from the window pulled him down into a deep, moist kiss.

"The lasagna won't be ready until 9:30. We need to take the edge off."

\* \* \* \* \* \* \* \*

Even in the pale light, he could see the glow from their recent lovemaking on her cheeks. She leaned over him to serve the lasagna and allowed her breast to rub on the back of his shoulder. Elliot smiled and poured the wine. The light coming from a pair of candles on the dining room table wasn't quite enough to illuminate the room, but the shine of the city helped as it came in through the glassed walls facing out toward the evening sky. Daylight had faded an hour ago, but the sky was still transitioning to night and cast a beautiful dark blue background to the west end of Montréal. The soft buttery sounds of an unknown saxophone musician played in the background. He closed his eyes and let the moment soak in. The smell of lasagna in the air, the tartness of wine still lingering on the back of his tongue, and the music floated through the condo like drifting campfire smoke. He forgot all about the case and savored the moment.

He opened his eyes to see Margie looking at him thoughtfully. He raised his eyebrows as a question.

"I have to tell you that I don't usually jump into bed in the first minutes of the first date, but I wanted this evening to be comfortable and fun. When I realized I'd put undo expectations on you with my forward proposition, I thought it best to get the physical thing out of the way so we can enjoy the rest of the night."

"You'll get no complaints from me. Mmm," he hummed as he took a bite of the lasagna.

"You're not just a pretty face and a sharp mind sitting on top of a great body, you can also cook. The lasagna is delicious, and done to perfection."

"Thank you. I would have preferred if it was a bit overdone, just saying."

"What are you trying to tell me?"

"Eat up PI. You'll need your energy later."

They finished their meal and retired to the living room where they drank wine, made small talk, and got to know each other.

"So tell me about the head shrinking business. What makes you want to get out of bed and go into the office every morning?"

"It's probably what you think it is. At a very base level, I spend my days meeting with people who need help. I find it extremely fulfilling. Regular physicians can claim their treatments save lives, the results are palpable and measureable. Psychiatry is different, our successes aren't so tangible. I'd prefer to say that we rescue lives, as opposed to saving them. What about you? Tell me about the case you're working on.""

"Rivka and I are trying to find the murderer of a teenage boy. "

"And how is that going?"

Elliot went on to tell her about Alphie and his aunt who hired him, meeting with Chalwell at the carwash, talking to the kids in the park, what Rebecca told Rivka, what the coroner said about Chalwell, Mamelon and the nature of his killing, Anderson, and Labrosse.

"This is way more interesting than listening to dysfunctional adults with Daddy issues. What's your take on this mysterious Mamelon?"

"You're the psychiatrist, you tell me."

"Let's assume that the whispers are true, that there is someone lurking in the shadows killing anyone who threatens the cocaine business in Montréal. I find the analysis from the coroner interesting. He told you Alphie's murder was performed with precision and care, that it was personal, and that he looked into the face of his victim as death took him. This indicates a psychopathy as opposed to a sociopathy. Only someone with a complete lack of empathy is capable of an act this heinous.

"This type of killing is about control. And, if he's killed as many as he's been credited with, without being caught, we can assume he is very intelligent. The complete lack of empathy, not driven by need but by design, and intelligent, makes for a dangerous combination. Mamelon could be your average Joe, the kind of man that has no outward signs of psychopathy, a chameleon killer. It will be interesting to see if Rivka finds any other killings that fit into this pattern. If so, you're dealing with the most dangerous type of killer. The type of psychopath that walks among us undetected, chooses his victims as part of a larger plan, and executes them in a manner that ensures he won't be caught. The fact that he gets a kick out of watching, that he enjoys it, makes him that much more dangerous. My advice to you is, trust no one, treat everyone as a suspect, and be very careful."

"I think your assessment is spot on. I think we know why Alphie was killed, because he was going to go to the police with his insider knowledge of the cocaine business. We're reasonably sure that Mamelon killed him, but who is Mamelon?"

"Do you think Chalwell could be Mamelon?" she asked.

"I don't know. I've always heard that serial killers are intelligent. I didn't get that sense from meeting with Chalwell. He could be Mamelon but he didn't seem to fit the mold for me."

"I can't argue with that assessment but I need to make a distinction. Most successful serial killers are intelligent. The dumb ones are caught early, so they never become well known," she said as she stretched her arms behind her head.

"All this mental stimulation is starting to work its way down into my body. What do you say we retire to my boudoir to finish this discussion?"

"I was going to tell you about Rivka's anxiety today."

"First things first PI. I always say, play before work."

## Chapter 27

Rivka stopped at the Langlois senior's residence, climbed the walkup to the massive front doors, and pulled one open. Just as before, she was hit with a blast of stale, warm air that had a faint odor of decay in it. She made her way to the edge of the grand room and looked for Rebecca. The red haired girl was nowhere to be seen, but she did see Theresa Chalwell sitting amongst a small gathering of senior's on the far side of the room. She held a book in her right hand and whatever she was reading seemed to be exceptionally entertaining. She would read a passage and immediately the entire group would burst into volley of laughter. Eventually Theresa looked up to notice Rivka at the door. She said something to the gathering and Rebecca emerged from the middle of it. She was sitting amongst them on the floor, out of sight. Rebecca made her way over to Rivka and they moved to the relative quiet of the kitchen.

"Rebecca, sorry to intrude without advance warning but I was on my way home and thought I'd stop in to ask you a question or two."

"No bother at all."

"When we met a few days ago I asked you if you knew a customer named 'Anderson'. We now know he's a lawyer and he has an associate named "Labrosse'," she went on to describe their physical characteristics.

"Does any of that ring a bell for you?"

Rebecca thought for a moment and replied negatively, "No, I'm sorry. I don't think I've ever heard of either of them."

"No problem, just trying to connect some dots."

On the way out she noticed Theresa still reading to the seniors, "I thought you said Theresa was the manager?"

"She is, but she does everything here. Cook, clean and wash when she's not out there lobbying for money or haggling with suppliers."

"It looks like she loves it," Rivka noted and felt a wave of regret pass through her when she said it. She realized that she also loved her job, until she left it.

* * * * * * * * *

Rivka, tired from a long day of heightened emotions and physical exertion, napped lightly on the couch, too tired to make her way to bed. She thought about how lucky she was that Lydia had come into her life. With all the angst that defined her life over the past weeks, Lydia was a gift.

The sound of Mrs. Johnson's dog barking next door got her off the couch to look outside. The dog was a yippy little thing with a piercing bark but it usually only barked when there was something to bark at. She heard Mrs. Johnson scolding the dog and beckoning it to come in.

"Hey, who are you? What are you doing back there?" She heard from the neighbor.

Rivka was jolted from her nap hangover and was alert in an instant. A dozen years of police training kicked in and she jumped off the couch and hit the light switch to turn off the only light in the living area that was on. She grabbed her gun from the counter and cautiously made her way to the windows at the back of the house. The gun, was un-holstered and in her hand when she quietly slid the patio door open and stood outside listening and watching for signs of movement. Because of the bordering golf course, there was no lighting in the back. It was one of the reasons she bought the house. She heard the sounds of Mrs. Johnson coaxing her dog into the house and then the sound of her closing her patio door.

She heard no unusual sounds, no movement, or no flash of clothing or snapping of branches that would indicate there was someone out there. With Ogrodnik already at the forefront of her thoughts, Rivka would take no chances. She knew firsthand how dangerous

Ogrodnik was and would not make the same mistake she made last time they met. At that time, she thought she could take him down without support. She knew he had been in the house and she didn't call for backup. That mistake had almost cost her life. She would not repeat her mistake.

"Emergency Services here," the voice on her cell phone answered after she dialed 911.

"I have an intruder in my back yard. I believe him to be armed and dangerous."

"I'll send a car," the dispatcher answered as she verified Rivka's particulars.

"Are you in immediate danger?"

"Unknown. I am a former police officer, I heard a sound in my backyard, and I'm now standing in the back with my gun in hand."

"Ms. Goldstein, I urge you to step back inside and wait for the police."

"Okay," she lied. She did not intend to hide away while the police were on their way.

"I'm dropping my connection now," said Rivka as she killed the call without giving the 911 administrator a chance to protest.

Rivka walked over to the Johnson's house and knocked on the patio door.

"Mabel. Sorry to bother you but I heard you calling out a possible intruder."

Mrs. Johnson looked down at the gun in Rivka's hand and stepped back. Rivka realized the awkward situation and quickly holstered the weapon.

"Rivka. Yes, I thought I saw something but it was Ripper that set me off. When he starts barking that way I know it's because there's something back there," she said nodding towards the golf course. Usually it's a skunk or raccoon so I don't like to leave him out, but when I opened the door to bring him in, I saw something lurking in back of your house. I can't say if it was man, woman or child but there was definitely somebody out there."

"Which way did he go?"

"Straight out the back to the left of the alder grove."

Rivka waved her flashlight in that direction but knew that whoever it was would be long gone.

"I called the police. They should be here shortly and they'll probably want to talk to you."

"Send them over and I'll tell them exactly what I told you."

"Thanks Mabel."

Rivka went back into the house and waited for the police to show. They came, took her statement, spoke to Mrs. Johnson, and then conducted a thorough search of the property.

It was well past midnight when Rivka got into bed and pretended to sleep.

## Chapter 28

Rayce flipped through the latest copy of '*The MotorCyclist*' to keep up on all the latest in motorcycle trends. He flipped through an article showing off the new breed of three wheeled bikes. Like most hardcore bikers, he did not consider a vehicle that ran on anything other than two wheels, a motorcycle.

His read was interrupted when his attention spontaneously shifted into high alert. He couldn't explain why his internal alarms had fired, and he couldn't say with any certainty that he heard, or noticed anything amiss. He just knew that something had changed in the normalcy of his riverside home. Years of field experience had taught him not to ignore his instincts so he turned off the reading lamp beside him and approached the large window facing out back. He edged up to the side of the bowed window and squinted to see out into the inky blackness.

He thought he saw shapes over by the tree line, no, shapes would be too specific a term for what he saw. It was more like different degrees of black against the darkened recess of the trees. He leaned into the window to gain better perspective and moved his head slowly from side to side in order to give both his direct and peripheral vision a chance to detect whatever might be out there.

The darkness exploded into light from a pair of strobing muzzle flashes. The fracture stars on the outer layer of the bulletproof windows immediately obscured his sight. He rolled off to the side and out of sight of the attackers in the yard. He knew that commercial bulletproof glass would prevent a few rounds from breaking through but it would not stop a deluge from automatics for long. He also knew that the large bay window in the living room that overlooked the backyard provided an unintentional kill zone for his attackers in the back. There were no rooms to either side of the living room to take cover in. His only option was to get to the back of the living area towards the entrance that led to the kitchen and rest of the house beyond. He crawled across the living room floor towards the back of the room and heard bullets zip overhead when the glass gave out.

The rain of bullets stopped for a moment and Rayce heard a voice yell. "Stand back!"

He took the opportunity to leap from his position in the middle of the room to find cover on the other side of the couch at the back of the room. He landed on top of the back of the couch and let his legs and body slide over the couch first so he could catch a glimpse of the activity in the backyard. The trees were lit up like full daylight as a plume of fire reached toward them. He'd seen that type of plume many times during his tours in the Middle East. It was the telltale flare from a shoulder mounted grenade launcher.

The grenade fired high and detonated as it hit the top of the window frame. Rayce did not see the back of the house get ripped out, nor did he see the wall of flame as it filled the room. The shock wave from the blast slammed the couch against the back wall with him in between. The couch may have shielded him from direct flame and blast but did little to stop the shrapnel that ripped through the flimsy fabric at bullet speed. He didn't feel that either as he was already out cold, lying on the floor with the couch on top and his shoulder and his head rammed through a newly ported hole in the wall.

Consciousness came slowly, like trying to stop a bad dream. Except in this case the bad dream was on the waking side of consciousness. Rayce was no stranger to pain, he had endured more than most men ever would, but he'd forgotten the terror that came with it. The fear one experienced when you don't remember where you are or how you got there. The fear when even the tiniest intake of breath sends spikes of pain through your body. It seemed like an eternity before he could piece together enough from his fractured brain to comprehend his situation.

He knew that the disorientation experienced from a grenade blast is enough to incapacitate a person by sheer sensory overload. The thirty seconds it would take to recover from that disorientation were often the difference in being able to protect oneself or become easy prey for a clean-up squad. The attackers would already be trying to gain access to the house to verify the kill. They knew that if the grenade didn't kill their target then the sooner they found him, the less fight he'd have left in him.

Rayce crawled through the entrance into the kitchen and staggered upright where he knew he could not be seen from the outside. He reached underneath the cupboard beside the fridge and found the toggle switch he sought. The resulting throw of the switch killed all power to the house and cast a shroud of darkness across the entire lot, now illuminated only by the flaming house.

He already knew what his play would be and that he needed to act fast to make it work. He did a quick check of his ability to function, everything seemed to be intact, and his hearing was starting to return. He could feel the burn of the shrapnel that found his back and felt the warmth of his own blood as it made its way down his back and into his pants. He couldn't afford to leave a trail of blood where he was going. He opened the basement door, grabbed an old hunting jacket that hung on a hook in the stairwell, put it on, and wrapped it tightly against his body to soak up any blood trail.

He closed the basement door behind him and, as he made his way down the darkened stairs, heard the side door crash in and men shouting muffled instructions. He staggered down the stairs and went past the vault and directly to a basement window on the west side of house. It was an old style basement window that hinged upward from the top. He opened the window and smeared blood on the lower windowsill. As he made his way back toward the vault he saw the frantic sweeping of a flashlight beam leaking into the basement from underneath the door and heard at least three distinct voices, one issuing commands, the others reporting back.

"Kitchen's clear."

More faintly, he heard a voice reporting from the front of the house, "Nothing in the bedrooms."

"Augie, you and Henderson take the basement. We have a minute thirty left."

Those were the last words he heard as he swung the heavy vault door open and entered.

# Chapter 29

*Sunday, August 27th*

"I had a good time last night," Elliot said as he poured a cup of coffee.

"You performed well."

"Well? No better than that?"

"Elliot, when it comes right down to it, it's a biological function. We female types, with our innies, were designed to have an itch in a hard to reach area. You males, with your outies, were designed with a tool that is perfectly suited to scratch that itch. You managed to do what every male in the history of men and women, has done since our evolutionary process developed sex. Taking all that into context, you did well."

"You really know how to woo a man with all your mushy words. Have you ever considered writing Valentine's Day cards?"

She let out an explosive laugh that made Elliot join her, "I might just keep you around for a while Forsman."

"I've got an investigation to get back to and I'm sure you have a whole lineup of heads to shrink."

"It's Sunday. I'll be spending the day heating my outside by the pool and cooling off my inside with a bottle of chilled Pinot. You're more than welcome to join me. "

"Maybe later. I have to stop at home to change clothes and then work on the case."

"Before you go, come over here, and give momma some sugar," she said as she pursed her lips.

## Chapter 30

Elliot, now back at home, was reviewing his notes on the case when he was interrupted by the annoying sound of the doorbell.

"Elliot Forsman?" The woman at the door asked.

"That's me."

"Sign here please to record that you've been served a restraining order to avoid contact with a Joseph Labrosse. The details can be found in the enclosed documents," she said as she handed Elliot an official looking manila envelope along with the signatory paper. He reached out to take the envelope and signed the register without thinking, still stunned that he was being served.

"Would you like me to explain the details of the restraining order found within the envelope?"

"No. I think I can understand them myself."

"We'd also like you to come back to the police station."

"Why would I do that?"

"It's a request from Chief Petit."

"So I'm not under arrest?"

"No."

"Do you know the nature of her request?"

"It's a private matter."

Elliot considered the unusual request for a moment and ultimately let curiosity guide his decision.

"I'll follow you there," he replied not wanting to be stranded downtown without a car.

Elliot arrived at the police headquarters on rue Sainte-Urbaine, an unimpressive building leftover from the 50's when square and functional design was considered the height of modernism and chic-ness. Directly across from the headquarters was the pinnacle of Montréal's artistic sophistication, Place des Arts, a major performing arts center, and the largest cultural and artistic complex in the city. Having the stodgy police headquarters exist so close to the opera house was a square peg. It was as if the city planning brain trust was trying to raise the cultural significance of the HQ building by allowing it to exist close to Place des Arts but in Elliot's mind, it didn't work.

He followed the female officer into the station and entered into a massive foyer. It reminded him of coming here the previous spring when he was summoned to meet the previous chief of police, Simon Doyle. That was before he knew that Doyle was complicit in multiple murders, that he had abused his power and, if it ever became public knowledge, would disgrace the entire department.

They rode up the elevator in silence watching the numbers above the door increment as the elevator climbed. The accompanying officer would not discuss the nature of the meeting, so he didn't bother pursuing it. He followed the officer to an empty room that contained a table and four comfortable looking chairs. The officer left and soon after, a slim and attractive, yet harsh looking, woman entered. Elliot immediately recognized her as Manon Petit, the new chief of Police in Montréal.

Elliot stood to greet her; she took his hand half-heartedly and motioned for him to sit back down while she remained standing. She looked down at the man seated before her as if trying to decide how to start. Elliot waited her out.

"I was promoted to this job three months ago," she started. "The first thing I took ownership of, was a file as thick as a phonebook that detailed everything known about the Ogrodnik case. And I've been burdened with it ever since."

She paced to the window and back without looking at Elliot. "I've been sparring with the mayor and district attorney, not to mention the press, about this file on a weekly basis. You and your actions have caused me no end of grief and I'm not happy."

"I haven't read the file but if it contains my statements from the interview, it's all true."

"It's not what's in the file, it's what's not in the file that concerns me. "

"If you've read the file you'll understand why there can't be full disclosure and, as I told Detective Renault at the time, if you want the entire story, I'll tell it. However, the media and my lawyer will be present. It's your choice."

"Yes, you've managed to tie our hands nicely. I'm not here to coerce a confession out of you Mr. Forsman, I'm here to warn you. You left a trail of a dozen bodies behind in the spring, bodies that we have no official explanation for. I won't let something like this happen again. Death and violence seem to follow you like a bad smell," she paced back and looked out the window. Elliot anticipated she had something else to say and waited in silence.

"I don't know what you're up to Mr. Forsman. I do know that Labrosse could have filed for assault, but he didn't. Perhaps he felt sorry for you. The restraining order might be a godsend for you. It might prevent you from trying to take matters into your own hands. Learn from this Mr. Forsman. I will not tolerate another body count under my watch. If you so much as look at Mr. Labrosse I'll have you locked up," she now stood directly in front of him and looked down on him like a boxer standing over a fallen foe, daring him to get up.

She left the room and the female officer came in to lead Elliot out.

# Chapter 31

Elliot drove from his meeting with the police chief and went straight to the office knowing that Rivka planned on being there.

"Elliot, good timing," she said as he entered the office. "Stella just sent me the fruits of our labor on the possible serial murders. We've pared the list down to 6 names over the past 5 years that fit our profile. There were another dozen that might fit our criteria but I didn't have enough info on them so I left them off the list. I've included the press summaries for the 6 as well as any relevant info we could scrape up out of the case files."

Elliot looked over Rivka's while she scrolled through the list. It was exactly what he was looking for.

*November 13, 2012.*
*Name: Reginald LeBlanc.*
*Address: 1324 rue Sicard, apt 227, Viauville, Montréal*
*White male, 27, found murdered behind shrubs in Parc Champetre. Cause of death, strangulation. The victims' hands were tied behind his back. The murderer was facing the man while he strangled him using his hands. There were no witnesses, motive unknown. Case unsolved.*

*June 2, 2013.*

*Name: Alain Dubois.*

*Address: 15234 Avenue Bourbonniere, Hochelga, Montréal*

*Black male, 39, found beside the rail yards near the docks past the end of Boulevard Pie-IX . Cause of death, loss of blood (from dismemberment). The victim's hands and feet were cut off while he was still alive. There were no witnesses, motive unknown. Case unsolved.*

The rest of the list read the same way;

-       *Throat slit while held standing up, case unsolved.*

-       *Suffocation from see-through plastic bag over his head, case unsolved.*

-       *Drowned. Held underwater in a 10-inch deep trough, case unsolved.*

-       *Tied to light standard and burned alive, case unsolved.*

Each of the 6 murders Rivka had chosen read the same way. Murdered in a personal manner, no witnesses, no motive, unsolved. Elliot didn't have the resources to investigate them further but he knew a guy who might help. He'd send them to Evan.

"You've seen what I've been up to, what have you been doing?" Rivka asked.

"Nothing much. If you discount the restraining order I was served this morning. Did I mention I also met the chief of police this morning. We had a friendly chat. She talked and I listened. Apparently she doesn't think much of my professional conduct."

"Don't leave me hanging partner. I want to hear everything."

They spent the next hour recounting the events of Elliot's morning.

## Chapter 32

Rivka's phone rang while Elliot was re-reading the murder summaries so she wandered off into the next room to talk.

"That was Stella," said Rivka as she re-entered the room.

"And…"

"She says Chalwell has a marker on his file."

"What's that supposed to mean?"

"It means he was considered a person of interest in a closed police investigation. When a police investigation leads to an individual who looks like he's doing something illegal but they can't find proof to support that theory, they put a marker on the file. That way, the next time an officer accesses the file they'll know that there's a story behind the person in question. In this case, Mr. Chalwell was suspected of being a drug dealer. Not just a drug dealer but a high level player in the Montréal drug scene."

"Whoa. How long ago was his file been marked?"

"Almost six years ago."

"Do you have any specifics?"

"It's probably better that we get someone who was there to answer questions. I know the leading investigator who worked the original case, Detective

Vince O'Brien. I worked with him a number of times when I was on the beat and he needed ground support."

"Will he talk to us?"

"I think so. We got along famously back in the day. He'd be nearing retirement now and no cop likes to sign off with a marker active."

\* \* \* \* \* \* \* \*

Rivka phoned the desk of O'Brien's office, got his cell number, and dialed it.

"Hello."

"Vince, it's Goldstein."

"Goldstein. Long time no hear. What's up?"

"I guess you know I'm no longer with the Force. "

"I heard that, it's too bad. Amyot's an ass; you should've taken him to court."

"It's all water under the bridge."

"I also heard you almost got the Stungun killer earlier this year."

"Almost," Rivka answered. The energy in her voice was suddenly gone.

"What can I do for you?"

"My partner and I are working a job and we found a marker in the file of one of your old cases."

"Which file would that be?"

"Jack Chalwell," Rivka heard the expulsion of air over the phone.

"You're fishing in deep waters Goldstein."

"We've been chipping away at the murder of a young boy and two things keep hitting us in the forehead. A carwash on St. Catherine and Descartes, and Jack Chalwell."

The voice on the phone hesitated for a moment before responding, "I'm off shift in 30 minutes. I'll be at the Griff."

# Chapter 33

Elliot was putting away his paperwork, getting ready to leave for the Griffon with Rivka when his cellphone buzzed.

"Elliot, it's Yves."

"Yves Renault, my favorite detective. I hope you're not calling to gloat about the poker game. If you are, get over it. That was a month ago and the first time you won money in a year. You are living proof that even a blind squirrel finds a nut once in a while."

"I'm not calling to gloat, but now that you mention it, I was quite spectacular that night wasn't I?"

"Well, if you're not calling to gloat, what can I do for you?" Elliot asked.

"I'm calling to tell you about an incident last night. It was out of my jurisdiction but an event like this gets a lot of air time around the station."

"What happened?"

"A man was attacked in his house last night by a number of heavily armed and well trained professionals. It looks like he survived the attack but that's just a theory."

"And why do you think that I'd care about that?"

"The man's name was Rayce Nolan."

Elliot went quiet while his mind tried to process this new information. He was trying to understand why Yves Renault would know about his relationship with Rayce. They'd gone to great measures in the spring to keep Rayce off the books.

"Elliot, you still there?"

"Why do you think I would know a Rayce Nolan?" Elliot probed.

"Give me some credit Elliot, I'm an investigator too. I did my homework after that fiasco in the spring."

"Who knows?"

"Who knows about Rayce Nolan? I haven't told anyone if that's what you're asking."

"Tell me about last night."

"The local police received reports of gunfire and explosions just before midnight last night. By the time emergency crews arrived on the scene the house was in shambles and there was nobody there."

"But you said you thought Rayce survived."

"Yes, they found blood inside the house, quite a bit of it, some on the basement window sill, but they didn't find any outside of the house. It's possible the attackers wrapped him up and took him away before the authorities got there but that wouldn't explain why they've seen out-of-towners staking out his house this morning. While the scene was being processed, the locals noticed a truck had passed the house a number of times so they pulled it over. The driver was Canadian ex-military, trained nearby with the VanDoos back in the day. He's an independent contractor, which to me says he's security for hire. If they had bagged Nolan, they wouldn't still be hanging around. All this is speculation of course, we don't even know if Nolan was at home at the time of the attack or if the blood was his. With any luck, forensics will be able to ID him by the blood. Do you know anything about it?"

"No. I'm stunned."

"So this has nothing to do with you?"

"No. I'm as much in the dark as you."

"I'm glad to hear you weren't involved. That's all you need is to get involved in another shit pile, especially when the new Chief has it in for you."

"You heard?" Elliot questioned.

"Heard? I heard it straight from her. She didn't like that I was involved in that shit storm you started in the spring and she really didn't like it when she found out that we're friends. She told me in no uncertain terms that if she ever finds out that I was collaborating with that 'Loose Cannon PI' that I'd be looking for work."

"Okay. Thanks for the heads up Detective Renault."

## Chapter 34

They parked close by and walked across Notre Dame to the Griffon bar. Elliot had passed by the bar many times and never noticed it before. The only signage was the painted image of a winged lion on a wooden board with the name "Griffon" underneath. Years ago, it would have been prominently displayed above the doorway to catch the eyes of drivers and pedestrians alike. Now the sign was barely visible, screwed into the wall beside the door. It told Elliot that the only patrons of this bar would be regulars, or people who came to see those regulars.

They entered and descended the three steps to the floor area as if the class of clientele in the bar were a few steps lower than the class on the street. The bar was a throwback to the days when many neighborhoods in Québec permitted local taverns. The taverns had all since disappeared, replaced by trendy bistros, brasseries, and pubs. Gone, along with the taverns, were the places where a patron was able to sit at a quiet bar and engage in conversation. The Griffon was such a place. The pub was one large room with an enormous bar sitting in the center of the right hand wall. Well-worn wooden tables surrounded the bar on three sides.

The interior of the bar had the look of age to it, from a time when industrial flooring and metal light shades were considered utilitarian, not stylish. At first glance, the establishment was clean and tidy, but it had an odor to it, a mélange of beer, food and a faint smell of something else. The something else was not specifically identifiable but it was an odor that anyone who'd ever been in an old bar would recognize. It was the smell of people over a long period, getting drunk, bleeding, smoking, pissing, and sweating. A smell that can't be washed away. Over the years, each successive coat of paint trapped the odor of the day in. By now, a dozen layers of paint stored the odor history of the bar and the people who frequented it.

An ancient Wurlitzer jukebox in the corner, dark and dusty. Its only purpose now was to look good and remind the patrons of the good old days when beer was cheap and worries were few. The twangy hum of an old country and western song could be heard in the background, the bass and the treble almost non-existent so it sounded like the black and white equivalent of stereo music.

Rivka saw Vince O'Brien exactly where she expected him to be, at the far end of the bar where he could face the entrance, sipping from a brown bottle.

"Vince," she said extending her hand.

"Goldstein, he said, taking her hand and nodded his head toward the two vacant stools beside him.

"This is my partner, Elliot Forsman."

"Forsman," he acknowledged in a ratchetty voice that seemed to catch momentarily on every syllable. He made no attempt to shake hands.

Elliot saw the remnants of a long career of police work and hard drinking in front of him. His hair, now completely white, still stood at attention on top suggesting he was ready, willing, and able. His posture told Elliot a different story. Slumped at the shoulders with head permanently stretched out long and forward, he looked beaten down and trod on. A man who had given up whatever dreams he had as a young man, someone who'd come to terms with the fact that he wasn't going to make a difference in the world.

Elliot noticed the cabinetry and mirror on the wall behind the bar was starting to sag. It had pulled out from the wall at the top that made it lean out a bit. It told Elliot there hadn't been any investment in this bar for many years. Like O'Brien, its best days were behind it, like O'Brien, it was waiting for retirement to tap it on its shoulder and take it to the next place.

"What can I do for you?"

"As I told you on the phone, we're looking for information on Jack Chalwell and the carwash on St. Catherine and Descartes."

"I've been thinking about what you said on the phone and came to the realization I shouldn't have called you down here. I haven't talked to the press or a PI about a case in 30 years as a cop, and I'm not about to start now. Sorry for wasting your time," he turned towards the bar and took a long swig from the bottle of Molson Ex.

Rivka looked at Elliot and raised her eyebrows as a question.

Elliot ignored his dismissal and probed, "What do you know about Mamelon?" He watched for a reaction hoping that he'd pushed the right button.

The detective paused his actions for a moment as if he remembered something from long ago. He raised his hand at the advancing bartender and looped it over the bar in front of them with his finger pointing down. It was the international gesture for '*another beer*'.

"You're chasing a ghost," he finally said. "I should know, I've been chasing that ghost for almost 6 years. I call him a ghost because I don't even know if he exists, let alone killed all those people," he took another long swig of beer that emptied his bottle.

"I'll be cashing in my ticket later this year. I'd hate to think I wasted almost 6 years of my career and never caught the bastard, so I'll tell you what I know, which isn't much," he whistled at the bar tender impatiently who had yet to bring the beer he just gestured for.

"The man you're looking for is the Canadian Pablo Escobar, if he is a man."

"What do you know about him?"

"What do we actually know? We know he controls 90% of the cocaine business in the Montréal area. We know he keeps a stranglehold on his territory and is ruthless when it comes to holding on to it. We know the Underground, the people who work in seedy bars and deal in back alleyways, attribute at least two dozen murders to him. We also know there is no evidence to support that attribution. That's it. That's all we know. Going on 6 years and we've never had more than a sniff of him."

"What's with the name Mamelon?"

"The nipple. It's not a name we gave him. It's what the Underground call him and, for lack of anything better, we use it. Some think that he's called Mamelon because he feeds the city, like a breast of coke. There's another meaning for Mamelon, it's not as common, but it's a French slang term for 'Boss'. It's all just speculation though; we don't know shit. He could be a fucken Leprechaun for all we know."

"You investigated Jack Chalwell, at the carwash. What happened?"

The craggy cop looked at them as if to say *'You shouldn't be allowed to see that file.'*, but shrugged it off. It didn't matter.

"He's a shrewd one, this Chalwell," O'Brien started. "He originally came under our scrutiny about five years ago when a street kid got busted with a few dime bags of coke. The kid, Ryan Bollock, was hauled in, sweated for a few hours and then was offered a deal if he told us what he knows, so he took it. He gave us sketchy details about an operation that used a car wash on the corner of Descartes and St. Catherine as the distribution point for the product. He didn't know specifics but he knew that the product came in on vehicles as they were going through the car wash and eventually made its way to the street dealers, like himself. Well, you can imagine we looked into this Chalwell pretty closely," he took long sip of the fresh bottle of Ex.

"What did you find?"

"He was clean, not a blemish on his record. We started following him, watched who came and went trying to get a picture on how the operation worked and more importantly, how to bust it."

"You had the kid's testimony though."

"No, we didn't. We found Ryan Bollocks' body two days after he talked to us, dumped in a back alley just off Nicolet Street. He had been tortured, his fingernails had been pulled, and his tongue cut off. The coroner said he drowned in his own blood. Later that same night, we found his kid brother in a park off Ontario Street with a baseball bat sized dent in the back of his head. Mamelon was sending a message. "

"Jesus. Message to who?"

"To anyone who was thinking about talking."

"So now you had two dead bodies, no testimony, and a likely suspect. Did you move in on him anyway?"

"You're damn right. We came down on Chalwell and the carwash like a hammer from hell. We tore everything apart, scoured their financials, looked at assets, drug detection, and checked their alibis. We were so far up his ass he couldn't wipe without moving us to the side."

"And…"

"Nothing. We didn't find a goddamn thing. His alibi was tight as a chef's apron. Not surprising, a guy this savvy wouldn't get caught without a story to back him."

"Nothing on the drugs either?"

"Not a thing. We don't expect to catch anyone operating at this level with the product, but we do expect to find trace. We power vacced the office and his home and didn't find even a minute trace of product. Detecting trace is not enough to bust anyone but it does tell us we're looking in the right direction. What usually gets these guys caught is the financials, their spending habits tip us off. We'll find lots of cash, they'll drive nice cars, take expensive vacations. Not Chalwell. He lived within his means. Every dollar in his bank account could easily be accounted for, given his income. We looked into the kids who worked the carwash, again, nothing that came back on Chalwell. We found drugs on some of the kids but just personal use stuff. Hell, these are teenagers live in Hochelaga; of course some of them are going to have drugs on them. "

"What happened next?"

"We watched, and sat on that operation for almost a year. Listened to every phone call, saw who he met with, read his email and saw nothing to indicate he was running an operation. The team was convinced that while a car went through the manual wash cycle one of the kids was picking up product and dropping off payment. We managed to get a mini cam in there for a few weeks before it was discovered; we saw nothing out of the ordinary. If one of the kids was making a swap he could be making millions as a stage magician."

"Maybe you scared them into shutting down the operation?" Elliot said as a question.

"If that was the case there should have been a ripple in the supply, but there wasn't. "

"Is it possible that the kid who got busted was lying the whole time?"

"It's possible. But if you were in there during the interview, you would have sworn he was telling the truth."

"I guess you didn't get anywhere on the murders?"

"No. Our only lead was the carwash story so once that didn't pan out, we had nothing. The murder cases went into the unsolved bin where a lot of our other street murders end up."

Elliot knew all about unsolved murder cases, his mother's still lived in a cold case file buried somewhere in the bowels of Police archives.

"You said you watched him for almost a year. What have you done since then?"

"We've backed off entirely. As I mentioned, he keeps a lot of kids off the street. He's somewhat of a leader in a community where nobody else wants to be. He donates to police charities, organizes community events, he looks out for the homeless.

He's a model citizen. Hell, even his wife's a fuckin saint; she manages an old folks home in a place where the government won't go near. The Force had no appetite to keep this guy under surveillance, he brings too much to the community. Not to mention the pressure the mayor was putting on the chief to wind it down."

Elliot didn't say anything for a moment while they digested the information.

"O'Brien, I know what the facts tell us, but what does your gut tell you? Is this man dirty?"

"I've lain in bed many a night thinking about that. Everything we have says that the initial testimony was bullshit and that Chalwell is clean."

"But…" Elliot led him on.

"But I know he's dirty. In a part of town where the way of life is living on the edge, he's just too bloody clean. Anyone that clean has to be faking it."

"Interesting. Tell me. How would someone run an operation this big, for so long, and not get caught?"

"We only know some of it, the rest is theory. It all starts with the people at the top, they have to be incredibly disciplined. They'd have a business plan that dictates that they're in it for the long haul and they'd execute it as such. The plan would be to make a shit pile of money, put it away somewhere without spending any, where it wouldn't be noticed, and then get out after a set period of time. And," he said emphatically to make a point. "And the operation would have to be completely compartmentalized."

"How would that work?"

"The money and the product are never handled together and they're handled by completely separate teams. The people who pay for product and collect money don't touch the product, and vice versa. They probably don't even know each other except at the very highest levels. The only people who handle both product and money, would be at the street level, the lowest level dealers who work in nickel and dime quantities. They would be foot soldiers and replaceable."

"You said you've busted some street level dealers. Couldn't you get them to give up their contacts and work your way up through the ranks?"

"No. They use an elaborate blind drop scheme so the handoffs never happen in person. This breaks the connection between different levels of dealers and eliminates what is usually the weakest link in the chain. If the guy who gets busted doesn't know who's supplying product to him, he doesn't pose much of a risk to the entire operation. And let's not forget the fact that you-know-who is lurking in the shadows, and everyone knows that if you wanna stay alive, you don't fuck with Mamelon."

"Why don't other dealers use a strategy like this?"

"It's a complex scheme that takes discipline and brains. It takes a lot of discipline not to flaunt your money. Hell, most of the players who get into this business get into it for the sole purpose of being able to flash their cash. It's a status thing for them, respect. Girl on each arm, travel with a posse in a big fuckin car, gold and diamonds. They might as well put up a sign saying 'investigate me'. There are plenty of intelligently run drug operations out there but they don't go to the same lengths as this one. This operation runs like a business on every level. We don't know what happens to the money but it's either being laundered locally or it's being funneled out of the country."

"This doesn't sound like a local operation. What type of people have the resources to run an operation like this?"

"Italians, Japanese, Chinese, Russians. All the big international organized crime mobs have the resources, but we think it's probably a well-backed local group. The big internationals all have their own distinctive MO's and none of them operates like this. As I said, this operation runs like a real business with a real business plan. Whoever put this all together was professionally trained and educated."

"So you aren't assuming that this is Mamelon's operation?"

"We don't know. Maybe he's just the muscle."

Elliot thought for a moment and then asked about his suspects. "In your investigation, did you ever come across a lawyer named Joel Anderson or business owner named Joseph Labrosse?"

O'Brien squinted towards the front window as if trying to see through the murky film of beer and age.

"No. I'm sure I'd remember those names if we came across them. Chalwell doesn't have any friends, he works, and he goes home. Hell, if I had a woman like that I'd go home too. I don't know what she sees in him but I'll tell you this, she didn't marry him for his looks. The only family he has, aside from his wife, are some uncles, aunts, and cousins down in the British Virgin Islands. He was actually born down there and he and his mother moved up here when he was in grade school. He goes down there a couple of times a year. It all looked pretty innocent when he was under investigation."

"Riv, anything else from you?"

"I'm good."

"Thanks O'Brien. You've been extremely helpful."

"If you find anything, let me know."

# Chapter 35

Once back in the office Elliot dialed a number he had committed to memory.

"Evan, we need your skills again."

"Speak my man."

"Before we get into it, did you hear that Rayce was attacked last night?"

"What do you mean, attacked?"

Elliot told him all that Yves Renault had relayed to him about the attack.

"Wow. I have no doubt there are people who want Rayce killed, but wanting it, and doing it, are two separate matters. I helped Rayce set up his perimeter alarms a few years back. There's no way anyone could come within a hundred yards of his house without him knowing about it. Whoever is behind this attack is well informed and highly skilled. Is there anything we can do?"

"I have a plan, it's just a hunch, but I'll know more after tonight."

"Okay. Keep me in the loop, if there's anything I can do let me know."

"Okay, back to the task at hand. Is it possible to hack into the computer over at Chalwell's carwash?"

"Anything's possible. What is it you're looking for?"

"We think the carwash is a front for a large drug distribution network in Montréal. So do the police. The problem is, after an investigation a number of years ago, the police came up empty. The kids working on the manual side of the wash seem to be a likely way to distribute whatever product they have but there has to be a way for Chalwell to communicate to his supplier and distributors. We know they aren't communicating using phones or email. The cops watched Chalwell for months and there was no sign of him meeting anyone to pass on orders and the like. He's been at this for over six years so whatever he's doing, it's working."

"So you want me to poke around on his work station to see if there's anything hinky?"

"Hinky? If hinky means incriminating then yes, find something hinky."

"Ok. Send me the address of the carwash and I'll poke around a bit. I don't suppose you know if there's any security at the carwash?"

"I noticed a sticker advertising the use of an OPUS II alarm system."

"OPUS II? This guy means business. OPUS II is one of the best security systems on the market. Does he keep a lot of valuables in the office?"

"Not unless there's a lucrative aftermarket for used wash rags. I didn't see anything of value when I was there."

"Let me look into it."

"Thanks Evan. One more thing."

"Really? We're taking this pro bono offer a little far aren't we?"

"Hey, you offered."

"Okay, what is it."

"I'm looking at a list of 6 names, each of them a victim of an unsolved murder. They're all different versions of the same story, no witnesses, no motive, and no closure. Because of the personal nature of the murders, I think they could be connected. Do you have anything in your bag of tricks that could find connections between them?"

"Send me the names."

## Chapter 36

Elliot thought about what O'Brien said regarding Chalwell. He knew that O'Brien's investigation didn't find anything on Chalwell's computer but he wondered if the police had a guy like Evan working for them.

Elliot heard his phone chirp as a text message came in, "Meet me tonight at my office. 8:00pm. I have something you'll want to see. Come alone. Joseph Labrosse."

He read the message and shook his head. The man requests a restraining order and now wants to meet? Alone?

He mulled it over before replying.

*He thought of two viable possibilities.*

*Labrosse was guilty, or at least complicit in Alphie's murder. In that case, I could be walking into a trap. Why would he set up a trap? The restraining order has already been issued so he doesn't have to worry about me badgering him anymore. He knows I don't have any evidence; in fact, it's unlikely any evidence even exists, so he has nothing to fear from me. If it is a trap, does he intend to kill me? He must know that even if I come alone I'm going to let others know that he's invited me, so he can't kill me without answering for it.*

*The other possibility is that he is not guilty. In that case, the request could be valid; perhaps he knew something that was of value, something that could point me in the right direction.*

He realized at that time there was a third possibility. *That he was guilty, but he wanted to confess. Maybe the weight of carrying this secret has worn him down. He wanted to unload his baggage.*

Elliot deduced that the only logical move he had was to meet Labrosse that night.

"I'll be there," he texted back.

## Chapter 37

"Lydia, so glad you're here. I've been waiting for you."

Rivka gave her a prolonged hug after Lydia stepped in and put her table down.

"You okay?" Lydia asked as she stepped inside and saw the darkened loops under Rivka's eyes. She looked past Rivka and noticed a cup of tea on the side table and an un-holstered gun beside it.

"I'm sorry," she said shaking her head. "I'm okay... no I'm not. I'm an effing basket case. Look at me. I don't even know what I'm doing," she said as she noticed the gun on the table, she wanted to cry.

Lydia led her into the living room and sat her down in the corner. "I'll make us some tea and then I want to hear what's bothering you."

The women spent a good part of the afternoon talking about Rivka and her challenges.

"Why don't I stay over tonight?"

"Would you? I don't want to sound needy but I'm totally freaked out. I feel like I'm losing it."

"I'd love to. By the look of the bags under your eyes, you didn't sleep much last night. I'll give you a nice relaxing massage. You should be able to nap after that, and while you nap, I'll make us something nice for supper."

"That sounds great, especially seeing how we never finished the last massage."

"I'll set up my table, you go get undressed."

Rivka gave her a long kiss on the lips before making her way to the bedroom.

## Chapter 38

Elliot pulled into client parking at Labrosse & Sons a few minutes before 8:00. As expected, his was the only vehicle parked in the street-front client lot. He saw a couple of cars parked around back but couldn't say which one, if either, would be Labrosse's.

The glass doors on the primary entrance were unlocked and he walked into the foyer area he had been in a few days earlier. He went straight upstairs to Labrosse's office and tried the metal door but it was locked. After knocking a few times he gave up and went downstairs to look around. Finding the warehouse area door also locked, he phoned Labrosse, but there was no answer.

He decided to give him some time so he settled down into a hard foyer chair and thought about the possibilities. He wondered if Labrosse had gotten cold feet, if maybe he had something to say and thought better of it. If that was the case, he might have missed an opportunity, the only opportunity he might ever get to know what happened. After 20 minutes there was nothing more to gain by hanging out at Labrosse's so he headed to Margie's.

* * * * * * * * * *

Elliot spent the next couple of hours at Margie's talking about their lives and eating leftover lasagna. It was a welcome distraction to have someone to talk to and he realized he'd forgotten how comforting it was to eat supper with someone else. As the light in the western sky started to ebb, he excused himself.

"Hope you don't mind if I skip out. I have a hunch about where my friend Rayce might be. I should follow it up, it's the least I can do."

"You do what you need to do PI. I've been looking for an opportunity to soak in a bath for an hour or two. Will you be out all night?"

"Is that an invitation to come back here?"

"There's a key on the counter in the kitchen, take it with you just in case you get an itch you want scratched."


Elliot drove out to the South Shore and timed it so that it would be dark by the time he arrived. If what Yves Renault told him was true, there'd be someone watching the house, so he drove slowly in order to enlist darkness as his ally. He parked his car in the overgrown driveway of an abandoned farm around a bend on the road near Rayce's, and then made his way along the river to his friends broken house. In the springtime, this route would be impassable but by the end of summer, the lower water had exposed a rocky shoulder that afforded him unfettered access along the river.

He turned inland when he got to Rayce's and groped his way towards the house. He knew it would be too dark for any surveillance to see him in the back, so he kept in the shadows as he neared the building. He stooped under the yellow warning tape that surrounded the open backside of Rayce's house and decided to crawl up in through the destroyed house rather than risk being seen on the side of the house trying to get in.

Once inside he felt, rather than saw, his way to the basement stairwell where he finally felt safe enough to turn on his flashlight.

He didn't waste time surveying the house or basement, Rayce was either in the hidden armory, or he wasn't in the house at all. Elliot presumed he was one of the few who knew about the hidden room behind the vault. During the Ogrodnik case the previous spring, Rayce had brought Elliot into the hidden room in order to arm themselves for a battle against a legion of mercenaries.

He pulled hard on the massive vault door to get it moving, stepped inside, and then strained to reverse the vault door momentum in order to close it fully. He knew that the hidden entrance to the armory would only open when the main vault door was fully closed. A giant push on the back wall of the vault started the hidden entrance to swing open.

Elliot stepped inside, "Rayce. It's Elliot."

He swept his flashlight across room exposing the shelving units he'd seen during the Ogrodnik case. The shelves were stocked with handguns, assault rifles, and knives of every type, just as he remembered. It wasn't until he was all the way in, that he saw a pair of legs on the floor behind the open door. He cautiously peeked around the corner behind the door, afraid of what he might find. The blood soaked body of Rayce Nolan lay on the floor, his face smeared with blood, but his eyes were alive and watching. Down by his side he held a handgun aiming up at Elliot.

"Rayce, it's me," he said as he lowered the flashlight to give the injured man a chance to see.

"Forsman," he croaked.

Elliot took one look at him and made the hasty diagnosis that Rayce was badly injured and needed more help that he was able to give him. The first task was to get him out of there.

"Can you walk?" he asked as he bent down to look more closely at his wounds but was unable to locate the source of the bleeding.

"I should be okay. Let's get out of here."

"How bad are the wounds?"

"Nothing a little thread won't cure. Did anyone see you coming in?"

"No. I came in from the river. My car is down at an old farmhouse around the corner."

Rayce nodded.

They managed to negotiate their way back to the car falling only a few times as they stumbled their way through the darkness.

"You need a hospital," Elliot said as he started the car.

"No. No hospital. They'll be watching. There's a private clinic out on the outskirts of Eastman; they know me there. Do you have a phone? "

"Here ya go," Elliot said as he handed Rayce his phone and headed toward the highway 10 south access road.

Rayce dialed a number from memory and listened for an answer. Elliot listened to the one sided conversation.

"Reservations," Rayce said and waited to be transferred.

"This is Rayce Nolan, I'm a client. I need a reservation this evening, full medical with surgeon."

Elliot heard the distant buzz of a voice on the other end of the conversation but couldn't make out the words.

"Yes, it's an emergency," Rayce answered.

"Client number 5018. You have my medical file on site. Do I have to remind you that discretion is vital?"

"No, I thought not."

"30 minutes."

Rayce handed the phone back.

Elliot had been watching Rayce during the conversation. He could see that the blood on his face was probably transference. There were a few scrapes on his forehead and left jaw but they were already scabbed over and didn't look to be serious. It was what he couldn't see that worried him. He could tell from the way Rayce had favored the right side of his back that there was some significant damage under his plaid shirt. The fact that he couldn't sit with the right side of his back touching the seat told him the injuries were still raw and sore. If they hadn't healed over in the 24 hours since the attack, it meant that they were substantial.

Rayce remained silent for most of the drive; Elliot could see him struggling to remain awake and alert. His pallid face was drawn, thinner than he remembered from only a couple of days ago, as if he had aged a decade overnight.

Elliot finally broke the silence, "Do you know who it was?"

"I have theories but, no. I don't know."

"What happened?"

"I thought I heard something out in the back of the house so I doused the lights and when I looked out in the backyard they opened fire. There were two men with automatic weapons and a third with a grenade launcher. They were military trained."

"So you've been holed up in the vault for the past 24 hours waiting for.... me?"

"No. Just waiting. I had water but I knew I'd need medical attention before infection set in. Whoever came after me will be watching. I was going to wait another day, sneak out at night and take my chances."

"No phone?"

"No. It was upstairs."

"Turn here into Eastman and take rue Martin. There's a small sign just past the old railway bridge that says 'Balmoral'. That's our place."

## Chapter 39

"Lie down there, on your stomach," she said shaking her head as she organized some instruments on the tray.

"How long ago did it happen?"

"Last night," he said between gritted teeth as his back stretched in ways that were clearly painful. "About 24 hours ago."

"What's your pain on a one to ten scale?"

"Just cut the shirt off, pull the shrapnel, and sew me up."

"I'll decide what needs to be done. Are you allergic to any antibiotics? "

"No."

"It's going to sting a bit getting the shirt off. It's stuck to the wounds."

He didn't say anything.

The surgeon cut the shirt up the middle of the back and started to peel the shirt from one side, the plaid pattern on the shirt barely visible through the blood soak.

Elliot heard the surgeon's intake of breath before he saw the reason for it. Half of Rayce's back, now exposed, revealed a moonscape of scars, pockmarks, and puckers, plastered across the width of the back and up into the shoulders as far as the shirt would allow to be seen. There wasn't a square inch of skin that wasn't disfigured in some way. The scars were old, they looked like they'd been there for many years, but they looked painful all the same.

"Jesus Christ," Elliot muttered.

The surgeon shook her head as she focused on getting the rest of the shirt off.

There were three obvious areas of concern, two on the upper right shoulder area, now caked with layers of dried blood and swelling. Elliot could see the end points of foreign objects still embedded, poking out of the oozing wounds. The other was on the lower right side, where a spear of wood was visible on both ends of a matching pair of wounds.

"You need a hospital."

"Can you fix me or not?"

"The damage to the underlying tissue is extensive. I can't guarantee you won't come out of this without permanent damage," the surgeon quickly followed that by saying; "you probably don't care though do you?" Elliot also understood that Rayce's entire back and torso were already disfigured beyond salvation.

"Get on with it," Rayce grunted.

At the surgeon's urging, Elliot waited outside the room. After almost an hour later, she came out looking drawn and angry.

"It's done. He's a few pints low and I'll give him some antibiotics but he tells me that once the IV's are finished he needs to get out of here. He didn't tell me why but I understand that this behavior is probably not unusual for a man who lives with those scars. He wants to see you."

Elliot nodded, not knowing what to say and let the surgeon walk away.

Rayce was lying on his left side, obviously cognizant of his right side wounds, with arm extended so as not to crimp the IV line.

"I have a cottage at 53 rue de la Plage on Lac Orford. It's a 10-minute drive from here. Go pick me up some clothes and come back. You'll find the key on top of the doorjamb. By the time you get back I'll be ready to go."

"Okay. Rayce, I need to make one thing perfectly clear."

"What's that?"

"I don't want you to think that every time a bully kicks sand in your face that I'll be here to bail you out."

Rayce body seemed to chug up and down, his mouth open, but no sound was coming out. Elliot initially thought Rayce was having an attack, or an epileptic fit, but it soon became apparent that he was laughing. He'd never seen Rayce laugh before.

\* \* \* \* \* \* \* \* \* \* \*

Elliot got Rayce set up at his cottage and then asked, "you want me to stay?"

"I don't need you, if that's what you're asking."

"No, I suppose you don't. Let me re-ask that question, do you mind if I stay over the night? It's already 3:00am and I don't want to tackle the 2 hour drive back home without a bit of shuteye."

"Suit yourself. The couch is yours and there're blankets in that closet," he said as he pointed to a closet at the far end of the room.

"What's your plan? Aside from getting healthy," Elliot asked.

"I don't have time to get healthy. I'm being hunted."

"You said you thought you knew who it was and then figured out it wasn't them. Are there that many people who want to kill you that you that you can't figure out who it is?"

Rayce stared through the blackened window at nothing in particular without replying. Elliot wondered if he had heard the question, or that he decided he wasn't going to answer.

Rayce got up from his seat at the table with some effort and took a bottle of Jack and a couple of glasses down from the top shelf. He poured out a couple of generous servings and started talking.

"You meet people, you work with them, eat with them, fight by their side, you share your life with them. And sometimes you never really know them until a certain set of circumstances are presented," he said as if talking to no one in particular.

"I had two soldiers in my unit over in Iraq, good guys, good soldiers. They'd lay their lives down for the unit, as we all would.

"They got mixed up with some locals in the drug trade. When I found out they were using, I tried to straighten them out but they were already in too deep," he took a deep swig and Elliot could saw his face contort slightly as the whisky found the back of his throat.

"Their usage made me nervous. You need to know if your comrades have your back. These two had changed and I didn't know if I could trust them anymore. I started watching them and became suspicious when they'd bugger off during recon missions for a couple of hours at a time. I noticed one day that the lug nuts on two of their tires had been recently removed. That's not unusual in that terrain, the mechanics would often replace wheels and tires.

But in this case two of the tires were dust covered from travelling around the desert and the other two were almost clean. I didn't know it at the time but they'd found a way to bring product back to the States. Pure heroin. It didn't take a lot of imagination to understand what they were doing. That night I confronted them. I told them I wouldn't turn them in if they stopped. You never want to see a fellow soldier go through a court martial, especially those that have fought by your side. They agreed to stop and told me they would reach out for help when they got back to the base. At that time, we were on a weeklong sweeping mission. We had a series of Iraqi cave systems mapped out and it was our job to see if they were hideouts, munitions depots, or just caves. The two users, Dan-o and Cropper, along with myself and another grunt, Rainman, went to investigate a cave system on the far side of the mountain. As we neared it on foot, we could tell from the wear on the paths leading to the cave that it was active. We did what we were trained to do, observe and engage," he stopped and took another pull from his glass, now nearly empty.

"The cave turned out to be a way station for travelling Iraqi troops. It was empty when we got their save for a teenage boy. We'd seen this arrangement before. They post a teenage boy or an old man at the cave to clean up and relay messages as troops pass through. I left the boy up top with Dan-o and Cropper to guard and watch for incoming. Rainman and I went down inside to look for intel. We came up an hour later and, against my orders not to harm him, they'd tortured and killed the boy. I got in Dan-o's face and then it all went sideways. Before I knew it, Dan-o had a knife in his hand and we got into a struggle. At the same time, Cropper had pulled his sidearm and shot Rainman. I was wrestling with Dan-o and ended up with a bullet in my back. They finished the job by shivving me in the belly. Rainman was dead and they left me to bleed out in the baking sun," he finished the rest of his drink and looked down into the empty glass.

"You can see I didn't die that day. At least not physically. The next Iraqi troop came through at some point and found me, more dead than alive, alongside the bodies of Rainman and the teenage boy. The boy had been tortured and his chest flayed open from belly button to throat," he filled another glass and topped off Elliot's.

"They brought me in and coaxed me back to life. I was much more valuable alive than dead. I was taken to a larger cave system where hundreds of soldiers came and went, it was an underground central command. They gave me a distinguished place, strapped to an inclined board in the central hub of the cave. I was tortured and brought back from the brink a dozen times. I was their living effigy of the infidel Americans. Every soldier who passed would spit on me, piss on me, punch me or butt their cigarette out on me. I spent 5 weeks hanging on to the brink of life until US soldiers stormed the caves and found me by chance. "

Elliot nodded to himself as he thought about the scars on Rayce's back and understood.

"During my rehab back in the States I fingered Dan-o and Cropper for drug trafficking and murder. They ended up dodging the murder rap on a technicality but were put away for 20 years for their part in the drug trafficking ring. I heard Cropper met his demise a few years into his term."

"And you thought it was Dan-o who attacked you last week?"

"I did at first. I've been looking over my shoulder since he got out three years ago. I always expected to see him show up on my doorstep one day, gun in hand and bent for revenge. I remember the look on his face when he was sentenced. I left the hospital that day just so I could be there. I've seen the look of blood lust and rage on soldiers when lives are at stake. That was the first time I've seen that look on someone outside the theatre of war. He was carrying a hatred for me that day that time wasn't going to diminish. The more I thought about it while lying in the armory, the less I thought it was him. Using a grenade launcher's not his style. He'd plan something much more personal."

"What are you going to do now?"

"Being hunted doesn't work for me. You said the police saw out-of-towners surveilling the roads looking for me. I'm gonna find one of those watchmen and see what he knows," he said as he finished the last of his Jack.

"Will you need a lift anywhere tomorrow?"

"Not needed. I've got a bike in the garage out back," he said as he stood up gingerly from his chair and his lips curled back when he attempted to stand tall. He didn't try to test his sutures again as he made his way to the bedroom, hunched over and canted to the side from the waist up.

# Chapter 40

*Monday, August 28th*

Elliot woke up to the sound of running water in the kitchen.

"I don't have much in the way of breakfast but there's plenty of coffee," Rayce said without looking up.

"Coffee's fine. What's your plan?"

"I'll be looking for my attackers today, until I find them, I'll be living here."

"If you don't mind I'll take this coffee to go. I should get back to town, I've got a case to solve."

Elliot didn't wait for a response. He picked up his cup and left the cottage without any further discussion.

There were no thanks offered from Rayce, nor any expected.

## Chapter 41

"Thanks for staying over last night Lyd, I really appreciate it"

"Thanks for having me, no pun intended."

"What's on your agenda today?"

"I've got a couple of client calls. Same old grind, as they say."

"Will you be coming back this aft?"

"No promises. I have a shitload to catch up on. I'll let you know though."

"If you're going home you could bring a change of clothes and stay over, just saying," she tried saying it casually but it came out rushed and needy. She found herself hanging on for Lydia's answer that never came.

"Help yourself to anything in the fridge and you'll find coffee and tea in the far cupboard. I'm going to jump in the shower," again she tried to put on a brave face and appear casual, but didn't succeed.

"Okay. I'll grab a coffee and be on my way. I need to get home and change so I might not be here when you get out," Lydia said.

Rivka took the opportunity to give her another prolonged hug and headed for the shower.

Lydia was busy making coffee when the doorbell rang. She peeked through the curtain in the front hall. A young woman was standing on the step that she immediately recognized as Rivka's friend in the Mont Tremblant photograph. She stripped off her top, down to the bra, and mussed up her hair.

"Can I help you?" she asked after opening the door.

The woman stepped back as if slapped, checked the address on the wall beside the door, and then looked back again at the half-dressed woman who opened the door. "Rivka, is Rivka here?" she stammered.

"She's busy right now but I'll take a message for you," replied Lydia with a bright smile.

"No, it's alright, I'll come back later. Tell her Angela…, no, I'll just come back later," she said clearly flustered.

Lydia closed the door and smiled as she put her shirt back on.

"Who was it?" Rivka yelled above the drum of the shower.

"Jehovah's, I sent them away," she yelled back.

Lydia pulled out her phone and texted a message. "She's ready."

# Chapter 42

Elliot brewed a real coffee when he got home. Rayce's instant coffee had filled a void in his gut but did little to satisfy his craving for a strong brew. As he carried his steaming cup into the den, he stopped in the entranceway. The door to his liquor cabinet was ajar. He remembered precisely when he last opened it, three nights ago when he poured himself a bourbon. He also remembered quite clearly struggling with the latch before he was able to close the door properly. With a quick check of the main floor, he found a number of items had been repositioned. Repositioned items would not raise an eyebrow in a normal family household, but in a house inhabited by a single person, they were obvious. The decisive factor was that cookie jar on the kitchen counter; the jar that always held a small amount of emergency cash was empty. Someone had been in the house. He did not notice the open liquor cabinet when he got home after meeting Evan two nights ago so it must have occurred sometime yesterday. His investigation was interrupted by an electronic rendition of the Mission Impossible theme coming from his phone.

"Hello."

"Elliot, Rivka here, I just got off the phone with Stella at the station. Labrosse was found murdered in his warehouse over in the Pointe."

"When did that happen?"

"The police got a call from one of the staff who arrived at work this morning. Elliot, they think you're good for it. The chief inspector is making a case to the Crown Attorney as we speak."

"That's bullshit. I didn't do it."

"They say you were there last night Elliot. They have you on security cam walking into the building at 8:00 and leaving shortly afterwards, at about the same time they think Labrosse was killed."

Elliot thought about those points for second "Damn-it. I've been played. Is there a warrant yet?"

"No, but it won't be long before it hits the street. Right now you're a person of interest. They'll want to talk to you even without a warrant. You better call your lawyer Elliot. This sounds serious."

"What else do you know about the murder?"

"They found him on the warehouse floor with two holes in the back of his head. Shot from close range."

"Not in his office?"

"No, it was on the main floor. They think it happened early evening, sometime between 7:00 and 9:00pm. The warehouse supervisor found him when he opened up in the morning."

"Are there any other theories?"

"They're still processing the scene but the only theory right now, is that you did it. They have you on the building cam entering the building just before 8:00 and exiting about 20 minutes later."

"He texted me yesterday. He set up a meet for 8:00 so I went to the office. When I got there, his office was locked, so I stayed for a while and then left. I thought he stood me up, but I guess he was already dead."

"The bullets were nine millimeter. They know you have a nine mil Glock registered."

"Lots of guns use 9 mil bullets. Besides, my Glock is stored upstairs in my closet," Elliot froze for a second as a possible scenario played through his mind. He thought about the break-in he had just discovered. He felt a chill slide up his backbone. He didn't believe in coincidences.

"I have to give this some thought Riv. If the cops come looking for me, tell them I've gone fishing up north for a week and I'm incommunicado."

"Elliot, are you sure you want to run? That'll make it look like you're really guilty."

"I can't clear myself if I'm in custody. See if you can find out what the Crown is asking for."

"Is there anything I should be doing?"

"There will be, I just don't know what yet. They'll likely be stopping by your place to look for me so I'll have to find a place to lay low until I figure this out. I'll call you later."

Elliot hung up and went upstairs to the bedroom closet. The weight of the box answered his question before he opened it. His Glock was gone.

He packed a bag for a few days along with his laptop, and locked up the house. Driving his own car wasn't going to work, so he picked up the keys to Jake's car and headed down the laneway to Mr. Forget's.

Francois Forget was no longer able to drive, so Elliot rented his laneway parking spot to store Jake's car while he was away at school. The Volvo fired up on the second try and he was gone.

Chapter 43

Elliot drove back toward downtown and veered north onto Queen Mary Avenue, went almost to the top, and then turned left onto Chemin Cote Des Neiges. He remembered there used to be a string of internet cafés on downslope side of Cote Des Neige that serviced the students of Université de Montréal. That was his destination. He slowed as he approached the University area and pulled into a parking lot that advertised spaces still available. His first stop was at a trendy looking place on the west side of the street named Ricardo's. Ricardo's didn't offer computers for public use but they did advertise free wifi for their customers. He spied a lonely table off to the side, claimed it by putting his laptop on it, and went to the front to get a coffee, all the while keeping an eye on his neglected laptop.

Before logging into his computer, he grabbed an abandoned newspaper from the table next to his and took a few minutes to unwind, and enjoy his coffee with a side of newspaper. He flipped through the pages and found a background story on the fentanyl crisis on the next to last page of the first section. He read that over the past three months more than a hundred deaths in the Montréal area were attributed to fentanyl overdoses. The story went on to explain the reasons behind the fentanyl crises.

*In an effort to maximize profits, the dealers were cutting pure cocaine with a filler compound and then to compensate for the less potent cocaine, they added fentanyl. Fentanyl was a synthetic pain relief drug that was both inexpensive, and potent. This also gave the diluted cocaine a kick that pure coke didn't have, and made it more addictive. It was a win-win for the coke dealers, more profit, and a captive clientele who were unable to free themselves from the call of the drug.*

*Cutting expensive drugs with less expensive products has been standard practice for drug dealers since the dawn of recreational drug usage. In this case, the consequences were frightful. Because of the flawed process of mixing in the fentanyl, a perfect blend was not possible. If too high a percentage of fentanyl were present in the cocaine, the results would be fatal. There was no way for users to know if the batch of coke they were about to use was lethal. Coke users were playing a game of Russian roulette and didn't even know it.*

Underneath that article was a related article about the gangs dealing drugs at the street level in North Montréal. Elliot read it with interest as he did with all gang related information. He'd been monitoring gang activity in Montréal for years and kept an extensive file on the active gangs in the area. His information came from news sources, his police connections, as well as a few inside sources that he had cultivated over the years. His sources weren't members of any gang, they were people who lived on the periphery of gang life and had their own personal reasons for wanting to talk about it. He snipped the article out and put it in his wallet for later addition to his files. His morning news and coffee ritual was interrupted by the Mission Impossible theme ringing out from his cellphone.

"Elliot here."

"Elliot, it's Sammy, your favorite burger flipper."

"What's up Sammy?"

"A couple of badges just came into my diner looking for you and walking like they had shit in their pants."

"I'm not sure what that means but go on, tell me more."

"An unmarked car pulled up and parked in the tow away zone right in front and I heard them banging on the JFK door upstairs. When nobody answered, they came in here asking about you. I told them I'm not your fuckin baby sitter and if they're not going to buy anything then get out and stop scaring away real customers."

"That should put you in their good books."

"Just thought I'd give you a heads up. They said you're wanted for murder."

"Did they show you a warrant?"

"The guy with the most shit in his pants waved a paper while he was talking but I didn't ask to see it. "

"Thanks for the heads up Sammy."

"Is it true?"

"Are you asking if I murdered someone?"

"Hey, I don't care if you offed someone if he deserved it, you know what I mean. I'm just wondering."

"Sammy, I didn't kill anyone. One of my suspects on the case I'm working was killed in order to put the blame on me. I've been framed."

"Those fucken cowards, is there anything I can do Elliot?"

"Nothing that I can think of Sammy. Thanks for the heads up."

Elliot looked down at the phone in his hand and cursed silently. If Sammy could call him then the police could track him. He knew that the police were obliged to respect privacy laws when it came to accessing confidential information without consent. He also knew that anyone in law enforcement would use whatever tools he or she had at his or her disposal when it came to making a collar, especially when murder was involved.

Before getting rid of his phone he made a quick call to Rivka.

"Riv, I hear the warrant's been issued."

"I just heard, you are now a wanted man," Rivka replied.

"What do they have on me?"

"They still have you on video, they've confirmed your prints are all over the place, and they found a gun in a sewer down the street. Testing still to confirm if it's yours and was used in the murder."

"Damn. Evan will be sending me some info on what he found in Chalwell's computer. I hope there's something that might lead us to Mamelon or the drug operation. They'll be actively looking for me now I'm going to get rid of this phone. "

"Where are you?"

"I'm at a cafe using their wifi. This will be my life until I can find the evidence to help my situation."

"Where are you going to stay tonight?"

"I'll think of something. It's probably better that you don't know. You won't have to perjure yourself if the police ask."

"Okay. Keep me in the loop."

He powered down his phone and spent the next couple of hours buying an unregistered phone and finding another café to set up shop in.

## Chapter 44

The first things Elliot did from his café based office was call Rivka and give her his new phone number and then call Margie to explain his situation. His conversation with Margie was brief and he kept it light by downplaying his situation. He didn't want to alarm her and he also wanted to see if he could stay over at her place if the situation demanded it. He could.

Elliot then called Evan to tell him his new number and to see if he'd made headway on Chalwell's computer.

"Evan, Elliot here."

"You have a new number I see."

"Yes, this whole case just got real hot. Someone set me up for murder and the cops are looking for me."

Elliot heard a low whistle through the phone. "Well, I do have info for you but I'm not sure it's going to get you through this jam."

"What do you have?" Elliot asked.

"Okay, let's start with the 6 murders. First let me explain my method so you can understand what it means."

"I'm listening"

"You've heard of Karinthy's theory of the six degrees of separation."

"You mean it wasn't Kevin Bacon?"

"Not quite," he laughed. "As you probably know, he theorized that any person on the planet can be connected to any other person on the planet through a chain of acquaintances with no more than five intermediaries."

"I've heard of it."

"If you just take a look at the numbers, the six degrees of separation idea seems plausible. Assuming everyone knows at least 44 people, and that each of those people knows an entirely new 44 people, and so on, the math shows that in just six steps, 44 to the power of 6, or 7.26 billion people would be connected to each other - more than are alive on Earth today."

"But it's still just a theory."

"It is, but the internet has partially enabled the theory. I have an app that will take any name I feed into it, and search for references to that name in pre-selected websites. It'll crawl through social media sites like Facebook, Instagram, YouTube, and Twitter and grab whatever data available on that person. It also looks at professional sites, dating sites, government sites, and even financial sites that track spending habits. There are hundreds of internet sites that keep, and offer for free, information on people and their habits.

"My app gathers information from those hundreds of sites and organizes it into a useable format. Two of the primary pieces of data it gathers are; people connections, friends, family, contacts, and the like. And place connections; workplaces, home addresses, schools, associations, and fraternities.

"But the people on the list I sent you are all dead."

"They are, but websites don't disable accounts automatically. If someone doesn't go into an account and explicitly disable or delete it, it is probably still active."

"Okay, back to the app you were talking about."

"So let's assume I've allowed the app to build a profile on a name and finds that person has 100 people connections and a connection to 10 places, schools, workplaces, bars and the like. This is what I call my first level discovery.

I then execute the app against every one of the 100 people connections, so I repeat the process that was just completed, 100 more times.

That leaves me with lists of people and place connections for each of the 100 names on my first level discovery. This is what I call my level two discovery. If each of the 100 people on the list also has 100 friends, contacts and relatives, I now have a total of 10,100 names in my database, 100 first level discoveries, and 10,000 second level. I can repeat that process as many times as I want. That said, it soon becomes much too computationally intensive to drill down through the lists. Even drilling down into the third level lists would take weeks of compute time. Assuming the same number of acquaintances, going to the third level would yield well over 1 million names. For your exercise, I only went down to the second level, but I went to the second level on all 6 names. In order to find commonalities between the 6 murder victims, I cross referenced the lists. Ideally, I was looking for someone who was connected to all 6 of the people on your victim list. That person would be the most obvious connection, and the one that you'd want to focus your investigation on.

"I won't keep you in suspense, there was no level 1 connection between all the victims. But remember, I also cross reference place connections. If all 6 victims went to the same high school, that might be an important piece of information. Again, there was no such level 1 place connection.

"Now the exercise gets a bit more arduous because I have to cross reference the second level connections, and we already know there could be tens of thousands of those. I won't bore you with the details but suffice to say, I have some skill in abstract number theory and how to manipulate large data sets.

"Don't leave me hanging Evan, I hear some good news coming."

"Three of the people on the list had worked at the carwash on St Catherine Street at some point in their lives. The three who never worked at Chalwell's carwash, had brothers, sisters or friends who did. The carwash is what I call the Bacon Bit. It is the most common element among the 6 victims.

"Wow. I'm not going to say I was surprised. That confirms what we suspected, the carwash, and Jack Chalwell, are at the very center of a major drug operation and the murders committed to protect it. Evan, you're a genius. "

"I'm glad you like those results, because you may not like the results I have on the carwash computer as much."

"What is it?"

"You asked me to hack into Chalwell's carwash computer and look for anything hinky. I couldn't get into the computer because of the security on his wifi router. I didn't have high expectations for the computer anyway. The cops didn't find anything five years ago and we won't find anything on it now, so I didn't beat myself up trying to break into it. I used one of my connections at the phone company, the same phone company that provides internet service to the carwash, and had her perform a few searches on the proxy logs."

"You'll have to slow it down for me Evan."

"Proxy logs? When you have a connection to the internet from home, you aren't actually connected to the internet, you have a connection to your ISP, or internet service provider, and they in turn, are connected to the internet. Follow? "

"Keep going."

"All of your web traffic travels along the connection to your ISP into a central server, along with the internet traffic from all their other clients. This central server, known as a proxy server, looks at the web page that you asked for, and requests that internet page on your behalf. When the web page is returned from the world wide web, the proxy server knows who requested it, and forwards the page to the correct home user. The proxy server keeps a log of every web page requested for all of their customers. "

"Makes sense. Did you find anything?"

"Maybe. After I discounted all the traffic going to sports, news, porn, email, and banking sites, I was left with only one recurring web site. It was an auto forum called World-of-Wheels.com. World-of-Wheels is one of the largest auto related forums in the world, there are over a million members. Any member who has a question about anything automotive related can post their question under one of the Forum topics and any other member who has an answer, or even an opinion on the matter, can respond. The computer at the carwash logs into that site at least once a day and often, more than once."

"That may not be unusual, he runs a car wash. Maybe he's a car enthusiast."

"Agreed. It doesn't necessarily mean anything so we need to drill down and see what he was doing on the auto website. One challenge is that the proxy server only captures the webpage that is requested along with date and time. It doesn't capture any of the activity that the user does on the website, like logging in and posting questions."

"So you don't know their usernames and there's over a million to choose from. There must be some clever way for you hacker types to find that info. No?"

"I don't know of a clever way, but there is a manual way. A person could log into World-of-Wheels and search within each of the topics for any posts within a minute or two of Chalwell's computer logging in."

"Explain it to me."

"My associate at the ISP sent me a dump of all the dates and times that Chalwell's computer went to the auto site. Someone with lots of time on their hands could start in one forum topic; jot down all the usernames who posted just after the time that Chalwell logged in. Then look at the next time in the login dump and do the same. When a username is found that logged into a forum at the same times as the times in the dump, you'll know it was Chalwell. If he's using this forum to coordinate pickups and deliveries, the information will be somewhere in those posts. "

"That makes sense. At a minimum, he'd need to ask for product and his supplier would have to acknowledge that request. If those assumptions are correct, we should also be able to find the supplier's username on the other end of the pipeline."

"Exactly. "

"So you're telling me that this is something I need to do?"

"I'm telling you that I won't do it. I'll send you the dump of all the dates and times and let you research them."

"Okay, how many forums are there?"

"I didn't count them, but my guess would be 300-400."

"Send it. I'll be buttoned down for most of the day, so I have some time on my hands."

Elliot thought about his next steps. It would likely take the rest of the day to go through the World of Wheels website. He thought about the other information Evan had given him. The 6 names Rivka had found were now linked to the Lav and Jack Chalwell. He wondered if those isolated murders would have been investigated differently if the police thought they were connected. He knew the answer, of course they would. Before he dove into the World of Wheels, he made a phone call.

"Jacques Bessette please," Elliot asked the coroners receptionist.

"Oui, Allo. C'est Dr. Bessette ici."

"Dr. Bessette, this is Elliot Forsman, we met last Friday along with my partner Rivka Goldstein."

"Yes, yes, of course I remember. What can I do for you Mr. Forsman?"

"This is an unusual request, but when we met, I got the impression that you were interested in doing the right thing."

"What is it you want Mr. Forsman?"

"When we asked if you'd ever seen the same MO used in Alphie Leduc's murder, you said you had not. What if I told you that we found another half dozen murders that have been committed over the past 5 years that may have been done by the same person."

"Forgive my skepticism, but you have to explain to me how you have discovered a serial killer that the police know nothing about."

"Rivka searched for murders in the Montréal area that were unsolved, no known motive, and had a personal slant to them."

"So you were looking for murder with completely different methods of killings but the commonality would be in the personal manner in which they were executed?"

"Precisely. We've gone as far as establishing that all the murder victims are connected to a drug operation centered around a carwash in east Montréal. What we aren't able to do is narrow down the list of suspects who may have committed the murders."

"And you want me to do what? Open up their cases again?"

"If the police, or the coroner involved in these murder investigations thought that they were part of a serial killer spree, they would have been investigated with a different level of scrutiny. No?"

"That goes without saying. I see where you're going with this. I'm not opposed to the idea of helping you Mr. Forsman but I just don't have the spare cycles. I've got three cadavers in my cooler that need examination and that number will likely be increased before the end of the day. It's just not possible for me to assist in this, at least not until my schedule opens up. I'm sorry," he said and ended the call.

# Chapter 45

Rayce gritted his teeth as the vibration from his bike coursed through his body and into his wounds. A painkiller may have decreased the pain but Rayce didn't believe in dulling his senses. He knew from experience that pain could be managed.

He took a route that headed towards his house but veered off early to take the bridge that led to the north side of the Richelieu River. He cruised along the riverside road until he was roughly opposite his place and then slowed until he found an opening in the trees that gave him the view he was looking for. He wasn't interested in a view of his property. He was looking for a spot that gave him a clear view of the ridge that rose about a half mile south. If anyone was assigned to watch his house without being seen, the top of the ridge is where they'd set up shop.

He pulled a case from the saddlebag along with a collapsed tripod and made his way to a flat spot down below the road that gave him the view he needed. It wasn't long before he was setup and scanning deliberately for signs of surveillance. On the fifth pass, he found what he was looking for. A splash of color where none should be. There was a person sitting in the shade of an alder grove, his knees up, elbows on knees, holding a pair of binoculars at the ready. He was wearing camo that would have made him nearly undetectable from Rayce's range, but he was sloppy. The man had a blue thermos sitting beside him, likely coffee, or soup, which gave him away.

Rayce checked his watch; it was 5:20pm. He packed up and sped to the other side of the river and along an access road that supported a series of locks for the canal. He travelled along the canal road that ran roughly parallel but about a mile south of his road. The canal was originally built in the mid 1800's and served as a major commercial route between the United States and Canada. Its only purpose now was as a leisurely way for recreational boaters to spend their weekends and holidays.

Rayce let his Harley rumble slowly down the dusty road until he found what he was looking for, a vehicle parked on the side of the road. It was old Ford Bronco that had seen one too many Canadian winters by the looks of it. The patching on the fender skirts was riddled with holes where the last remnants of metal body had rusted away. He passed the truck without stopping and then angled his bike in behind a thick stand of raspberry bushes. It didn't take long for him to steal his way back to the truck and take up post behind some nearby trees.

His plan was simple; he'd find a hiding spot and wait for someone to relieve the watchman. Rayce's assumption was that there'd be at least two watchmen to provide around the clock surveillance on the house, if not three. If these guys were military trained they'd be working a strict schedule. A lifetime of rigid military discipline is not easily forgotten. If there was only two watchmen then 6:00pm seemed like a probable time for the next shift change. He settled down into stakeout mode and let his senses take over. He'd often stayed out for days on recon missions while in the military and learned that all five senses were needed to be effective in a stakeout. He set his sight in a fixed position and focused on nothing in particular so that the only thing that would catch his attention was movement. He allowed his thoughts to retreat into the backdrop of his position. He felt the damp earth he knelt on and the smell of the plant growth around him. He listened to the sound of the breeze filtering through the trees until all of his senses were tuned into the natural pulse of his surroundings. Anything disturbing that pulse would be detected immediately. In this tuned-in state, time was meaningless, just as it would be for a rock or a tree.

He felt the oncoming vehicle long before hearing or seeing it. It parked not far from the rusting Bronco;

Rayce didn't have to look to know where it was. He allowed the new guard to walk by without incident, no more than two dozen feet from his crouched position. The watchman on the ridge was expecting to be relieved so he needed to let that happen. His mind drifted out of surveillance mode and into high alert. Recon was over; it was time for action.

It wasn't long before he heard the relieved watchman making his way back through the brush. He was making no efforts to conceal his progress; his job was finished for the day.

"Hands where I can see them," Rayce barked as he stood up from his crouch and pointed a handgun at the passing watchman. His command sounded terse and strained as his wounds protested when he stood up.

"One more warning is all you get pal. Hands where I can see them."

The watchman bowed his head in resignation and put his hands up on top of his head. Rayce quickly patted him down and took his backpack.

"Put these on," Rayce said as he threw the man a pair of nylon cuffs and watched as the man slipped them on and tightened them with his teeth.

Rayce stood in front of his captive and gave him a long look. The man in front of him looked to be in his late 40's. He had a small gut overhang on his hips and his face was just starting to jowl. He had the look of someone who was once fit and strong but time had started to soften him.

"I'm going to ask two questions and I'm expecting two answers. Who are you? And who hired you?" he asked as he started rifling through the man's backpack.

The watchman remained silent, and defiant.

Rayce shrugged his shoulders and rolled his eyes as if to say '*You really want to go there*?' but thought better of that approach and instead replied,

"Look pal. If I thought you were one of the men who attacked me, we wouldn't be talking right now. You'd be face down on the ground with my knife in your ear telling me everything you know. That said, you're still going to tell me everything you know."

The captive watched Rayce for a moment and decided that sacrificing his well-being wasn't worth whatever he was being paid.

"My name is Gord White."

"That answers question number one."

"I was hired by a guy I was in the service with, a man named Robert Sauvage."

"Start at the beginning and tell me everything," he rumbled.

The captive watchman took a deep breath and started, "I got a call from Sauvage yesterday morning. I hadn't heard from him in years. We were in the forces, we came up through boot camp together and were both stationed at the St. Jean base, not far from here. He asked me if I wanted to make some easy money and told me what I'd be doing. I need the money, so I said yes."

"If you haven't seen him in years why would he call you out of the blue?"

"He probably heard that I took early retirement a few years ago and that I was looking for work."

"What did he ask you to do?"

"Sit up here on this ridge and watch your house. If, or when, someone approached the property I would call him. With that phone," he said pointing his chin towards the phone that Rayce was now holding.

"What do you know about the attack on the house down there?"

"Nothing. I assumed Sauvage knows but I didn't ask. I didn't want to know."

"Is Sauvage the brains behind this operation?"

"Not a chance. He's a foot soldier, nothing more. He's just a cog."

"Any idea who's running the show?"

"No."

"How can I find Sauvage?"

"I don't know. He might be in the phone book, I never checked. You've got his number in that phone though," as he pointed at the phone Rayce had in his hand.

Rayce stepped away from the interrogation and thought about what he'd just heard. He looked back at White and considered him for a moment.

"Do we know each other?"

"We've never met but I know who you are," replied the watchman. "I had my bike in your garage last summer."

"Are you the guy with the 77 Commando?"

"That was me."

Rayce nodded as he remembered the job, "you wanted your heads rebuilt."

"That's right," the watchman confirmed.

Rayce holstered his gun, pulled out a knife that was half as long as his arm and stepped towards his captive.

"I have a family," he protested hoarsely.

Rayce said nothing and reached down for the man's arm with his free hand saying nothing but commanding the man's attention with his eyes. He brought the knife up and cut the man's ties.

A quiet "thank you," was all the man could muster.

Rayce watched as the man gathered his things and stuffed them back in the backpack.

"You were in the military. What are you doing now?"

"Nothing. Looking for work. I'm having a tough time adjusting to civilian life."

"Civilian life can be a tough nut to crack," Rayce said as he thought about his own life experience when he left the military. The military has great intentions to re-integrate vets back into society after they leave the service. In many cases, the issue was that the very things that make a soldier, a soldier, prevent them from being productive in civilian life. He knew that a lifetime of learning to live within a structured military environment is not easily undone. When a struggling vet reaches for the support that was always there and finds nothing, he sometimes becomes lost. In his own case, he was lucky, he had financial means, and he'd had Sarah Soucy. The woman who would later become Sarah Forsman, Elliot's wife. Without those two things in his life, he would have become lost.

"Look White. This gig is up for you. Go home to your family. You don't want to be around when I find your employers."

## Chapter 46

"Riv, it's me."

"What's up partner? How's life on the run?"

"Not nearly as exciting as you'd think. I talked to Evan this morning about Chalwell."

"Was he able to hack into the computer?"

"Sort of, he was able to get a list of login times for a car forum from the workstation at the carwash."

"Car Forum?"

"Yes, he couldn't access the workstation but he was able to get access to the ISP browsing logs. After he discounted all the regular browsing like news, sports, and porn, he found only one site that was browsed on a regular basis, a discussion forum for automobile enthusiasts. The challenge is that the ISP records only contain the webpages that are requested, not what they actually do on the website, so I've been correlating any posts that were created in the minutes following our workstation logins."

"Sounds like a lot of work. Are you getting anywhere?"

"I think we have something. I went through all the forums, alphabetically, and jotted down the usernames who posted within minutes of the first login time from the log that Evan sent me. I'm looking for a forum that has a username who regularly posts a thread soon after the login times in Evan's log file.

"I eventually found the username in a forum called 'CarWanted'. The user 'SoapBox66' posts an average of once a week, always within minutes of one of the login times from Chalwell's computer."

"What's in the posts?"

"Exactly what you'd expect. SoapBox66 posts that he's looking for a vehicle. The vehicle is inconsequential, a late model Honda Civic, a well-used Ford Bronco, he's all over the map. But, in every post there's a number written out, never more than one. Here's an example where he's looking for a 2010-2012 Camry, sports package, leather interior six cylinder, etc. I believe the number 'six', spelt out, is the key. Every post by Soapbox66 has one number spelt out. If my theory is correct, he is telling his supplier how much product is needed. The 'six' probably refers to how many kilos he wants."

"Interesting. So Chalwell posts a question under the name Soapbox66, like a blind drop. He puts it out there and whoever is watching for Soapbox66 posts, will read it. And then he'd have to acknowledge it."

"Exactly. Not only acknowledge it, but also include details about the delivery. And that's exactly what a user named 'HarleyMan' does. He responds to every SoapBox66 post with one of his own. Look at this one:

*'For Sale: $10,200. 2012 Honda accord coupe, metallic blue exterior, 90,000km. Black leather, sunroof, heated seats magnaflow exhaust system, a/c fully functional also has a custom side skirt. Full description available online at www.FernsCarDepot.com. Photos available tomorrow at 10:00am'.*

"Every HarleyMan response has the description of a car, a date and time specified. That's enough to setup the drop. They don't specify a location, but they don't have to. It's always at the Lav."

"I think we have something Maven. When was his last post?"

"Soapbox posted yesterday morning and used the number 'five' in the post. HarleyMan replied last night that he has a blue Honda Civic for sale. Full description available online at www.FernsCarDepot.com. Photos available tomorrow at 10:00am."

"So tomorrow morning a blue Honda Civic will be delivering 5 kilos to the Lav. What does the Lav do with it?"

"I'm not sure, but based on O'Brien's lack of success finding trace, I'd say the coke is passed on to someone else quickly. The Lav is likely just a transfer point. "

"What do you need me to do?" she asked.

"Can you run down info on Fern's Car Depot? Let's find out what we're up against."

# Chapter 47

"Margie. Qué pasa?"

"A man of languages, how interesting."

"Linguistics is just one of my many talents."

"What is it you think you just asked me?"

"That was Spanish for what are you doing."

"Sorry, you just asked me 'what's up'. Do you still want me to answer?"

"Okay, how about this. What are you doing and, can I come over and do it with you?"

"No."

"No what?"

"No, you can't come over and do it with me. I'm playing solitaire on the computer, if you play it with me, it's no longer solitaire. So the answer is no. If you asked if you can come over, the answer is 'yes', but we'll have to find something else to do."

"I'm sure we can think of something but I have to warn you, I'm on the lam."

"So the police are actively looking for you?"

"Yes, apparently they found my gun in a sewer near Labrosse's. I'm in deep shit."

"I've never harbored a criminal before. Is there any chance you're going to tie me up and gag me?"

"Not likely."

"That's too bad, but come over anyway."

\* \* \* \* \* \* \* \*

Elliot lay in bed thinking of the case and the way it had unfolded. The sounds of Margie's post coital slumber provided a comforting background of white noise. Perfect conditions for deep thought. He told his lover that he was in a tight spot but downplayed how tight it really was.

In complex cases, he often envisioned the case as if it was a Rubik's cube. Each of the small colored squares was a piece of evidence, a scrap of information. At the beginning, all he had were a few scraps of data, each one a different color with no alignment between them. As he gathered more data and started making connections between the pieces of information, the cube started to take shape. The colors started to consolidate so that instead of visualizing dozens of disconnected squares of different colors, there were half a dozen groups of the same colors. Elliot knew that when all the squares within a color group aligned and the groups of colors connected, the case could be broken.

When he envisioned this case in his mind's eye, the cube was incomplete. He considered the facts surrounding Alphie's murder and the drug operation. He now knew that Jack Chalwell and the

Lav were at the center of the drug operation. He also had suspected that the lawyer, Anderson, was somehow involved in Alphie's murder as was Labrosse, the business owner, before he was killed. But, with nothing more than an unsubstantiated meeting between Alphie and the lawyer, evidence was non-existent. Elliot's skill in reading their body language counted for nothing in a court of law.

He also knew that Chalwell could not run an operation this big by himself, so he must have partners. *Was Anderson a partner? Was Labrosse? If so, why would they kill a partner just to frame me? Why not just kill me instead?* He wondered.

*Were any of these men the one they call Mamelon?* He asked himself. His hypothesis was that neither Anderson nor Labrosse was Mamelon, but that was just a theory.

He came to the conclusion that he had no idea who the partners were, and the detached manner in which the operation communicated amongst each other would make it difficult to find them.

Rivka was busy tracking down the people at Ferns' Car Depot. They would be the suppliers. They would also be the people behind the fentanyl crisis. If the suppliers have been operating for as long as Chalwell's operation, he assumed that they too, were extremely careful, and that their operation would be compartmentalized, just as Chalwell's was. He decided to put that train of thought on hold until he heard back from Rivka.

The cube thus far, was not nearly complete. He thought about the meeting with Labrosse, Labrosse's murder, and being framed for it. His gun was stolen before the failed meeting with Labrosse, so someone had gone to great lengths to plan the murder and pin it on Elliot. Labrosse petitioned for a restraining order, received it, and then texted Elliot for a meeting. It was obvious now that Labrosse was already dead when he received the text. Whoever killed Labrosse had sent the text. It seemed likely that whoever planned the murder had also convinced Labrosse to get the restraining order. If that was the case, then the murderer was someone Labrosse knew well. *Was it Anderson?*

There were still many questions left to answer, and Elliot's time was running out. He didn't have the luxury of sorting through clues and building a solid case. He needed to act and needed to do it quickly. With an open warrant for murder, the police were ramping up their search for him. He knew it was only a matter of time before they caught him.

Now that he'd mentally summarized his situation, he understood how bleak it was. He could do nothing about the murder charge, the evidence was overwhelming, and he was going to jail. His only hope was to build some goodwill with the legal community so they might show leniency.

He had options when it came to the drug operation and Alphie's murder. He now knew enough detail to smash the drug operation. People would go to jail and put a stop, however brief, to the drug supply. He also knew that Chalwell had probably insulated himself so that he even if he were caught, it would not result in the kind of sentence he deserved. The Mamelon angle would not see justice, there was likely no evidence connecting Chalwell, or anyone, to Alphie's murder, or any of the other victims. The same probably held true for the suppliers.

Out of desperation, he came up with a plan. He didn't like hasty plans, especially when the outcome was so unpredictable, but circumstance forced his hand. His plan was to stick a bee up Chalwell's ass and see how he reacts. Maybe Chalwell would make a mistake that he could leverage. His plan was to intercept the drug delivery scheduled for 10:00am tomorrow morning.

Margie was still snoozing soundly beside him so he quietly got out of bed and made a phone call from the kitchen.

# Chapter 48

"Whataya want."

"Sammy, it's Elliot."

"Okay, sorry about my rude answering, I use it to scare off telemarketers. So, whataya want?"

"I'm looking for some help."

"You came to the right place my friend. What is it?"

"Before you say yes I have to warn you that what I'm asking for is against the law."

"Against the law as in, I could go to jail?"

"Yes, and throw away the key."

"Is it dangerous?"

"Moderately."

"I'll do it."

"I haven't told you what it is yet."

"Elliot, I helped you out 4 months ago. I got beat up pretty good, almost lost my thumb, and racked up the tail end of my truck. And ever since then, when I'm working at the diner, it's all I can think of. I'm serious. I flip fucken burgers for a living. I ain't no goddam psychic, but I'm pretty sure that when the big man calls and I'm circling the drain on my death bed, I won't be regretting those burgers I didn't flip because I was helping my friend. I'll do it."

"First hear me out and then decide. I'll need a wheelman, someone to drive a car that will be involved in a crime. I'm going to steal a drug dealer's stash."

"That's it? I thought you said it was dangerous?"

"It is. The guy we're going to rip off has already murdered for far less."

"Fuck him. This fucker's out there poisoning kids and ruining lives. I'll do it."

"Does your cousin still work at that chop shop?"

"I don't know what you're talking about."

"Do you think you can get a beater with a bogus plate? I'll pay for it."

"I'll ask him. It shouldn't be an issue. If I have to, I'll drive my jeep."

"That bucket of bolts still runs?"

"Smooth as a jockey's ass."

"We can't use anything that'll be traced back to us. The cops will be watching my house and JFK, so pick me up at 9:00 tomorrow morning in front of l'Oiseau café and I'll fill you in. One more thing, do you have a handgun I can use? It doesn't even have to work, I need it for persuasion purposes only."

"I've got a couple of old guns stored in the basement. If you don't need it to work I'll dust one off and bring it with me. Do I need a disguise?"

"Sure, can you dress like a 50 year old fry cook with a waistline the size of a small planet?"

"You didn't tell me I have to lose weight."

"Okay. Tomorrow 9:00. We'll go through the plan. "

## Chapter 49

Rivka had received the background info on the auto garage that supplied Chalwell's drug operation and sent it off to Elliot's cell as a text. Fern's Auto was a garage in Verdun owned by a numbered company. The police knew it to be a hangout for Hades Henchman and suspected there were illegal activities going on, but without proof, there was no reason to shut it down.

Her thoughts were interrupted when a call came in on the JFK phone.

"JFK Investigations."

"Elliot Forsman please."

"He's not here right now. This is his partner speaking, perhaps I can help you."

"Your name is?"

"Rivka Goldstein."

"Ms. Goldstein, this is inspector Bertrand, Montréal Police."

"What can I do for you this evening inspector?"

"Do you know a Rebecca Boyle?"

"Yes," she heard her words catch as visions of the red haired girl flashed through her mind.

"Her body was found this evening in an abandoned warehouse on Cremazie."

"What happened?" she asked, not really wanting to know.

"We found her in the warehouse. Her hands and feet were nailed to a wall. Cause of death was as a result of a nail through the heart but not before she suffered for some time."

*"She talked to me,"* Rivka thought. She felt the blood rush to her head and her breath shot from her lungs, leaving a hollow, empty space inside. *Rebecca is dead because she talked to JFK.* She wanted to get away, to run, and not stop, to find a place to curl up and wither away. *I am responsible for her death.* She knew she couldn't hide. What chased her was something inside, something dark and sinister, part grief, part anger, and all guilt.

"Ms. Goldstein, are you still there?"

"I'm here," she replied hoarsely.

"Inspector, how did you know to phone me?"

"We found your business card," he replied as if reading her thoughts. "It was stuffed into her mouth," the inspector paused a moment before adding, "are you able to come down so we can take your statement?"

"In the morning," she said flatly and ended the call.

Rivka sat down to process what she'd just heard. She breathed deeply in an effort to relax the tightness in her chest. A deep despair found its way into her; she fought to keep it at bay, to push it from her thoughts, and lost.

# Chapter 50

Rivka lay in bed, pretending to sleep. Sleep had been elusive the past few months, but none more than this night. Even the pills didn't help. She wanted to call Elliot and tell him about the murder but didn't think she was capable of retelling the story without breaking down. She'd call him in the morning when her mind was fresh and her resolve hardened.

She rolled the events of the past few days in her head, not because she wanted to, because she had no choice. Her brain was hyperactive and there was no shut-off switch. She knew that her runaway thoughts were irrational, and that many of them were imagined, but she couldn't stop them. Occasionally, she would slip down towards the place where sleep lived, only to be pulled back from the brink of slumber into a state of alertness by even the most insignificant stray thought.

Finally recognizing she would not sleep, she decided to get out of bed and make tea. She wondered if there was a bad late movie on that would bore her into slumber. She put on a robe and mechanically picked up her gun. It wasn't until she reached the living room that she even realized she was carrying a loaded weapon. The realization of her current instability slammed into her. The weight of despair pulled her down onto the couch and paralyzed her with a sense of helplessness. She came to the understanding that she was nowhere near ready to function normally. Tears welled up and she shook violently. She wanted to call for help, to call Elliot, or Dr. Maller, but that would show a weakness she didn't want exposed. Her mind raced through her options, stuck in another loop she could not break out of, a loop of imagined scenarios and desperate thoughts that were borne from a wounded mind. She wasn't fit to work, her carelessness had caused a young woman to be killed, and her personal life a failure.

Lydia had not phoned this afternoon as she said she would. Rivka looked over at the front vestibule and saw the empty hook where Lydia's jacket used to hang. The tightness already in her chest squeezed harder. Lydia would not be coming back. A wave of depression swept over her as she realized that she'd managed to scare off another one. Those close to her would think she was weak and unbalanced. They were right.

She looked at the gun in her hand and realized that she had already chambered a round. She wondered *why not? Who would care? Angela is no longer part of my life. Lydia certainly wouldn't care, she*

*told me she loved me but her actions told a different story.
My partner Elliot? Maybe, but not for long. He has his
own problems to deal with. With Elliot going to jail, JFK
would close down. I would be out of work, again. How will
I spin this into something positive with my mother? I
can't. Worst of all was Rebecca. She'd still be alive if it
wasn't for me. I failed trying to catch Ogrodnik and I've
failed in my duty to Serve and Protect.*

She fantasized about the escape she held in her
hand, a one-way ticket out of desperation. It would
be the period at the end of a story of disappointment
and failure. She considered the downside of taking
her own life, and couldn't think of any.

A change in the quality of the thin light that
seeped in through the back windows snapped her out
of her trance and caused her to look up. It took her a
moment to process what she saw, the moonlight
filtering in through the trees created a shifting mosaic
of greys on the windows. It was the pattern on the far
left window that held her attention. Unlike the
random movement of tree branch shadows on the
other windows, the shades of grey seemed to move
with a purpose. Like an unprocessed negative in the
developer bath, an image started materializing out of
the inky shade. At first, it was just an area of darker
grey and, as the boundaries became sharper, the
shape started to come into focus. She watched

transfixed, neither afraid nor curious, she was oblivious to such sensations in her damaged frame of mind.

It came at once, without warning, she jerked out of her reverie and directly into vigilance. Whatever her current mental state was, years of police training took over and assumed control of her actions. The shape was that of a man, a large man, outside her house and bending forward to peer into the darkened room. Thoughts of Ogrodnik flooded into her. She would take no chances this time. Her Beretta, already in hand, roared. She emptied the clip through the window as the darkened figure outside staggered back and fell. She leapt off the couch and stared out through the shattered window. The crumpled form of an enormous body lay motionless on the lawn. Ogrodnik had escaped death before, so she took no chances this time. Afraid to go near him, she ran back into her room to get the spare clip for her gun, grabbed the phone, and called 911. Her heart, still hammering from the adrenaline rush, threatened to jump from her chest but she managed to call in the incident. She breathed deeply a few times to gain control of her emotions and advanced out into the living area and past the glass of the shattered window, gun leading, and bullet chambered.

She expected to see the big man coming back to life, crawling in through the broken window, with a bloodied chest and a scornful sneer. But there was no movement. The body still lay where it had fallen. She now heard activity from the neighboring houses. Mrs. Johnson was calling her name while dialing for help. Sirens in the distance came in answer to her call but she found no strength to respond to Mrs. Johnson's queries. She stood with gun in hand, pointing through the window at the body on her lawn. Ready to empty another clip if the form so much as moved. She stayed in that position until the police arrived and took the gun from her hand.

"Ms. Goldstein. Are you alright?"

She nodded. "He was trying to get in. I shot him. His name is Ogrodnik. He came to kill me," she said to no one in particular.

"Please, have a seat Ms. Goldstein," an officer said as he she was led to the couch while the others busied themselves containing the scene.

"We have a trauma counselor on the way Ms. Goldstein. She'll stay with you. Is there anyone we should call?"

Rivka looked at the officer blankly, "My partner, call my partner," and then added, "Call my therapist too, Dr. Maller" and she recited the numbers.

It wasn't long before the entire property was overrun with police and support units.

Elliot and Margie saw the strobing lights of police activity as they neared Rivka's house.

"I'm going to drop you off before we get there, I can't take the chance that the police on site don't have my description."

"Okay. I'll meet you back at my place," said Margie as she got out of the car and hurried over to the house, now completely immersed in the red and blue brilliance of law enforcement.

Rivka stood up when she saw Dr. Maller and went directly to her.

The psychiatrist held her and let the moment pass. She felt Rivka take a deep breath and heard the breath catch in short spurts as her body trembled deep inside.

"Elliot?" Rivka asked when she pulled back to look into her doctor's face.

The psychiatrist shook her head and replied, "He can't come here," and swept her eyes to the side to indicate that, with so many police on site, he couldn't take the chance. Before the psychiatrist could ask any questions about the situation, Rivka started talking, as if she had to get the words out before they injured her.

"I saw a man in the back trying to get in. I shot him. It was Ogrodnik."

"It's over now Rivka," is all Dr. Maller said. Over Rivka's shoulder, she saw an officer outside trying to get her attention. The officer was beckoning for the psychiatrist to come outside to the crime scene.

"Rivka, I have to speak with the officer. You sit here with the councilor and I'll be back in a moment," she said as she passed off the shaken PI to the police council.

Based on the twisted angles of the limbs, Dr. Maller surmised the body had not yet been moved. The entire scene was in the process of being photographed and measured out. She advanced to the officer who'd called.

"Dr. Margie Maller," she said, and then added, "I'm Rivka's psychiatrist."

"Detective Lamarche. Thanks for coming out Dr. Maller. Are you able to confirm the identity of the body? Ms. Goldstein calls him Ogrodnik but we didn't find any ID on the body."

"I can't but if you allow me to take a photo of the face I can verify it quickly enough," wanting to protect Rivka from seeing the body again.

Detective Lamarche signaled an officer to expose the face.

Dr. Maller took a photo of the face and sent it off immediately to Elliot. While waiting for the photo to be transmitted Detective Lamarche added, "as her psychiatrist you should know that a young woman named Rebecca Boyle was found murdered this evening. It seems she was working in some capacity with Ms. Goldstein and JFK Investigations." Their conversation continued along that narrative as the detective filled in Dr. Maller on all the murder details relevant to Rivka Goldstein and Rebecca Boyle.

The psychiatrist moved over to the side of the property where she couldn't be overheard and dialed Elliot's number.

"How is she?" Elliot asked immediately upon answering.

"She's shaken, but unharmed. As per the phone call from the police, she shot a man who was trying to get into the house. The investigating detective wants to verify that the man is Ogrodnik. I sent you photo of his face."

"Okay, gimme a second," he replied as he pulled up the photo on his phone.

"Margie," he replied, "I've never seen this man. It's not Ogrodnik."

The ramifications stunned the psychiatrist as she processed Elliot's words.

"Elliot, there's something else. Rebecca Boyle was murdered tonight. They found her body nailed to a warehouse wall."

"Damn it!" he barked, "she was killed because she talked to us," he said quietly as if he was talking to himself. "Nailed to a wall?" he then questioned in disbelief.

"Think crucifixion," replied Margie. "It's a classic example of betrayal symbolism."

"I'll call you later. When Rivka finds out about the man she just shot she could go sideways, I don't want to lose her," she said tersely, closed the connection and walked back to the detective.

"It's not Ogrodnik?" the detective restated.

"No. I don't know who it is, but it's not Ogrodnik."

"Merde," the detective muttered. He took out his phone and called someone as he walked away.

* * * * * * * * * *

Margie phoned Elliot to tell him she had taken Rivka to the hospital after it was apparent she'd be better off with some professional care. While she waited for Rivka to stabilize, she phoned Detective Lamarche.

"Detective Lamarche, Dr. Maller here. I just wanted to thank you for the way you handled a very delicate situation this evening. My patient, Ms. Goldstein, is now receiving the attention she needs. Being involved in two murders in one evening would test the mental stability of even the most hardened character but I think she'll be okay. Do you know who the man was?" she asked the detective.

"Yes, it was Simon Lemieux. We know of him. He frequents the shelters in this part of town. He has a record for vagrancy but nothing more sinister than that."

"Do you have any theories about why he would be lurking in Rivka's backyard?"

"None. The only unusual thing about him was the $400 we found in his pocket."

"That's a lot of money for a homeless man."

"It is, but I doubt we'll ever find out where it came from. He certainly can't tell us."

"What's next for my patient?"

"We've taken all of the statements that we need. We'll process them along with the scene and write it up in a report. As you said, being involved in two murders is highly unusual so we have to assume that there's more to this story than we currently understand. Ultimately, her fate in this matter lies with the Crown Attorney's office. As you know, Ms.

Goldstein is a former police officer and well thought of in law enforcement circles. I fully expect she'll be allowed to go free on her own recognizance, but for the time being, we'll post a guard at the hospital."

"Thank you Detective Lamarche."

## Chapter 51

It was late, well past midnight. Elliot called Margie to see how Rivka was doing.

"How is she?"

"As well as can be expected, she's sedated and sleeping soundly. It's been a rough day for her. She was wallowing in guilt for Rebecca Boyle's murder and then she shot and killed an innocent man."

"If there's any guilt to be had, it should be mine. I'm the one who recruited Rebecca. And I'm not sure how innocent this man is. He's not Ogrodnik, but my gut tells me he's not as innocent as the police think he is. I'm back at your place, are you coming home soon?"

"I was hoping you'd be there. I need a massage something terrible."

"Sounds good. When you get here I'll work the knots out of your shoulders."

"It's not my shoulders. I was thinking about you massaging the inside of my thighs with your hips."

"You over-sexed strumpet. Do you never stop?"

"Maybe if you did it right I wouldn't be so needy."

"Ow. Didn't you learn in head shrinking school that the male ego is a fragile thing?"

"Don't fall asleep on me, I'll be there soon.

Chapter 52

*Tuesday, August 29th.*

Elliot fetched the morning paper from Margie's mailbox; he still liked reading a paper version of the news. It had none of the currency of online news, yet he felt a comfort he could not explain when flipping through the pages. Perhaps it was the tactile feedback the paper provided, as if the news was more real if it was in print. He also liked that newspapers presented information in a consistent manner. The placement of a story in the newspaper and the size of the font made it easy to identify important stories. He knew from experience that only the highest profile stories got page one treatment. Page one stories of violence and death invariably had elements of compassion, family misfortune, or celebrity.

The major headline on the front page of the today's paper was about a husband and wife who died from a drug overdose leaving two young children behind. Fentanyl overdoses were killing people and the public demanded action. The police answered with evasive clichéd responses. It was obvious to Elliot that they had no answers.

Elliot wondered what would happen to the children of the parents in the story. If they were lucky, a relative would take them in and raise them as their own. If no relatives stepped forward, they'd probably be split up and sent to foster homes. Either way, the tragedy in tales of drug abuse was often not in the people who died, but in those they left behind.

A story in a thin column on the second page caught his attention. It was about the death of a man in the south shore community of St. Jean, home of a Canadian military base. The man, Robert Sauvage, was a decorated veteran of the Canadian Forces. His body was found at the bottom of a ravine beside a jogging trail. The police said they hadn't ruled out foul play yet, but speculated that he might have lost his footing and broke his neck during the fall into the ravine. Elliot had never heard of the man but instinct told him that this was no accident. He knew Rayce was out there hunting his attackers and wondered if this death was connected to Rayce. If it was, Elliot had no doubts the man had given up his secrets.

Margie came downstairs, hair still wet and buttoning up her blouse.

"I've got an 8:30 this morning. What are you up to today?" she asked.

"It's probably better I don't tell you. I intend on breaking the law this morning."

"With a warrant out for you aren't you breaking the law just by being here?"

"I guess I am, but I won't tell you anyway. The less you know the better."

"How mysterious. Are you able to tell me if you'll be here for supper tonight?"

"Don't count on it."

"Where will you be staying tonight?"

"I may come back here if it's all right with you. I'll let you know either way," he answered, clearly preoccupied with whatever was on his mind.

"Okay. I gotta go," she said as she pecked him on the lips and left for work.


Elliot's preparation for the upcoming drug heist was interrupted by his phone. He didn't recognize the number but knew that only a handful of people knew about this phone so he answered.

"Hello," he answered cautiously.

"Mr. Forsman, Dr. Bessette here from the city morgue."

"Dr. Bessette. I didn't think I'd be hearing from you again."

"I wasn't intending to call, but events last night changed my mind about helping you."

"Can I ask what it was that changed your mind?"

"I got a call late last night to look at a murder victim. A young girl by the name of Rebecca Boyle. I believe you know her."

"I do. At least my partner does. I heard what happened."

"It didn't take much imagination to realize that her murder would fit nicely into your theory about a serial killer on the loose whose MO was to kill with a personal flair. So I treated her autopsy as I would as if her murder was connected to the others. After identifying the cause of death, I performed a thorough trace analysis."

"I vacuumed her clothes, scraped her nails and a full body skin swab. Within the trace I found 4 distinct hair sample types. Three of them were Caucasoid and one Negroid. Only one of the hairs had the root structure needed for DNA analysis so I sent it off to the lab. It was one of the Negroid hairs. That analysis takes a few days so we won't know the results until it comes back.

"So it's possible to discern African American hair as opposed to Caucasian just by looking it is?

"A microscope is needed, but yes, it is possible. Hair by itself, without the root structure intact, does not tell us a lot, but it does tell us a couple of things. We can tell which of the three human racial classifications it comes from, Caucasoid, Negroid, or Mongloid. And we can match it, by close examination, to other hairs from the same person by comparing the cuticle, the cortex, and the medulla.

"After examining the trace hair found on Ms. Boyle, I packed up my microscope, along with samples of the hair I found, and visited the evidence storage room at police HQ. 4 of the 6 cases you sent me also had collected Negroidal hairs. None had the root structure needed for DNA analysis but I was able to compare the hair I brought from Ms. Boyle to the Negroidal hairs from the other 4. Mr. Forsman, they were indeed from the same person."

"So you were able to connect 4 murders, plus Alphie Leduc's, to a single person?"

"That is correct. Mr. Forsman, I need to get some sleep, it's been a long night and I'm running on fumes, but when I wake up I'll formalize my research and get it into the hands of the police for further investigation. By the time the DNA results are ready, the police should be fully engaged. You said you have a likely suspect."

"Yes, an African American man by the name of Jack Chalwell. I'll send you his name and address."

## Chapter 53

"Hop in."

"Thanks Sammy. I appreciate it."

"What's with the glasses?"

"I don't expect the guy to recognize me but my picture was on the front page of the paper after the Ogrodnik case. I'll wear these just in case," Elliot said as he adjusted a pair of thick, black framed glasses.

"What, you're Clark fucking Kent now?" Sammy asked.

"I've got a part to play so I'm going to dress for it."

"Okay, so what's the plan?"

"The supplier is driving a blue Honda Civic and is going to make a drop at 10:00 this morning at the Lav. We want to intercept him on the way."

"Okay. You want me to run him off the road?"

"No. He's leaving from Fern's Auto Garage on Bannantyne Street in Verdun. He'll almost certainly be taking the Atwater Tunnel to the drop. We'll pick him up when he leaves and make sure we're the car in front of him when we go through the tunnel. I want you to allow him to get real close behind you and then slam on the brakes so we have a little rear-ender. When we do, I'll jump out of the car and get in his," Elliot said.

"What happens if he's packing?"

"He won't be. If my theory is correct, he'll be a mild mannered accountant type. The type of person nobody would look at twice, especially if you're looking for a drug dealer."

* * * * * * * *


"There he goes," said Sammy.

"Okay. Stay out of sight; we don't want to tip him off."

"Ya ya. I got it. I've seen this fuckin movie before."

About a half mile before getting to the tunnel, Sammy accelerated in front of the Civic. Elliot looked at the driver and confirmed his suspicions; the driver looked nothing like what you'd expect to see for a drug dealer.

As they drove through the tunnel, Sammy slammed on the brakes and the Civic behind skidded to a halt but not before he clipped the back end of Sammy's beater. Elliot got out and casually inspected the damage. He waved at the Civic driver as if to say no damage and walked to the Civic passenger door. The Civic driver leaned across the center console to speak as Elliot opened the door.

Elliot slid into the passenger seat and exposed his handgun, keeping it down below dash level. Before the driver could say anything Elliot grunted, "If you don't want your brains all over the window, shut up and drive."

Sammy was already on his way and now out of sight.

"Go straight up Atwater and turn right on St. Antoine, There's an abandoned parking area underneath the Ville Marie, I'll tell you when we get there," Elliot said as he directed his hostage.

"You can have my wallet; it's got a couple of hundred bucks in it."

"I don't want your fuckin wallet asshole. Drive."

The driver complied without hesitation.

"The access on the left, turn in there," directed Elliot.

"Over there behind that stanchion."

The driver pulled in behind a cement stanchion and put the car in park.

"What do you want?"

"You know what I want. Hand it over and you can leave unharmed."

"I don't know what you're talking about"

"Look pal. I'm here to take your product. If you aren't going to give it to me then I'll get it myself. If that's the case, then I don't need you."

"Do you know who I work for?"

"Some assbag bikers who've gotten fat and lazy," Elliot said as he cocked his gun.

Hearing the click of the cocking mechanism told the driver it was time to cooperate. The man opened the door and squeezed underneath the car. Elliot followed him and watched from the side as he struggled with something up in the bowels of the undercarriage.

He heard a latch disconnect and the bottom of the muffler swung down revealing what looked like a number of book-sized packages. The driver reached in, removed five packages from the false muffler, and then snapped it back into place. He dragged himself from under the car and left the packages on the ground.

"That's all of them"

"Give me your phone. Now, hands behind your back. I want to make sure we're not followed," he said as wrapped the man's wrists with duct tape and tossed the phone beyond a fence at the back.

Elliot stuffed the packages into a knapsack and jogged around the corner and onto the side road where Sammy was waiting. He thumped on the trunk and Sammy opened it using the release. Elliot tossed the backpack in and climbed into the car.

So?

"All good"

"What's next?"

"My car's back near l'Oiseau. Let me off there. I'll follow you to the long term parking on Mountain Street south of St. Catherine. I want you to drive in and go down to the bottom floor, park the car and leave the keys on top of the front driver's side tire. I'll be waiting for you outside."

As they drove home, Elliot interrupted the silence as they both thought about what they had just done.

"One more thing Sammy. I need you to go down to the land registry office and get the original blueprints for a building."

"What's the address?"

"Gotta pen?" he asked and then gave the cook the address of the carwash.

"Okay. What should I do with them when I get them?"

"Email them to me."

# Chapter 54

A massive iron gate rolled to a close after two motorcycles rumbled through and around back of the house. They added to the herring bone array of parked bikes and headed directly into the house.

"Okay, we're all here, let's start. As you know, we've been ripped off and Manny thinks he knows who did it," said the biker called Chunks. "Manny, tell everyone what you told me this morning."

"I thought I recognized the guy during the rip-off but couldn't place his face. It wasn't until I got back here and gave it some thought that it came to me. Remember the big deal in the news back in the spring about the PI's who found the Stungun killer but he ended up getting away?"

A few of the bikers nodded and one of them answered, "There was a man and a woman team interviewed on the news, yeah I remember them."

"The man, Elliot Forsman, was the same guy who ripped me off."

"Fuck off, what's a PI doing ripping off drugs? How did he even know about our operation?"

"All I know is that it's the same guy. I asked our source down at the cop shop to pull his background.

Get this, he's wanted for murder! Apparently he whacked some guy named Labrosse."

"You got a picture of him?"

"Yeah, here's a still of him from the news station interview."

"I don't recognize him."

"Well, I do. This is him except he was wearing thick, dark framed glasses when he ripped us off."

"That's his disguise? What, he thinks he's Clark fucken Kent? Well we're gonna stick some kryptonite up his ass," said Chunks as he addressed the rest of the bikers.

"You want us to go after him?" one of the bikers asked.

"Damn right. We need to get him before the cops do. If he's picked up, he'll use the product, and his knowledge of the drug operation, to make a deal. What else you got on this guy Manny?"

"House in Westmount, office is on Sherbrooke and Marlowe. His known associates are a son in the UK, his partner, Rivka Goldstein. She's in the psych ward at the General, and a friend, Sammy Golbis."

"That's it? Three known associates? No other family? No other friends?"

"That's what the report says."

"Poor fucker, we're doing him a favor by whacking him. Okay, we need to watch for his credit cards, phone usage, and any places he frequents."

"I want someone sitting on his house and his place of work. Remember, he can't stay at home so I want to know where he's staying. If his partner is in the hospital he might decide to camp out there, so put someone at the partners house. Look at his charge and ATM cards. If he frequents a place for lunch every day, I want to know about it. And don't worry about the airports, the cops will be all over that," he barked, and the bikers moved out.

"And boys, priority number one is to shut this fucker up, permanently, before the cops get him. Second priority is to get our product back."

## Chapter 55

Rayce lay in bed, using time, and rest to heal his injuries. He forced himself out of bed, took his antibiotics, and prepared to change the dressing on his wounded side. The information he extracted from Sauvage had cost him. Sauvage had been tough, tougher than Rayce anticipated, or perhaps Rayce was not as healthy as he thought he was. Another consideration pushed into his thoughts, that maybe he was just getting old. He didn't dwell on it.

He looked at the open sutures and cursed silently. He didn't mind self-suturing, he'd done it many times in the past, but it was the location of his wound. Accessing the open injury with needle and thread would be challenging if he were healthy. Now, with limited flexibility due to his injuries, it was all but impossible to reach his lower back. He discarded the needle and used an adhesive backed bandage to cover the open incision. The type of bandage he had in his hand was designed to cover cuts and scrapes, not pull two sides of ragged flesh together, but he made do.

Even though he just woken up, he lay down again to rest; he needed to get his strength back. Sauvage had told him about the mercenaries that were hired to kill him. Rayce didn't know much about the operation, or who was ultimately behind it, but he was certain Sauvage had disclosed all he knew. Rayce knew firsthand about ways to extract information from unwillings. He'd been on the other side of those discussions and understood the limits of resistance and how to reach human breaking points. He sometimes hated himself for some of the things he knew, but he also recognized that he couldn't change that, and that as long as they were a part of him, a part of his memories, he would use them.

He closed his eyes and let fatigue take him. He didn't drift off to a lazy slumber; sleep came upon him like a bird of prey and dragged him into a deep, dark place.

*He shielded his eyes from the brilliant light and squinted to keep out the blowing sand stinging his face like a thousand needles, finding its way into his ears, his nose, and his eyes. He crouched behind a rock face to find shelter, and found the mouth of a cave instead. He had no choice, he was compelled to enter, the cave called for him. His eyes adjusted to the darkness and he saw a boy, no more than 13, strapped to an inclined board in the center of a cavernous underground room. His chest was completely flayed open, exposing his organs, his lungs breathing, his heart still beating. He clutched a bloody keffiyeh in one hand, and gazed at Rayce with a look that begged 'help me'.*

Standing around the boy were members of his old unit, Dan-o and Cropper. Beside them were his mother, his father, and his uncles. All held bloody knives in their hand, all now staring at Rayce.

Rayce yelled 'No' and pushed them aside so he could reach the boy. He unstrapped the dying boy and laid him gently on the ground. He tried to pull the skin back over the boys open cavity, but was unable to. He could see the flaps of skin hanging from the boy's side but when he reached for them, was unable to find purchase, as if the flaps of skin were not quite substantial enough to exist. He turned his attention away from the boy and mounted himself onto the board, tugging to secure the straps. When he looked up, he saw that Iraqi soldiers now surrounded him, brandishing a variety of instruments meant to cause him pain. They were smiling and laughing. He yelled at them to hurt him, to maim him, to torture him, that he deserved it. He closed his eyes and screamed.

When he opened his eyes, he was in his parent's backyard. Standing around the barbeque pit were his parents and uncles. They were talking amongst themselves too low for Rayce to hear, but the way they'd look back at Rayce during their discourse told him they were talking about him. The delicious smells of roasting meat found his nostrils and he walked towards the barbeque pit, and his family. They shouted at him to stay away, that he couldn't come closer. They told him that his face was disfigured;

they ridiculed him, and shouted that he wasn't a hero. He felt his face for disfigurement and felt none. He pulled a large knife from his belt and looked at his reflection in the blade. He saw a face that was a moonscape of pockmarks and puckers. Not a square inch of his face was unmarked. He felt shamed.

He turned his back on his family and started walking, it was night now and the air was cold, but he continued walking with no destination in mind. Eventually the grassy fields turned to hills, and then mountains, and still he walked, and still, it was night. When, at last the morning sun broke, he saw that the ground was frozen and snow covered, and he felt cold. He headed for a cabin off to the side and entered without knocking. There was a woman inside, a beautiful woman in a nurse's uniform. She told him he could live here now, that this could be his home. He replied saying, "I can't live here. My face is disfigured. I'm not a hero."

She replied. "Your face is not disfigured," and handed him an ornate mirror with a long silvered handle.

Rayce looked in and saw that the woman was correct; there was nothing wrong with his face. He wondered why his family would tell him that.

"You are right Rayce, you are not a hero. There are no heroes. A hero is what one person sees in another. You can never see it in yourself."

*Rayce thought about what Sarah Forsman said and knew it was true. "Are you expecting company?" he asked.*

*"No. Why do you ask?"*

*"I hear motorcycles coming."*

*Rayce got up and opened the door. Blinding sunlight hit his face, and it was hot, so hot. He realized he was sweating profusely.*

Rayce woke up with the sun beaming in through the bedroom window directly on him. His bed clothing was drenched with sweat, but he felt refreshed. More refreshed than he'd felt in days. He crawled out of bed, and opened the fridge in search of cold water. He was thirsty. He felt parched and dried out on the inside and he drank deeply.

He thought about the dream. Something in the dream had woken him, something important. He knew that the memory of dreams faded quickly so he wasted no time recalling it. The dream, like most dreams, consisted of a few accurate details connected loosely by a nonsensical storyline. The portions about the boy, his parents, the Iraqi soldiers, and Sarah Forsman were all true, and for him predictable. They had walked, uncalled for, in his dreams for longer than he cared to remember. The motorcycles he heard just before the end of the dream kept coming back to him as something important. Not just motorcycles, they were Harleys. A sound he knew all too well. He remembered hearing two motorcycles in the dream, two Harleys. One of them, not just a Harley, but it had the distinctive sound of a Harley Knucklehead. The same type of bike that the Henchman they called 'Tiny' rode. A rare bike anywhere, but especially in these parts.

He didn't waste time overthinking the situation. The sound of two Harleys cruising by the cottage had woken him. Rayce was a man who didn't leave things to chance. He grabbed the Sig Sauer P320 off his nightstand and, as an afterthought, put the silencer in his pocket. He made a quick survey out of each window before exiting and headed straight for a thick grove of cedars fifty yards from the cottage. The worst place he could be when the bikers came for him was inside. If they caught him inside, his chances for survival would be slim. Once concealed, he settled down to gather his thoughts and form a plan.

He worked with the assumption that his dream was not false. That a couple of Harleys had rumbled by, that they were Henchmen and they were after Rayce. How they managed to find him he didn't know. At this point, that didn't matter, what mattered was for him to stay alive. He put himself in their position and thought about how he would approach their task. He would have slowly rumbled by the cottage and confirmed location and setting for possible attack strategies. He would park his bike up the road, out of sight, and come back on foot to execute the plan.

He planned for the worst case, the men they sent would be armed and dangerous, and that their intent was to finish the job that started 3 days ago. The forest around him held many places to hide and many ways to approach the cottage. His immediate concern was finding where the bikers were, and the path they'd use to get to the cottage.

He settled down into surveillance mode. He set his sight in a fixed position and focused on nothing in particular so that any movement would catch his attention. He felt the damp earth beneath him and the smell of the forest around him. He listened to the sound of the breeze filtering through the trees and the distant echoes of humanity out on the lake. He tuned his senses to the natural pulse of his surroundings so that anything disturbing that pulse would be detected.

He heard them long before he saw them. They were coming in from on top of an escarpment a hundred yards behind the cottage. A wash coming down from the escarpment offered easy access to the back and provided a viewpoint of the entire property. Coming down from the ridge would have been Rayce's strategy too. Now that he knew which direction they were coming from, Rayce hunkered down farther into the bowels of the cedar branches and waited.

He saw the two bikers appear at the top of the escarpment and kneel down to survey the cottage terrain. They stayed up top, motionless, for over 10 minutes, looking for activity in the cottage and ensuring they weren't walking into a trap. Finally, convinced there was no danger, they advanced. The smaller biker came first, one-step, and pause, another step, another pause. The larger biker stayed up top, gun at his shoulder, ready to shoot. It took many minutes for the advance biker to make it to the bottom of the ridge and find cover behind a tree. Now that he was safely down, he trained his automatic weapon on the cottage while the big biker, the biker known as 'Tiny', came down the wash.

Rayce had a plan. Knowing the bikers would be focusing on the cottage, he wasn't worried about them finding him until the cottage proved empty. He would not be in the cedars when they came out.

Rayce waited them out as they took their time advancing, and ultimately, storm the cottage. As soon as they entered Rayce sprinted out from his place of concealment and headed up the road, knowing there were no sightlines from the house. His plan was to attack them when they were not so focused. He'd get them when they were relaxed and their adrenaline rush had ebbed. That's when they would be the most vulnerable.

He easily found their bikes stashed behind an old shed and took up a position that would maximize his chances of a clean, swift victory. Once again, he settled into surveillance mode, again, he became part of the surrounding eco-system. He turned off his internal clock and waited. The bikers must have been thorough in their exploration of the cottage, garage, and surrounding environment. Rayce waited in silence for over an hour before he heard them coming.

"Let's take a quick run over to the Knowlton Pub. We'll have a couple of beers and come back later," said Tiny.

"Sounds like a good idea, I'm fucking parched. I wouldn't mind seeing that waitress again."

"Which one? The one with the nice smile?"

"I dunno. I never looked at her face. The one with the perky tits and the nice ass."

"I think I remember her. Was she the one who balanced a full tray of beer in one hand and made change with the other without putting the beer down? Now that's a fucken woman."

"That's what it's about for you eh. How much beer a woman can carry."

"Look, they all have woman parts. You seen one snatch you seen 'em all. But how many can balance a tray like that? Hell, there must have been a dozen beers on that tray. And they were fucken quarts, not your pint bottles," said the big man.

Rayce watched as the two men had now put their weapons away and were in the process of pulling their bikes out of their hiding places.

"All the same? What the fuck you talking about? Every pussy has a personality. Just like people, except they're useful and they don't talk back. You probably think they're all the same cuz you only ever had one. It was probably a drunken old broad with fucken yeast and shit."

"Fuck you, motherfucker."

Rayce used the ensuing laughter as his cue. He stood up from his place of hiding and ran towards the closer of the two bikers, the smaller one, with gun extended, pointing at Tiny. Two steps, two bullets, center mass in the big biker. He staggered off the side of his bike and fell into a heap.

The smaller biker was still struggling to get his gun out when Rayce hit him with a head butt to the side of his head. Ten pounds of skull-armored head made a formidable weapon. Rayce's forehead caught the biker on the right temple, beside his eye. He felt the structure of the biker's orbital bone fail as his head caved in. The biker was out cold, Rayce hoped he wasn't dead. It's not that he cared about the bikers' life, he did not, but Rayce had questions and the biker would have answers. A quick check told him that the biker was hurt badly, but still breathing.

Rayce went through their saddlebags and pockets while he waited for the biker to come to. He was obviously in need of medical attention but that wasn't part of Rayce's plan. Rayce found nothing of value so he sat down and waited the biker out. Eventually the biker stirred, Rayce came to his side and helped raise his level of consciousness.

"Who hired you to kill me?"

The biker, having trouble focusing his gaze, took a moment of staring at Rayce before the words came.

"You're the bike dealer."

"Tell me something I don't know. Who wants me dead? And why?"

"You're the bike dealer," he repeated, still groggy.

"Look buddy, if you want me to give you some pain to focus your attention, I can do that. But you're not going to like it."

The biker, now understanding his situation, and feeling the pain of a crushed skull, was coming out of his grog.

"We were sent here to get a PI. A guy by the name of Forsman."

"You weren't here for me?"

"No. We didn't know you were here."

"Why did you think he was here?"

"We saw his cell phone ping at this location Sunday morning. The boss sent us out to take care of the PI. He ripped us off."

"Okay, so you were sent out here to kill Forsman because he ripped you off. Let's talk about me for a second. Why did the Henchmen finger me? Who tried to kill me? And who hired the killers?"

"We were hired to go to your garage and verify who you were. The guy described you and said if we threatened you, and you backed down, you weren't the guy."

"Who hired you?"

"I don't know. Even the boss doesn't know. The job came in through corporate."

"Corporate? The Henchmen have a corporation?"

"We call it corporate. Henchmen leaders are businessmen. They don't ride bikes and party. They're lawyers and bankers. I don't know who they are, only the generals know them."

"You have ranks too?"

"Sort of. We have generals, lieutenants, members, and guests."

"Is Chunks a general?"

"Yeah."

"Why does this guy want me dead?"

"I don't know. All I know is that he wanted us to finger you and he'd send in his own muscle afterward to do the job."

"So you don't know anything else?"

"I'm just a member. I don't know shit."

Rayce, thought about sparing the man's life. Once he weighed the facts his decision was made, the man was a criminal, responsible for who knows what, but certainly part of the drug operation that was killing dozens of innocents. And he was here with the intent to kill his friend, Elliot Forsman. No, letting him live was not the wise choice. He raised his handgun and finished the job.

Rayce broke down his gun into pieces, wiped his prints off them, and distributed them into the bike's saddlebags. Rayce never kept a weapon used to kill someone. Weapons were cheap but once they became evidence, they could be costly.

"Gaetan, Rayce here."

"Rayce, que puis-je faire pour vous?"

"I've got something for you."

"How hot is it?" the man asked as he switched to English.

"Let's just say that it's not something you want to be caught with."

"What is it?"

"Two hogs, fully decked. One of them is a 47 Knuckle."

"Nice. That should be easy enough."

"You'll have to take the owners with you."

"They won't be needing them any longer?"

"Not in this lifetime."

"Where are they?"

"They're waiting with their bikes."

"Are they messy?"

"Not too bad. They're outside so it won't be an issue."

"Where are you?"

"My place out in Orford?"

"I'll send Steve now."

"I'll wait till he gets here."

## Chapter 56

Now that the cafés were closing and Elliot was forced from his 'laying low' spots, it was time to execute the next phase of his plan. He dialed Margie.

"Hello," she answered a sleepy voice.

"Did I wake you?"

"What kind of question is that? Of course you woke me, it's after 1:00 in the freaking morning. You think I'm a vampire?"

"Every fiber of my being wants to make a snappy answer to that question using the word sucking, but I won't. Just calling you to tell you I probably won't be going back to your place tonight. I have some errands to run."

"You're running errands at this time of night?"

"Yeah, I have to drop by Chalwell's carwash and Labrosse's export business."

"That sounds highly illegal."

"When in Rome," he replied without explanation.

"Should I be lining up bail money for you?"

"Nothing says '*I love you*' like bail money."

She ignored his glibness and continued. "You're not going to sleep tonight?"

"Doubtful. I have to stay off the streets so I might duck into Rivka's for a few hours. I'll play it by ear."

"Can't this wait for the morning? You cruising around at 1:00 am in the morning sounds like a recipe for disaster."

"Believe me, I'd rather not have to do this at all, but my time is running out. I need to gather evidence while I still can. Tomorrow might be a shit show."

Elliot parked a block away from the Labrosse & Sons building and walked in from there. He knew there was an access door in the rear of the building that didn't have line of sight from the street out front. Even though it was after 1:00 in the morning, he needed to be careful. If the police stopped him, he would be arrested; he couldn't afford to be apprehended before he had what he came to get. He walked by the warehouse with no apparent interest in the building so he could safely approach the building from the rear without raising any alarms.

Once his approach started, experience told him that the best method is to walk up to the back door as if he owned the place and work the lock without looking around to see who might be watching. He was relieved when he got to the door to see that the lock was an older Schlage. A good solid lock, but definitely pickable. Elliot inserted the bump key and torsion bar and 10 seconds later was in.

His destination was the shipping bay near the back of the warehouse and let his flashlight show the way. He found the same type of Schlage lock on the warehouse entrance and minutes later was playing his flashlight across the shipping area. On the left wall, farthest from the shipping door, there were dozens of arcade games in various states of repair. The arcade games did not interest him. On the wall adjacent to the big shipping doors, he saw a lineup of a couple of dozen crates on skids; they all looked similar so he inspected the manifest on the crate nearest to him.

The destination on the label was J3T Industries in the British Virgin Islands. The enclosed manifest listed the serial numbers of a dozen devices, all described as Telecommunication Equipment. He took the manifest and moved to the next crate. It didn't take long for him to determine that all the crates were part of the same shipment. All containing Telecom equipment, and all going to J3T Industries in the British Virgin Islands. He wanted to open the crates and find the drug money he believed was hidden inside. Ultimately, he had what he came for, and would let his lawyer work through the legal system and allow the police to search the crates.

He checked the clock in the Volvo and saw that he only took 15 minutes at Labrosse's. He wasn't pressed for time but wanted to minimize the time he was out on the roads. Every minute he was out in the open was a minute he could be found and caught, by the police, or the Henchmen. He didn't know if the Henchmen knew who ripped them off, but he assumed by now they knew it was himself. He'd been 2 steps behind at every step of this case, this would be no exception.

He used a different parking strategy at the Lav. He parked on the street just around the corner from the Lav and walked through the parking lot watching for activity. The entire lot was dark and quiet; the only light came in as weak shine from the streetlights on St. Catherine Street. He slowed his walk through the lot while a car passed on the facing street and then he angled over to the gap between the office and boundary fence.

Evan had already told him that the OPUS II alarm system was top of the line. There was no stealthy way into the building so he didn't even try. He smashed the door window with a hefty rock and slipped his hand inside to unlatch the door. He quickly edged over to the walled Marlin and cursed silently as he slipped and almost fell in a small puddle of water at the base of the coat rack. He risked turning on his flashlight to look at the floor and noticed that a small puddle of water extended underneath the adjacent wall. He pushed on the wall and it seemed to flex inward, as if it wasn`t part of the office`s exterior frame, no matter, he didn`t have time to explore it further.

He was startled by a voice coming from the broken door, "Who are you," the voice barked.

He said nothing as he whipped around to meet his discoverer. The voice sounded again, "I will repeat the question one more time and know that I've already dispatched a police call."

It was then that Elliot clued in that the voice was coming from the OPUS II alarm system. He had triggered the alarm and the OPUS II service was responding remotely. He exhaled and proceeded with his task, ignoring the OPUS II voice.

He pulled the photo underneath the marlin from the wall and bolted from the building. He knew the police would be responding in a matter of minutes.

Within 30 seconds he was in his car driving away from the Lav, it was only then that he took a look at the photo. The picture he held was illuminated briefly every time he drove past a street light but it was enough for him to validate his suspicions. He already knew that Chalwell was the skipper in the photo. Now he knew that the 2 tourists posing in front were the lawyer Anderson, and his partner in crime, Joseph Labrosse.

## Chapter 57

Elliot checked the time and decided that he'd rather not intrude on Margie at 2:00 am. He wouldn't be able to sleep anyway so why impose his sleeplessness on someone else. He wasn't too far from Rivka's house so he'd take advantage of her empty house and lie low until he could blend in with the morning rush hour.

A car in her driveway would be a dead giveaway for anyone driving by, so he parked his car on a dead end street a few blocks from Rivka's and walked through the golf course and into the backyard. He paused at the edge of her backyard and watched the house for a few minutes. A sheet of plywood covered the window through which Rivka had shot the homeless man. The shards of broken glass at the base of the plywood caught the moonlight and threw it back at Elliot. The house stood, dark and empty, like a tombstone of wood and glass.

He advanced to the house and used his key to get in through the garage and the rear access door. The house was silent; the only sound was the soft purr of cool air pouring through the vents.

Elliot crept quietly to the edge of the large living area and stood on the threshold looking into the room without entering. The nearly full moon shone in through the windows and cast an intricate shadow of the treetops across the floor. A gust of wind caused the shadows to sway back and forth in a ghostly dance. He watched and listened for a few minutes without moving. Slowly, as if compelled to do so without conscious direction, his hand moved to the handgun, still tucked into his waistband. It settled on the butt and stayed there, as if it knew on its own not to make even a slight rustling noise. The only sound he now heard was the beating of his own heart, which had increased significantly since he stepped into the house.

Elliot had always been a believer in what people refer to as gut instinct. He understood that the whole of his senses was greater than the sum of its parts. He had heard or seen nothing to be concerned about, nor had he smelled or felt anything. Yet his brain screamed danger. At a subconscious level, his mind had taken all the sensory information that his body fed it, and interpreted it into something that couldn't be perceived at a conscious level. He waited for the danger to reveal itself, a creaking floor or rustle of fabric, but none came. The only signal his senses returned was the sight of the tree shadows dancing across the floor.

Not one to ignore the significance of the message, he backed away slowly from the threshold of the room. Careful not to make even a sound, not even a muted breath. Once his hand was on the doorknob of the exterior access door, he threw it open and bolted back the way he came. He ran down the hedge line and into the woods bordering the golf course behind. He didn't slow down as he darted through the sparsely wooded area as fast as the shifting light would allow. After a couple of hundred yards, he zipped to the side and slid to a stop behind a large boulder. Trying desperately to catch his breath without making noise, he dared to poke his head off to the side to see what, if anything was behind him. He scanned back and forth across the wooded terrain and absorbed the dark of the night. He saw nothing, he heard nothing, and nobody had chased him. The house still dark and no sign of life. Perhaps it was his imagination, he thought. Now emboldened, he stood and rebuked himself. If he was going to complete his task list, he needed to be more aware and mentally alert. He could not allow his thoughts to run away with the truth. He was about to turn and leave when a light in Rivka's living area flicked on. It bathed the area immediately behind the house in a weak glow, like a stage might look from the back row in a dark theater.

A figure walked in from the bedroom hallway and approached the window looking out towards the golf course where Elliot stood. Even though the figure was 150 yards away, he could see the silhouette quite clearly. He saw a large man and the nap of a long scraggly beard showed clearly against the lighted room behind. Cradled in his arm was a rifle, no, thicker and shorter, it was a shotgun. The stout figure watched out the back for a few moments and then headed towards the front door.

If Elliot had any doubts before that the Henchmen knew he was the one who ripped them off, they were now gone. Not only were the police looking for him, he now had the Henchmen pursuing him. The police would take him into custody and he'd eventually end up in prison. The Henchmen were not bound by the same rules. They would mete out their own brand of justice. They would torture him for the location of the stolen drugs and then kill him.

# Chapter 58

Elliot's options of where to lay low for the remainder of the night were few. His only viable place of safe refuge would be at Margie's. He decided to stay off the highways going into downtown and instead, took Sherbrooke all the way in.

He cruised by the JFK office being careful not to look at it or slow down. He saw what he expected to see a half a block east of Marlowe. An unmarked police car parked on the opposite side of the street from JFK with a couple of heads slumped down in the front seats.

He continued driving east on Sherbrooke and then shunted down one block to Boulevard Maisonneuve, towards Margie's downtown condo near Stanley Street. He slowed to a stop as he approached Crescent Street, one of the hubs of Montréal nightlife. He slowed to a stop when a knot of drunken revelers blocked the street while they argued about whether to cross the street or go back the way they came and the the light turned red. Elliot lost interest in their drunken banter and turned his attention to the bars and pubs on Crescent. The pulsating beat of dance music pumped from the nearest pub and he noticed the bopping mass from within had spilled from the dance floor area and out onto the patio.

He knew that the three major cultural ideologies in Montréal would be found within the gyrating throng. The English speaking Anglos, the pro-Canada French, and the French Separatists. The Indignant, the Indifferent, and the Incensed.

In day-to-day life, the three groups acted like mistreated puppies, defensive and on edge, ready to growl and snap at the first sign of misunderstanding. None of that mattered where the music pulsed and drinks flowed. The mob he watched were there to exorcise the thread of underlying tensions that run through their lives. This is where they come to dance, to mingle, and to drink. Their sweaty ballet driven by sexual hunger and fueled by alcohol. Their eyes alive, heads thrown back, and faces locked in rapture. The crowd moved like a ritualistic Rhumba to purge their demons, hopping, twisting, and grinding.

He remembered a time, not many years ago, when members of these disparate ideologies would not mingle freely. He sensed that the hardliners from all sides had softened over the years. The younger generations seemed to have developed a broad mindedness that their parents may not have had. Elliot was optimistic, and hoped the flames of intolerance would not be re-ignited by an ambitious politician trying to establish a reputation. The light turned green and he left the night scene behind, along with all thoughts of Quebec politics. He had more pressing matters on his mind.

Elliot crawled into bed beside Margie knowing there would be no sleep but wanting the comfort of a warm body and a soft bed. It might be a long time before he experienced either again.

"I knew you'd come. Did you get what you were after?"

"I think so."

"Did you find evidence that will absolve you in Labrosse's murder?"

"No. There is no evidence," he looked at her, smiled and kissed her forehead.

"Go to sleep, we can talk in the morning."

It wasn't long before he heard the soft murmur of Margie's breathing. He wished he could sleep but knew that there was too much to think about for him to achieve a blissful slumber.

He had the invoices from Labrosse and Sons, and the photo that connected Anderson and Labrosse to Chalwell, as well as the info on the drug operation. He now turned his thoughts outward and looked at the entire case in his mind's eye.

He thought about Alphie and his murder.

He thought about photo from the wall and he thought about the murders of Joseph Labrosse and of Rebecca Boyle.

He thought about all the murders attributed to Mamelon, all the drug overdoses due to fentanyl, and the lives that were turned upside down because of it. And he thought about the Montréal drug ring that operated through Chalwell's carwash.

These facts were the foundation he would build his new mental Rubik's cube on. These were the anchor points that all other evidence would hang from.

He harvested all that had happened over the past week and listed the events mentally. He assembled the new facts and rotated them in his mind, looking at them from every angle. As he pieced together the case, his cube started to materialize again. The cube was not quite complete but there were extraneous pieces of data that didn't fit. It was as if he was assembling a jigsaw puzzle and, without his knowledge, someone had removed a few pieces and replaced them with dozens of similarly colored, but incorrect pieces. Even though the puzzle was almost complete, none of the remaining pieces would finish it, and even if he found the pieces to complete his cube, there would be unexplainable leftover shreds of data.

He ignored the extraneous pieces of data and focused on what he knew. He then took stock of his situation and his next actions. He quickly determined that his situation was unchanged. He was going to jail, Chalwell was getting away with murder, his drug operation was walking away with a fortune, and the Henchmen's illegal operations would continue. He came to the grim conclusion that all his investigative work was for naught. He had accomplished nothing except get himself in grave trouble with the law.

Even though he intercepted the drug delivery and knew how the operation worked, he could do nothing about it. He wondered if the justice he sought was not justice at all, but revenge. He played with the idea of going after Chalwell and killing him. He was already facing a lifetime in prison so adding another body to the count probably wouldn't mean much. He dismissed the idea on principle; even though Chalwell deserved nothing more, he wanted justice, not revenge.

He considered his next steps. He could turn himself in and hand the stolen product over to the police along with the story of the drug operation. That wouldn't change the fact that he's going to prison but his cooperation might reduce his sentence. It also wouldn't change the fact that Chalwell would get away with murder, literally, and that he and his cronies would walk away with the riches they made selling drugs and killing people. Exposing the drug operation might stem the flow of product for a short period but would likely not blow back on Chalwell. He'd protected himself far too well. He would already be in the process of shutting down the operation, there wouldn't be any more deliveries, his own actions had seen to that. It also wouldn't accomplish much with Chalwell's suppliers. He had no doubt they were busy getting rid of any evidence that might cause them trouble and were already in the process of recruiting new distributors. Their fentanyl poison would still infiltrate the streets. Innocents would still die.

His current scenario was not palatable, so he put those thoughts aside and turned his attention to his mental Rubik's cube and the extraneous, unexplained pieces of data.

The more he thought about the events of the past week, the more he suspected there were other forces at play. The colored squares that existed on the periphery of his mind's eye bothered him. The disconnected colored squares represented recent events that were not directly related to the case, or were they? Their only commonality was that they all occurred with Elliot at their center, framed for a murder he did not commit. Rivka, seemingly on the road to recovery after her Ogrodnik ordeal, was pulled back in deeper than she could escape from, and Rayce, attacked and almost killed by unknown assailants.

He thought about what Rivka told him about her anxiety episodes and when she saw the flowers at Alphie's funeral. That event by itself wouldn't be noteworthy, but why those particular flowers at that particular time? He thought about how she saw a big man in her backyard and shot him two nights later. Again, it wouldn't be unusual that a homeless man wandered to the edge of a golf course on a nice evening, but why on those two nights, at those two times? In addition, to have it happen to a man large enough that she would mistake him for Ogrodnik, and where does a homeless man get $400? Again, taken individually, none of those events would be unusual, but given the context of the date, the time, and the person involved, the odds of them being coincidental seemed unlikely.

He thought about the attack on Rayce. The fact that the Henchmen had scouted him out the day before the attack made it a well thought out, coordinated operation. The question was, was it coordinated to occur at the same times as both he and Rivka were wrapped up in their own struggles?

Finally, he thought about himself being framed for murder. Labrosse was a partner in the drug operation. *Why wouldn't they just kill me*? He thought. That way they keep their partner alive and eliminate the only person on the planet who has been able to crack open their operation. Mamelon and the drug operation have killed dozens of people over the years without conscience or consequence. They would not shy away from killing one more. *What did they gain by framing me? And why at this particular time?*

On the surface, all these events were unconnected, but if he panned back, away from his mental Rubik's cube, the other events started coming into focus. He used a method astronomers sometimes used to discover new planetary objects. At times, the light coming from a distant celestial object is so faint that it is not visible with a telescope, but minor fluctuations in the paths of visible objects near the unseen object give it away. It seemed to him that there was an unseen entity influencing events. He had no direct evidence suggesting that such an entity existed but the manner in which events unfolded around it were proof that it was real.

It would be impossible for Elliot to say how long he was in a state of mental retreat. If he stopped to think about it he would have guessed it would be hours, but to think about time would have forced his mind up a layer, he would not do that. Time did not exist while he was in this state of deep contemplation. Much like a chess master who tries to envision consequences of possible moves, Elliot altered bits of information and allowed his mind to ripple the effects of that change through the case.

It wasn't until he had the epiphany to shift his focus on the extraneous events that they started making sense. He always considered the extraneous events as if they were centered on him, but once he viewed them with Rivka at their center, they started slotting into place. He let his thoughts manipulate the colored scraps of information taking care to discard any assumptions he had made during the course of the investigation and inserted new information based on the facts that he knew. He played out hundreds of possible scenarios, testing his assumptions as he went, and slowly, gradually, a new image started to form in his mind's eye. The image was unique to his experience. The original cube was now complete, the facts about the drug operation, Chalwell, Anderson, and Labrosse would not change, but the other, previously disconnected facts had formed a second image.

The extraneous pieces now fit into a second structure he'd never experienced before. He marveled at its intricacy. For lack of a better description, he imagined the case as a cube within a cube. The original cube, whole, and solid, encompassing all the evidence and events related to Chalwell, his many murders and the drug operation. The second structure, translucent, but substantial, completely encompassed the first cube. He studied the manner in which the outer structure interconnected with the original cube and eventually came to understand the depths of deception that had surrounded him.

It was a revelation that instantly jolted him out of his meditation, sit up in bed, and force his eyes open. A quick glance at the bedside clock told him he'd been in trance for nearly four hours. He heard a change in the soft breathing of Margie next to him as his lover stirred, oblivious to the fact that Elliot had come to a major break in the case. He slid out of bed quietly, but failed in his attempt not to wake her.

"Where are you going?" she asked while trying to stifle a yawn.

"I've got a busy day. I have a few things to do before I turn myself in."

Margie turned to look at him, "you told me that you couldn't turn yourself in because nobody else could prove your innocence. Has something changed?"

"The only thing that's changed is my understanding of the situation. Rivka is in danger. If I don't turn myself in, she will be killed."

"What? By whom? How did you come to this conclusion?" she said now sitting up in bed.

"I've thought the situation through. I'd rather not give up. I'd prefer to stay out of jail and see if I can prove my innocence. I won't lie to you, I'm in a tight spot. My only play is to turn myself in. I fully expect to see time in prison."

"But you didn't kill Labrosse. You can't admit to something you didn't do."

"I'm not admitting anything. After I build out the rest of the story on the drug operation, my lawyer will use it to negotiate a better plea deal."

"It sounds like you're giving up."

"No. I'm making the best of a bad situation. When I put all the options on a scale and weigh out the pros and cons, there is no decision to make. If I don't do something soon, Chalwell and the entire drug operation will be gone. They'll take their money and start a new life somewhere far away. I'm talking about the money they built on the dead bodies of all those drug overdoses and the suffering of their families. My freedom doesn't stack up against the justice that these assholes deserve. "

"I know all about your over-developed sense of justice, but is there no other way?"

Elliot shook his head no without answering directly.

"I know it's only been a week but I'm kind of getting used to having you around."

"Is that sentiment I hear? Did you just say that you love me in Maller speak?"

"I wouldn't put it that way. I think we may be an emotional match. The way we interact causes a chemical reaction on the brain that we perceive as pleasure. "

"Dim the lights and let the soft music play, you old-fashioned romantic," Elliot smiled. "Are you going to visit me in jail?"

"Are you asking if I'm I going to sit in front of a plexi-glass window and speak through a phone receiver that's been licked, kissed and sneezed on by the bottom 10% of societie's dregs?"

"That answers my question."

"Now if you can arrange a conjugal visit I might think about it."

"How is Rivka?" he said changing the subject.

"She's somewhere between not bad, and okay. I don't think she's a suicide risk but I have her on merry-meds just in case. I also don't think staying in the hospital is best for her right now. I'm going to visit her this afternoon, if she hasn't taken a turn for the worse I'll recommend that she be discharged today."

"Good to hear it. I'm going to make a coffee and prepare my day, do you want one?"

"Not now, I need to jump in the shower."

# Chapter 59

*Wednesday, August 30th*

It was just after 6:00 am when Elliot turned on the coffee maker. He needed the coffee as he hadn't slept well. Even though there were tasks for him to complete before he turned himself in, he took the time to plan out the day. He sipped his coffee and sat at the table with his plunder from the previous night. He had the manifests from Labrosse's warehouse and he had the photograph taken from Chalwell's carwash.

He picked up the photo from the carwash and looked at the two tourists posing with the marlin. As he had already verified, he recognized the tourists. The tourist on the left was a younger version of a man he knew, his hair was mostly intact and much thicker, but there was no doubt that he was looking at Joseph Labrosse, the man he was accused of murdering.

The tourist on the right was a younger version of the lawyer, Joel Anderson. This was the proof he was looking for. He already knew about the connection between Anderson and Labrosse. He also knew that the Lav was the distribution point for the drugs which implicated Chalwell as a priciple in the drug operation. The manifests would give the police a paper trail that would allow them to tie the drug money they find, back to Labrosse.

The photo was the missing piece that tied the three together and proved without a doubt that Chalwell, Labrosse, and Anderson were involved in the Montréal drug ring. Not just involved, these three would be the principals.

He heard the shower turn on upstairs and decided this would be a good time to complete his next task. He'd rather make this phone call without Margie in the room.

"Dupree Motor Garage."

"I'm looking for the owner."

"Speaking."

"We've never met but I have a business proposition for you."

"Who are you?"

"I was hired to hit your car yesterday."

There was a momentary pause at the other end of the line.

"What the fuck are you talking about?"

"I'm talking about you, your operation and the product that was stolen yesterday morning."

The garage owner was silent for a moment while he processed the situation.

"Who are you, no bullshit."

"I was hired as the wheelman on a drug heist yesterday morning. We caused a little fender bender in the Atwater Tunnel and my associate hopped into your car. He ended up with 5 bricks of blow."

"What do you want?"

"I know where it is."

"So. You calling to brag or what?"

"I'm calling to offer you a deal. I'll give you the pickup place and you pay me the money this guy stiffed me out of."

"Who hired you?"

"I got picked out of a bar. I didn't know the guy, I guess a mutual acquaintance sent him to offer me the wheel job."

"He stiffed you?"

"Yeah. He promised me 5% of the take and then tossed me a grand and told me to fuck off. He said that's all I earned."

"A thousand dollars is a pretty good payday if all you did was drive."

"What can I say, I'm a man of fucking principles. We agreed on 5% and that's what I want."

"So…"

"I'll tell you where the coke is and you can make up the money I'm missing."

"How do I know you're not bullshitting me?"

"I know about the ripoff don't I?"

"So if you know where it is why don't you get it and sell it?"

"Sell it. To who? As soon as that product shows up on the street your guys will trace it back to me and I'm a dead man."

"True. Okay. Where is it?"

"In a car that's in a long term parking garage."

"Why would they tell you anything if you were just a dumbass driver?"

"They didn't tell me. When we were waiting for your car yesterday morning he got out and talked to his employer. He didn't realize the back window was open so I heard most of his conversation."

"What did you hear?"

"He told the guy on the phone that he'd leave the coke in a car in the storage garage on Mountain."

"Which car?"

"I don't know. The way he talked it was a car they had pre-arranged to be there."

"Did he say who the employer was?"

"I think he called him Chaswell."

"You mean Chalwell?" he blurted.

"Yeah, that could be it."

"So the product is in a parking garage, in an unknown car. How do you propose we find it? You think we're going to break into every car in the garage?"

"No. The guy, Chaswell, is going to pick it up later today. He's bringing cash and he'll leave it in the car when he takes the drugs."

"What time?"

"It'll be around noon, some time between 11:00 and 1:00 this afternoon. The guy who hired me will pick up his money after 1:00 so they're not found in the same place at the same time."

"How do I know you're not setting me up?"

"How can it be a setup? You go there and wait for Chaswell. When he shows up and makes the exchange you get him, the product and his payment. If he doesn't show, you lose nothing."

"What's the garage?"

"What about my money?"

"If we get our stuff back I'll give you your money. Now what's the garage name?"

"How do I know I'm not going to get stiffed again?"

"Consider it honor among thieves. I'll tell you what. If this goes down like you say, I'll pay you from the money he's bringing. If he doesn't bring cash, you get nothing. If he doesn't show up, I better not find you."

"It's on Mountain, just south of St. Catherine. Call me when you have the money."

Elliot looked up to see Margie standing in the entranceway with towel in hand. She had a puzzled look on her face and he could tell she was busy processing whatever she may have just heard.

"What are you up to?" she finally asked.

Elliot didn't know how long she had been standing there so he kept his answer short and vague.

"It's called justice," he said as he started gathering his things. This was a conversation he wanted to avoid.

"Don't try to hide behind the noble idea of justice. I recognize revenge when I see it," she said flatly as if issuing a challenge.

Elliot stared at her for a moment before deciding that he wouldn't engage her on the challenge, "I should be going."

He walked to her and stooped to give her a kiss but at the last second she turned her face and his lips landed on her cheek awkwardly.

"You can leave my key on the counter," she said as she wiped her cheek and turned away.

## Chapter 60

An orderly knocked once and entered the hospital room. "Morning Ms. Goldstein," she said with a smile that made patients feel less as if they were in the hospital and more that they were in a posh hotel.

"Morning Glenda, and, as I've already told you, my name is Rivka," she replied, still in bed.

"That's good to know Ms. Goldstein."

The orderly first fussed with the IV drip and then fluffed up the pillows that didn't need fluffing. Glancing once over her shoulder, pushed a note into Rivka's hand.

Rivka looked up and the orderly was moving her eyes to side indicating she was trying hide the note from the prying eyes of a guard. She opened the note and read it quickly, *"Riv, we need to talk and I can't risk being seen by the guard in the waiting area. Room 3011 down the hall is empty. I'll wait for you there."*

She made the effort to get out of bed and asked the orderly to help her with the wheeled IV stand connected to her arm. Doing her best *'I'm sick of this hospital and I don't want to be here'* impersonation as she sauntered past the waiting area and down the hall, IV stand in tow. She entered room 3011 without looking back.

"Elliot, what are you doing here?" she whispered loudly.

"We need to talk, and I couldn't phone you. How are you feeling? You're looking better."

"Thanks, I'm feeling much better. The last few days have been a roller coaster for me but I have my head in a better place right now. What's up?"

"I'm turning myself in today."

"Did you find the evidence you're looking for?"

"No. There is no evidence, but I have a plan. I'll take my chances in court. My lawyer, Moe Greenspan, thinks we'll have enough to at least reduce my sentence."

"That's your plan? Go to jail?"

He peeked out into the hallway to ensure there wasn't anyone coming. "Listen closely, I'll be phoning you in about an hour, and this is what I want to discuss," he said as he closed the door and explained his plan.

# Chapter 61

"Okay boys, we've got a line on the rip off yesterday. It was Chalwell," said Chunks as he entered the main room.

"Chalwell was behind this? That fucker's dead. What else did he say?" said one of the Henchmen at the table counting, stacking, and banding paper money.

"I got a call from some loser who claimed he was the wheelman yesterday. The wheelman was short changed on his cut so he's rolling over on the guy who hired him."

"What's he want?"

"He told me where the drop is going to happen and wants his original cut if it goes down like he says."

"You going to pay him?"

"Fuck him. I don't pay snitches."

"What's our play then?"

"We'll take the truck down into the garage where the pickup is supposed to happen and wait for it. The guy said Chalwell is supposed to pick up the product between 11:00 this morning and 1:00 this afternoon. We'll be there waiting for him. Freddie, Clem and Franco, you're with me in the truck. Bring some heat with you. Rico, I want you out front as the lookout. Watch the entrance and let us know when you see anything. Let's leave now and get there early. I'll fill you in on the way."

"What about our other boys. You want me to call them in?"

"No fuckin way. The PI ripped us off and knows our operation. There's no guarantee he'll be at the parking lot so as long as he's alive, he's a threat. "

# Chapter 62

Elliot dialed Vince O'Brien from his car.

"O'Brien?"

"Speaking."

"This is Elliot Forsman, I have some info you'll want to hear."

"You're a wanted man Forsman."

"I am. I know you've heard this story before but, I'm innocent."

"Yeah, sure you are. If you're calling for help I can't offer you any."

"No. I have information about a drug deal going down tonight."

"I'm listening."

"I'm not sure where it's going to happen yet but I do know that there are going to be heavy hitters from the Montréal drug scene and there's going to be product involved."

"Where you getting your info?"

"I've got a source inside. He's going to text me when the drop details are finalized."

"Who are the heavy hitters?"

"I don't have names. I just know that some of the leaders will be meeting for a drop."

"Mamelon?"

"I don't know. Maybe."

"So what's my play?"

"I need you to have a task force on standby. You won't have much time, when I get the text, you'll have minutes to get to the scene and catch them red handed."

"Minutes? You don't even know where the drop will be. "

"It'll be close to downtown."

"So you want me to ask for overtime for a dozen men on the word of a known felon at large with sketchy details about a mysterious drop with no names. I need something to tell the Captain."

"O'Brien. You've been after these guys for over 5 years and don't have a pot to piss in. I'm offering you their heads on a platter and you're worried about excuses to your boss. I'm sure you'll think of something."

O'Brien said nothing and Elliot knew he was thinking up a story he could sell to the Captain.

"Be ready to roll in a couple of hours. Like I said, when you get my call you'll have minutes to respond."

## Chapter 63

Elliot looked down at the phone in his hand and thought about the decision he was about to make.

He had taken human lives in the past; four months ago, he shot two men. There were others, before that, that he didn't dwell on. For the two earlier in the year, there was no decision to make, it was him or them. If he had been unable to pull the trigger, he would have been killed.

It was different this time. He was about to commit to a course of action that would result in men being killed. Although he wasn't on the trigger side of the gun, he may as well be.

He weighed the pros and cons in his mind. If he did not execute his plan, if he did not make the phone call he was about to make, Mamelon would go free, Chalwell would not receive justice, and the drug operation would sprout up again somewhere else. On the plus side, there was still a chance that he could prove his innocence and stay out of jail, albeit a small one.

If he executed his plan, he would go to jail, no questions about it. To offset that, Chalwell, Mamelon, and the Henchmen would get what they deserved. Some more harshly than others, but justice would be served. He wanted to believe that there were no considerations of payback in his plan, that his motivations were altruistic, but knew this was not true. For the people behind the drug operation, the ones who profited from other's deaths, extreme justice was the only answer. He wasn't about to let the legal system fumble this one away.

In the end, his decision was already made. The scales of justice leaned too heavily to one side. His personal situation was secondary. He would sacrifice his chance for freedom, his friendships, and even his business, if that's what it took. He would make the phone call that would set in motion a series of events culminating in death. Now that his mind was made up, he probed his own feelings about the decision. He looked deep down inside to the place where man's most base principles lived. What he found did not surprise him, it only strengthened his resolve.

Elliot's phone chirped and he saw that a text had just come in from Sammy. He read the short message, "H.H. are inside."

That was the signal he was waiting for before executing the next phase in his plan. He dialed Rivka's number.

"Rivka speaking."

"Riv, it's me Elliot."

"Glad you called. I thought you'd have dropped by to see me by now."

"There's a warrant out for my arrest. They're probably watching you to see if I show up."

"I guess I can accept that as an excuse."

"Sorry about not making it to your place the other night. I couldn't take the chance that one of those officers wouldn't make the connection between me and that outstanding murder charge. Margie tells me you're doing well considering everything you've been through. Are you?"

"I'm functional now but still a mess. I killed an innocent man Elliot. That doesn't just go away."

"I hear you. When are you getting out?"

"Probably this afternoon, and looking forward to it. There's really no reason for me to stay in here. I can take it easy at home better than I can in this place, and the food is better at home. Two days here and I actually look forward to the morning bowl of gruel, it's fresher than the lunchtime gruel or the supper gruel."

"I can tell you're on the mend, you're starting to get your sense of humor back."

"Dr. Maller has me on happy pills. I think I'll be okay to go home, as long as I stay away from other people for a few days. I'll feel better when I get back in the pool so I can really work myself out for a couple of hours. I need the physical release. "

"That'll be tough to do if you don't want to see other people."

"I know the owner down at the gym, he dropped a key off for me so I'm going to have the place to myself tonight."

"I'd say break a leg, but knowing you, you might. "

"Have you heard from Rayce? Last I heard he had survived an attack at his house."

"Yeah. I saw him yesterday. He's in bad shape. He was going to admit himself into a private clinic. My guess is he'll be out of commission for months."

"That's too bad. What about you? How is the case? Have you found Alphie's killer?"

Elliot explained how he intercepted the drug delivery, and how there was no evidence to convict Chalwell, his drug operation, the Mamelon murders, or implicate the Henchmen who supplied the product and cut it with fentanyl.

"Wow. So you think your only option is to turn yourself in?"

"Yeah. I don't like to wave the white flag but I don't have any other options. I'll pick up the drugs early afternoon, drop them off with Moe, and turn myself in. I'll document the entire case, and my theories, and Moe will use that, along with the drugs, as part of a plea deal."

"Pick up the drugs? Where are they?"

"When we took them from the courier, Sammy got an old car and parked it in a long term storage garage on Mountain south of St. Catherine. He left the keys on top of the front tire. I'll stop by later, pick the stuff up and take it to Moe. "

"Good luck Elliot, I'll come visit you in the Crowbar Motel."

# Chapter 64

Elliot sat at Le Caché Café sipping his third coffee. He had the skaggy, hollow feeling that he got when he drank too much caffeine. His table looked out onto St. Catherine Street, but not directly at the window. Knowing that he'd be there for a couple of hours, he didn't want to have his face framed in the window on one of the busiest streets in Montréal.

He would have rather be waiting somewhere else but his options were limited, he didn't know where the police or the Henchmen might be looking for him. Besides, Le Caché was close to station 10, the police station where he planned to surrender.

He checked his watch again. It was one minute later than the last time he checked, 10:50am. Sammy had texted him at 9:12 saying that an SUV with four beards inside did a couple of drive-bys and then entered the garage. A black Toyota following it, parked across the street from the garage entrance a couple of hundred yards south. That would be their lookout.

Sammy was parked a half block north of St. Catherine Street on Mountain, about a block north of the garage entrance. The incline on Mountain Street offered him a perfect view of the garage entrance and, with the aid of binoculars; he had a clear view of the entrance of the garage, the vehicles that entered, and their passengers.

At 11:04 Elliot's phone chirped and he received the message, "Chalwell and a passenger just drove by slowly." When Chalwell went into the garage, Elliot would phone O'Brien, but not before. He couldn't afford to scare anyone off prematurely. The thundering sound of a couple of Harley's caught his attention as they rumbled down St. Catherine's in front of his cafe. Elliot leaned forward in his chair to get a look at them and, as he feared, they were wearing the Henchmen colors. If they continued driving past the café, he was in no danger, they were just a couple of biker's doing what biker's do. They did not continue driving past.

Both bikes stopped beside Elliot's Volvo comparing its license plate to the numbers on a scrap of paper held by the lead biker's. The lead biker nodded and they both looked around to take stock of the local neighborhood. The bikers scanned the street side businesses and both settled their gaze on Le Caché Café. It didn't take long for them to formulate their plan. One Harley accelerated to the corner and turned on the street that would take him in behind the café. The other biker made a U-turn and pulled into a parking spot out front of the café.

Elliot cursed and peeled through his options. He quickly determined they were few. In desperation, he made a quick 911 phone call to report an armed robbery in progress at Le Caché Café. He then hurried back to the hallway that led out to the laneway behind the café block. The other biker would almost certainly be coming in through the rear doorway so leaving from the back was not an option. He grabbed an unused chair from one of the tables, ducked into the woman's restroom, locked the door behind him, and wedged the chair up underneath the door handle. He needed to some buy time because he didn't want to phone O'Brien until he got Sammy's text. He watched his phone in anticipation of the text but none came. He sat in the restroom straining to hear the sounds of commotion from the café. None came, he wondered if the biker's did a quick pass through the café and after not finding their quarry, made off to continue their search elsewhere. His hopes were dashed when the handle on his door jiggled, followed by forceful knock. "Excuse me," a rough voice sounded.

Elliot dialed O'Brien without hitting send.

The knock repeated, this time louder. "Excuse me. Is anyone in there?"

He heard muted words exchanged outside the door followed by a mighty crash as the door flexed in. The hinges rattled but held.

Elliot couldn't wait for the text. He hit the dial button on the phone.

The door crashed again and the lock wrenched out of the doorframe. The wedged chair slipped back a couple of inches but caught on the rough floor. The door was now open about an inch, enough space to allow gloved fingers to reach in and get a better grip on the door.

"O'Brien speaking."

Elliot put the phone down on the floor and grabbed the wooden plunger from behind the toilet. He gave the fingers a whack with the handle and they recoiled with a sharp curse.

Elliot leaned in to put his weight against the door and yelled, "O'Brien, hear me out," at the phone now lying on the floor. "There's a long term parking garage on Mountain, just south of St. Catherine. The main entrance is on Mountain and there are access doors on the north and south walls. They have a spotter sitting in a black Toyota half a block south of the main entrance, you'll need to take care of him first."

Just as he finished his monologue, he was driven back against the far wall as the door burst in. Elliot saw two burly bikers in the doorway, breathing heavily. They were not smiling. The biker on the left reached inside his jacket for what Elliot expected was a handgun, but stopped in mid pull. As he looked to the front of the café.

"Police de Montréal. Démissionner. Stand down, where is the man who called in about a robbery in progress?" came a voice from somewhere in the front of the café.

Elliot wasted no time and yelled at the approaching voice, "My name is Elliot Forsman. I'm wanted for the murder of Joseph Labrosse and I want to turn myself in."

Elliot watched as the biker slipped his gun back into the holster and feigned to be a concerned citizen.

"He's in the bathroom. I think he has a gun," the biker shouted at the approaching officers. The lead cop pulled the bikers aside for questioning while the second officer trained his gun on Elliot and forced him onto the floor,

While he was being cuffed Elliot looked down at his phone lying on the floor near his head and saw that Sammy's text had come in during the excitement of the past few minutes.

## Chapter 65

Elliot offered no responses to the officer's queries as he watched the city pass by from the back seat of the cruiser. He wasn't worried, he'd already accepted his fate, and whatever lay ahead for him. He wondered if O'Brien had heard his entire discourse as his phone lay on the floor. He wondered how events had unfolded at the garage. He wondered if justice had finally been realized. Would he feel satisfaction, or would he just have a hollow space inside where empathy once lived.

The cruiser pulled into a lot around the back of an old brick building and parked in the rear. He was led in through the back entrance, and directly to a long counter that separated the public access area from the private area where police officers' conduct their business. The officer leading Elliot by the arm turned him in to face the counter and the officer behind it and, before he could say anything, Elliot proclaimed in a loud voice.

"My name is Elliot Forsman. There's a warrant for my arrest for the murder of Joseph Labrosse. I'm here to turn myself in but I am innocent," he announced in the direction of the officer on the other side of the counter. The words came out flat and hard and seemed to bounce off the cement walls without the weight or drama he had envisioned. The officer looked up at him momentarily and turned his attention back to his paperwork.

Elliot was immediately escorted into a waiting room where they filled out the requisite forms and filings. The room had no bars, nor did it have a metal bed and toilet, but Elliot recognized a cell when he saw one. He'd heard it was often a relief, a cathartic experience, when a person turned himself over to the law. That the weight of carrying the knowledge of being wanted was debilitating. Nothing could be further from the truth in his case. He turned himself in for a crime he did not commit and there was no hope of clearing his name. Evidence was non-existent and, the only people, aside from himself, who knew he was innocent were most likely dead.

He hoped he'd get news of how events unfolded that evening. He'd done what he thought he needed to do. He's set in motion a chain of events that would bring justice to those who had evaded it for so long. The only person who would not realize justice, was himself. It was a sacrifice he was more than willing to make.

Some hours later, now lying in a cell not sleeping, Elliot heard the familiar voice of Moe Greenspan, his lawyer, from somewhere down the corridor. A guard opened the door, stood him up and led him down the hall, in handcuffs, to a breakout room similar to the one where his personal information was recently taken.

"Moe, it's good to see a friendly face."

"Have a seat Elliot, we have a lot to discuss. "

"Have you heard any news about the bust in the long term storage?"

"Nothing official. Whatever happened there, it's big. An eye witness says he saw them pull two bodies out of the garage. I'll let you know as soon as I know something."

"Okay. You received all the material I sent?"

"Yes, I have the shipping manifests from Labrosse & Sons that identify the company in the British Virgin Islands. I agree with your theory that this is how the drug money is being funneled out of the country," the lawyer said.

"I have the photo from the carwash that ties Labrosse, Chalwell, and Anderson together. I also have the blueprints from your friend that confirm the existence of a tunnel between the carwash admin building and the carwash bays. And finally," he said as he looked at his notes, "I have your summarized report stating how the drug operation worked."

"Good. Is there anything you don't understand?"

"Given that the Lav was the center of the drug operation I was surprised when you told me that there was no trace coke found during O'Brien's initial investigation."

"That's because the product never stayed at the Lav. It would be taken from the Henchmen delivery car from underneath and passed into Joel Anderson's car directly behind it. The Lav was just a transfer point," answered the PI.

"That makes sense. And the money was handled by a completely separate arm of the operation, Labrosse's Telecom company."

"and all the profit went to the Caribbean company, J3T Industries," Elliot added. "Without a money trail to follow, the police could never crack the case."

"I think I'm good for now Elliot. I'll package everything up and present it to the Crown to see what it buys us."

## Chapter 66

Elliot lay on the bunk, eyes closed, brain still wired. He thought about Mamelon and all the people he'd killed over the years. He thought about the Henchmen, Chalwell and the drug operation who had been ruining lives and lately, killing people in alarming numbers. He held no remorse for them, they'd made their choices, and now they lived with them, or died because of them.

His contemplation was interrupted by the sound of the primary door opening down the hall. He heard the thud of safety boots on concrete as the guards walked towards his cell. They were not sauntering as if on patrol, they had a destination in mind, and it was Elliot's cell.

"Against the wall Forsman, hands up and legs spread," Elliot complied, more curious than afraid. One guard cuffed his hands behind his back and then led him out, the other guard watching from a distance. They led him into an interrogation room further down the hallway, fastened him to the desk, and left him there. A few moments later Manon Petit entered.

"Coming to wallow in your victory? You finally got your man."

She didn't reply, just stood above him, waiting him out.

"I just talked to Detective O'Brien. He tells me that because of a tip he got from you, there was a major drug bust tonight. He tells me they have enough to put away the leaders of the Hades Henchmen. He just got a warrant to take apart their known locations, including a garage on Bannantyne Street in Verdun.

"So you're coming here to commend me?"

"They busted five bikers from the Hades Henchmen in possession of cocaine, and found two bodies in the garage. A highly respected financier and a business owner from Hochelaga, but I think you know that already. What I don't know is why they were there, or why you set them up to be killed. I do know that you are now here, in my cell, with at least one murder charge that you won't be wiggling out of. And when I find out how you managed to place these two citizens in harm's way to meet your own warped sense of justice, I'll be charging you with their murders also."

"I have no idea what you're talking about."

She looked him over trying to decide to if she should humor the man or walk back to her office.

"At approximately noon you phoned Detective O'Brien to tell him that there was a drug deal going down in a long term storage garage on Mountain.

You told him about a lookout that was watching the front entrance and that if they covered the three entrances, they would catch the suppliers red handed."

"You'll get no arguments from me on those points. Did they manage to bust anyone?"

"You know damn well what was going to happen, that's why you turned yourself in, so you couldn't be implicated in the aftermath."

"So they made the bust, that's great."

"Our men went in and caught four Henchmen in a car with 5 kilos of cocaine in their trunk. They were armed and one of the firearms had been recently discharged. Further investigation led us to two bodies in the lower level. The first body was a lawyer named Joel Anderson, with a single gunshot to the head from close range. The second man was Jack Chalwell, a philanthropist and respected businessman in the community of Hochelaga, as well as a supporter of the Montréal Police, and I should add, a personal friend of the mayor. Mr. Chalwell was beaten to death. I saw the body myself, his upper torso and shoulders were purple from being pummeled, and his face was non-existent, just a mass of raw flesh and broken bone."

"So you made the bust and have taken the bad guys off the street, that's awesome. Now all the fentanyl deaths will stop, you'll be a hero Chief Petit."

"Just because there were positives that came as a result of your manipulations does not excuse you for murder. When you are involved, people die Mr. Forsman, and that's going to stop here and now."

"Have you wondered why two respected businessmen were in that parking garage?"

"I'm waiting for you to tell me."

"I have no idea. Maybe they were part of the drug deal."

"My sources tell me that Mr. Chalwell was one of your suspects in the murder of Alphie Leduc. You've already killed the man you thought was his partner, and you've found a way to kill your other suspect. I want to know how you knew that deal was going down and what Mr. Chalwell and the Mr. Anderson were doing there."

"I'm an investigator; I see, I hear, I deduce."

"Names and places Mr. Forsman."

"Not possible. I can't give up my sources." Elliot wasn't about to hand his only bargaining chip over to the person he could trust the least. When the story was assembled and evidence compiled, Moe would offer it up as part of a plea deal. There was no way Chief Petit was going to come out of this with all the glory and leave Elliot in jail.

"Then don't expect any leniency in court."

# Chapter 67

Rivka let the water run over her and wash the stress from the past weeks run down the drain. It'd been days since she last exercised and it felt good. Two hours in the pool got her to the point where pure exhaustion would put her asleep by the time her head hit the pillow, her pillow. The last two nights in the hospital had not been restful, she had slept a lot, but it just wasn't restful. She looked forward to her own bed.

She thought about how Dr. Maller managed to change her frame of mind. She realized now that many of her troubles of the past month had been imagined, head up her backside, as Dr. Maller would say. Then just when she thought she was starting to get a grip on her emotions, it all went sideways. First, she started imagining she saw Ogrodnik at every corner; she walked around the house with a loaded gun without realizing it and ended up shooting an innocent man. It seemed so long ago now. Had she really contemplated taking her own life? She thought about how Dr. Maller brought her to the hospital and talked her off the edge. But it wasn't until Elliot visited her in the hospital that she found herself again. Had she not heard from him, she'd still be struggling in recovery, but the information he brought was exactly what she needed to hear. It all made so much sense, Lydia, the man in the back yard, the flowers at the funeral, and the attack on Rayce. Elliot had tied them all together and come up with a plan, a plan that would only work if he turned himself in and went to jail.

She wrapped her hair in a towel as she walked around the stall entrance back to her locker, wearing nothing else but a contented, but weary look. As she rounded the corner, she flinched visibly and her knees sagged. She caught herself and forced her legs to straighten and stand tall.

"Ah. Ms. Goldstein, how I've missed you," said the pre-pubescent voice of the giant in front of her.

She stood her ground without speaking, processing the bleakness of her situation. Nothing behind her but an empty shower stall, and face to face, not thirty feet away was Ogrodnik, flanked by a couple of well-armed heavies.

"Nothing to say? Surprised to see me? Yes, I've been patient, waiting for events to unfold, for plans to be executed. Waiting until your comrades were safely out of the way and when you were at your most vulnerable. "

The giant turned toward his guards "You two can wait outside. Ms. Goldstein and I have some unfinished business to take care of."

They hesitated for a moment not wanting to turn away from the denuded female form, but a second look from the massive killer cemented their decision and they left without further ado.

"Look at you, standing there in all your glory, and what glory it is. Magnificent, and not a shred of modesty. Not even a reflexive attempt to cover up, but why would you. You've been the object of men's ogling your entire life, I'm sure you are quite used to it."

"What do you want you sick fuck?"

"Come, come. I want you, of course. I want to consummate our love so I can take your life and find peace within myself. After that, you'll be mine, and mine alone. Your only consolation will be that you'll live a long and cherished life, in my memories."

Ogrodnik noticed her glance at the aisle where her locker was, roughly halfway between them and off to the right.

"Please, don't think about expending your energy unnecessarily," he said as he pulled a gun from his pocket. "As you can see, I found your locker while you were showering, this gun will be of no use to you," he said as he ejected the clip and tossed them both to the side.

The other hand pulled out a stungun "It's time I reprised the Stungun MO one more time. This time it won't be for the purposes of deception, the police will know it was me as soon as your body is discovered. No, I consider this as a symbolic thumbing of the nose at those who chased me for so long."

"You won't get away with it, every cop in the country will be looking for you."

"True, but with the help of my sentries outside, your body won't be found until I'm long out of harm's way. And with your protectors safely out of the picture, nobody will be looking for you. Tell me, did you enjoy your time with Lydia Morgan?"

"I found her out a couple of days ago."

"Nice try my dear. If that was the case you would not be standing in front of me now, with a look of surprise on your face and, quite literally, your backside hanging out," but even as he said it he questioned his words. His intended victim was not exhibiting the look of shock and disbelief he expected.

"You heard exactly what we wanted you to hear," Rivka shot back.

"Sorry, I cannot take your words at face value. Your partner's in jail, your muscular friend is unable to help you and you stand here in front of me with no more hope than you have clothes on. The 'proof' as they say, 'is in the pudding'."

"Your entire plan to alienate me, to take Elliot and Rayce off the board, and to drive me crazy was discovered days ago. You wanted to manipulate events in order to isolate me and force me into a defenseless position. We gave you exactly what you wanted, and we let you think you were in control. Checkmate Ogrodnik."

"If you're stalling for time it will not work. Your time has come," he said, no longer sure of himself but intending to finish his plan.

Rivka quickly surveyed her surroundings. The changing room consisted of rows of lockers on each side of a wide, open area. Each row of lockers had a bench running down its length to facilitate the changing of clothes. Ogrodnik stood 30 feet in front of her, close to the center of the open area. Ten feet to her right was the bench for the first row of lockers. Just as Ogrodnik stepped towards her, she took two long strides towards the bench and pulled a handgun from its hiding place taped beneath.

"If I didn't know about your plan, then why would I have planted guns all over this room?" she spat out.

The look of surprise on Ogrodnik's face turned quickly to shock as she fired a round that struck him in the shoulder, hitting the joint and rendering his left arm useless.

"That one was for Elliot, and this one's for me," she said and lowered her aim down to his knee and squeezed off another shot. Ogrodnik's knee buckled when the bullet smashed through the knee joint and sent him crashing to the ground, not even able to lift his injured arm to cushion the fall. The big man's head bounced off the concrete floor and, despite his attempt at being stoic and strong, he whimpered and groaned. Rivka watched as he slowly rolled over to his back trying, and failing, to hide his pain.

Rivka said nothing as she trained her sights on the big man's head. Thoughts of her kidnapping assaulted her, screaming at her to pull the trigger. She thought about his victims, and the shattered families he had left behind. She thought about Elliot's father, and finally she thought about her niece, lying face down in a dumpster, despoiled and broken, like a discarded doll at the landfill.

Rivka jumped as the door slammed open and one of Ogrodnik's thugs appeared in the entrance. She rolled to the side and raised her weapon, but did not fire. Her instinct to shoot was interrupted by the stance of the sentry, there was something unusual about the way he stood in the doorway. The guard did not raise his weapon, just looked toward her from the odd angle of his head. She watched as he fell forward hitting the floor face first, already dead. Behind him, standing in the shadows, was the silhouette of a man in the doorway. She thought she saw his head nod, as if to say *'He's all yours'*. As the door closed she watched a muscular torso turn to leave, canted to the right, as if compensating for injury.

## Chapter 68

Elliot lay in his cot listening to the sounds of restless humanity echoing across the cemented hallways. This would be his home for the coming months until his trial was finished. The facility lacked the massive multi-level central atrium found in maximum-security prisons but there was no mistaking that he was in jail.

One thing he was thankful for was that he had no cellmate. That was probably because he was considered a dangerous killer, and that another inmate might not be safe with him. He knew that would change when he went to prison.

What he was experiencing now was the start of the de-humanization process that all imprisonment facilities employed. He knew the process and understood the reasoning behind it; Detainment Concepts was one of the courses he taught during his 20-year tenure as Criminology Professor at McGill University. He wouldn't be assigned a number until he was sentenced, but little things like wearing drab jail garb, the indignity of using a toilet without privacy, and queuing up in the cafeteria line to receive the daily nutritional staple were all part of the process. It was a process refined over many decades and meant to detach convicts from their individuality, to grind them down, and mold them into a herd mentality so they could be controlled.

He had made the sacrifice to throw himself at the mercy of the court in order to achieve justice. He didn't regret that decision, he'd do it again if he had to, but he realized he wasn't prepared for institutional life.

The noises from dozens of sleeping men prevented him from escaping into the refuge of his own sleep. Snorting, rasping, farting sounds echoed down the halls while he lay awake on his foam slab. The bleached-out odor of filthy men that hung in the air was just another facet of the new reality that he wasn't prepared to deal with. Elliot didn't fear his situation, he feared getting used to it, to becoming so de-sensitized to this miserable place that he forgot how appalling it was.

His mind drifted to the case and the decision he had made, but he didn't dwell long on that subject. He was mentally exhausted from his ordeal of the last week so he pushed the case out of his mind until his lawyer, Moe Greenspan, visited in the morning.

He recalled the phone call he had with son Jake earlier in the day. He had downplayed his situation, he told Jake they had a good case to present and that he expected to be out of jail before too long.

Elliot had been in the Remand Center for less than a day and already he missed the life he left behind. He knew Rivka would come to visit soon and looked forward to hearing about her ordeal with Ogrodnik. He wondered how often she would visit. He wondered the same about Margie. Would she visit at all? Not likely, they were probably finished, his own actions had seen to that.

Oddly enough, the person he thought about most was the old man standing on the sidewalk, selling his produce and talking to everyone who passed by. He didn't even know the man's name, yet felt the crush of regret when he realized he wouldn't see him again. The old man would not be alive by the time he got out of prison.

Elliot closed his eyes and pretended to sleep for the rest of the night, hearing every rustle, scratch, and grunt from the surrounding cells.

# Chapter 69

*Thursday, September 1st*

"You have a visitor," grumbled the guard as he unlocked the cell door. The guard led Elliot to a small room with a single chair and a desk against the wall. He saw Moe Greenspan on the other side of the plexiglass partition and sat down to face him.

"Good morning Elliot."

"Morning Moe."

"How was your first night in incarceration?"

"Very pleasant. I've spent the night kicking back in my new brick and steel condo overthinking my situation. Were you able to get a pulse on what they have planned for me?"

"You'll have your bail hearing tomorrow. The water cooler chatter I hear is that the judge is leaning toward granting you bail, albeit, a large one, something in the half million-dollar range. I have to tell you that he's getting pressure from the chief of police to deny bail and hold you. She says you're dangerous and a menace to society."

"Not unexpected. We have a history," he said not wanting to go into the details of her feelings on the Ogrodnik case.

"I prepared a summary with the details of the drug operation and how you managed to bust it open. We cannot mention anything about you orchestrating the meeting between the bikers and Chalwell. That would not end up well for you."

"What will you do with the summary?"

"After the bail hearing I'll get an audience with the prosecuting attorney and the judge if he'll agree, to tell them your story. They already know that you'll be pleading innocent to the Labrosse's murder charges and that you will claim you were framed. I think, with that seed of doubt already in their minds, when I tell them about how you single handedly brought down a drug ring that has been killing people by the score, they'll be charitable."

"What do you think that means in terms of time spent in prison?"

"Difficult to say without knowing who the prosecutor is. You're in a big or small scenario. Murder 1 comes with a mandatory life sentence. If you're convicted of murder in the first, no amount of good will on the drug operation will save you. You will do full time. If the murder charge is reduced to a second degree, we'll be able to deal. "

Elliot shook head. The reality of serving time in a prison was starting to scare him. "Life is a long time," he murmured to himself.

"We'll do our best to reduce to murder 2. But I caution you, even if that happens, the prosecution will want a conviction. It looks good on their record. They will want you to plead guilty so they can claim a victory. Pleading guilty will mean serving time."

They spent the next hour chatting about Elliot's options and their approach in court before packing it in for the day.

"Thanks for the pep talk Moe, I guess we'll see each at the bail hearing."

## Chapter 70

Elliot lay down on his slab of foam and tried to tune out the sound of the TV mounted on the wall outside of his cell. He wanted, and needed sleep but his mind was much too active. After a few hours of pointless rumination, he was interrupted by the midday repast they called lunch. He looked at a lone chicken leg sitting in the largest of the three dividers on the metal tray. There was no effort to make it look appetizing; it was sustenance only, just like the frozen veggies and instant mashed potatoes beside them. He took a few bites of the leg before pushing the entire tray away and returning to his bunk. All he could think about was the coming trial.

"You have another visitor," said the guard as he unlocked the cell door. The guard led Elliot to a different small room with the same single chair and same desk against a similar looking wall. Rivka was on the other side of the glass, looking spectacular and sporting a huge grin.

"Afternoon partner," she said and through her smile. "How's life in the big house?"

"I've got a cozy room with a beautiful view of a ventilation stack. I'm finding it quite restful, thanks for asking."

"I brought you some soap-on-a-rope."

"Not funny."

"Why are you smiling then?" she asked.

"Because it's good to see you."

"I gotta say, I'm disappointed in your prison garb, I was expecting to see you in a bright orange onesie."

"They're called overalls, and I'm not in prison yet. I haven't seen you this cheerful since before the Ogrodnik case started. Moe tells me you're a celebrity. He said your picture was on the front page of every newspaper in town."

"I have been busy. It's all a bit much right now. Interview requests, calls from friends and family, some from cops I haven't heard from since I left the Force. "

"The girl next door who brought down a serial killer."

"Yup, just like we planned."

"How's it feel? Like, inside."

"It feels, liberating. It feels good," she said with a contented smile on her face.

"I'll never forget the feeling I had when I told my sister, we both cried. She cried because her daughter's killer was finally caught, but more than that, she cried because she knew that it was eating me up inside."

"That's great," he replied and looked at her beaming smile. "So, you didn't kill him. I wondered how you'd react when the moment came. Congratulations, you have risen above your most base instincts. You are human."

"I thought about it, believe me. "

"What are they saying about Ogrodnik? Will they get him for all the murders?"

"They're certainly going to try. They still have the box of trophies that he planted at Amyot's cottage, that, along with my testimony, will be enough to put him away for life."

"Has Amyot reached out to you?"

"No. And I don't expect him to hear from him. Calling me would be admitting he was wrong. He'd never do that."

"Tell me how it went down."

"As we expected, Ogrodnik wouldn't show himself until he believed Rayce was unable to help, you were in jail, and that I was at my most vulnerable. He took the bait, hook, line, and sinker. I swam for a couple of hours, looking over my shoulder on every lap, but, as anticipated, he didn't take me in the pool. It's too wide open. Someone could have come in.

"Once I got into the shower, I was shaking so badly I could barely keep hold of the shampoo. I really didn't know if he was going to show up or not. When I came out of the stall, rounded the corner, and saw him standing there I almost lost my shit. I managed to play it cool and listened to him blather on. They say we need to face our fears in order to conquer them, but I don't think whoever came up with that theory could have imagined facing Ogrodnik with nothing but a towel on her head. At some point during his dialog, he realized I wasn't afraid of him and he started to doubt himself, that's when I knew I had him. I went for the gun that I'd taped underneath the closest bench and didn`t take any chances, not after last time. I'd already decided that if I got the chance, I was going to shoot him. I gave him one in the shoulder for you, and took out his knee with a second shot. That was payback for my leg. It scared the hell out of me when the door slammed open and one of Ogrodnik's guerrillas appeared but I quickly realized that it was just Rayce taking precautions. I guess he figured that if Ogrodnik had gotten the upper hand, he'd buy himself a few moments if Ogrodnik saw one of his own at the door. How'd you manage to get Rayce involved?"

"I already figured out that Ogrodnik was behind the attack at Rayce's, so that morning I sent Rayce a text telling him about our plan and that there was a good chance Ogrodnik's mercenaries would be with him. The same mercenaries that attacked him at his house."

"It's over Elliot. More than three years of me obsessing about The Stungun Killer and it's finally over. I don't remember the last time I felt so... so unshackled," she said with a contented smile. Neither spoke for a minute or two as they both replayed the saga in their heads.

Rivka finally broke the thoughtful silence by asking, "Elliot, I can't understand why Chalwell would kill his friend Labrosse. And why did he want you framed? Why not just kill you instead?"

"Mamelon didn't kill Labrosse, Ogrodnik did. The MO for the Labrosse killing was all wrong, two bullets in the back of the head. That's the MO of someone who doesn't get a thrill from the kill. "

"I still ask the same question, why just not kill you?"

"Let me back up a bit. We already talked about Lydia's role in this and how she worked for Ogrodnik and planted a listening app on your phone to record your conversations."

Rivka's jaw tightened as she remembered Lydia asking to borrow her phone the first day they met.

"So Ogrodnik knew about our investigation into Alphie's murder and the progress we were making on the drug operation. Ogrodnik was looking for a way to isolate you, so he allies himself with Chalwell and offers him access to the information he is getting through Lydia in exchange for influence into Chalwell's activities. It wouldn't take too much pressure for Chalwell to get Labrosse to meet with me, attack me, and petition for a restraining order. Ogrodnik shows Chalwell that our investigation is getting close so he serves up Labrosse to take the fall, and gets rid of me at the same time. One less player in the drug operation means the money split is that much more. Ogrodnik wouldn't want me dead anyway. He'd want me to know what was happening, but be unable to do anything about it."

"Well done partner. We were hired to find Alphie's killer, so what should I tell our client?" she asked.

"I fully expect the DNA evidence that the coroner sent to the lab will confirm everything we already know. That Jack Chalwell is a serial killer and that he killed Alphie to stop him from disclosing what he knew about the drug operation. You can tell Marie Bernard that her nephew did not die in vain. His intention to go to the police set in motion a series of events that resulted in bringing down a major drug operation and preventing more deaths from with their tainted product. You can tell her that justice has been served and that Alphie died a hero," he answered.

"With Chalwell gone, what happens to the unsolved murders? Will the police admit they screwed up that they allowed a serial killer to roam the streets for over 5 years?"

"My guess is nothing. Moe said he expects the police will want to suppress that part of my testimony. They'll probably ask you to do the same. The greater public doesn't know about Mamelon, or his legacy of death, so why make it public knowledge now. It'll just make the cops look more incompetent than they already do. For those who have heard of Mamelon, why give them license to misbehave? Let them believe he's still out there, watching and waiting."

"You're right, the threat of Mamelon will still carry a lot of weight with the drug underground," she said and paused for a moment before changing the subject. "I hate to say this, but we were fortunate in the way it all played out in the garage. If Chalwell and Anderson hadn't decided to meet with the Henchmen, they'd still be alive to fight it out in court. And, the Henchmen would be setting up business somewhere else to sell their fentanyl laced product."

Elliot looked at her impassively through the glass without answering but knew that his silence told

Rivka that something was amiss. He could not lie to his partner, so he said nothing.

He watched as her wheels turned, processing the information she actually hadn't heard but now knew to be true. He observed as her face went through the gamut of micro-expressions that told him what she was thinking. The subtle nod of her head as the truth dawned on her. The twisted half-smile flashed across her face, as the ramifications were realized, signaled contempt. Finally, her eyebrows flattened and lowered as a simmering anger settled in.

She looked directly at Elliot and asked in a low, measured voice, "You phoned me at the hospital and we talked about you stashing the stolen drugs in the long term storage garage because we knew that Chalwell and Anderson were listening. Why were the Henchmen already there waiting for them?"

Elliot considered the question and his response.

"I think you already know the answer," he finally replied not wanting to say the words.

"So what, you are no longer concerned with abiding by the law. You've appointed yourself as supreme judge and executioner?" she said as she stood and backed away from the glass.

"I did what I had to do."

"You orchestrated the deaths of two men, and you used me to set them up," she replied pronouncing each of the words individually and emphasized the word 'me' in a raised voice.

"They were guilty."

"The law determines who's guilty, not Elliot Goddamn Forsman," she spat out the last words.

"The law is broken. Men like OJ Simpson have already proven that. If you have enough money and influence, the law can be subverted. Chalwell, Anderson, the Henchmen. The whole fucking lot of them would have walked," he said his voice now matching the intensity of Rivka's. "I was not about to let that happen. They got what they deserved."

"This is bigger than Elliot Forsman's ideology of justice. As soon as citizens start taking the law into their own hands, we devolve toward anarchy. The law has its warts, but we can't ignore it," she said and turned away from the glass. Elliot said nothing. After a few paces she turned back to Elliot, "If this is where JFK is heading, you can go there without me, we are no longer partners," she said, voice now low, flat, and menacing, her mind made up.

Elliot, uncertain how to reply, stared blankly through the glass. He watched as she picked up her purse from the desk and fished out a paper from within.

"I got this yesterday; I've given everything to Moe already. Congratulations," she said spitefully as she slapped the paper out on the desk in front of Elliot and then left without another word.

Elliot shoulders slumped and head hung down as he watched her leave. He took a deep breath and silently questioned his own motives. *No matter*, he thought, *the die was cast, I cannot not undo my actions.* Eventually his curiosity took over and he leaned toward the glass to read her note.

*"Rivka, I offer no excuses. I am who I am. I was hired to do a job, and I did it. I'm not asking for forgiveness, if I were you, I wouldn't consider it either. My only regret is that I didn't know who my employer was. Had I known it was Ogrodnik, the Stungun Killer, I'd have turned down the job, and turned him in.*

*I don't want to bore you with any emotional tripe so I'll get to the point. If you understand what I do, then you'll know it's not unusual for someone in my line of business to be involved in blackmail. By force of habit, I always try to record my professional conversations. Please find enclosed a USB key with a copy of my conversations with Ogrodnik. He talks quite freely about his plans to murder Labrosse and pin it on your partner. I'm no lawyer but I'm pretty sure it'll stand up in court.*

*PS. It was never supposed to get personal, but I have no regrets. Another place, another time, who knows?*
*All my tainted love, Lydia"*

# Chapter 71

Elliot, back in his cell, lying on his foam slab, wondered why he wasn't more pleased by the events of the past couple of days. The drug operation was crushed, the suppliers were on their way to prison, Alphie's murder solved, and the serial killer who murdered him, Mamelon, received the justice he deserved. On top of all that, his own murder charge was being withdrawn and he'd be back at home tomorrow.

He should feel triumphant, like a hero coming home from war. Yet all he felt was the emptiness of a hollow victory, and regret for sacrifices made.

He'd used his partner, without her knowledge, in his single-minded pursuit of justice. Rivka, his partner, his confidant, his friend, no longer. He forfeited a budding relationship with Margie, without considering other options. The thought that depressed him even more, was that if he had to do it all over again, he'd do the same thing.

He came to the realization that he was like one of the junkies that Chalwell made a living from, except his fix was not drugs, but his blind pursuit of justice.

Like the junkie, he is driven in his quest for the next needle, controlled by the need to satiate a gnawing hunger, and possessed by a craving he neither wants, nor understands. And then, once the needle tracks, and the damage done, he feels an overwhelming sense of despair, knowing that his pursuit for the next fix is not far off, and the cycle will begin again.

His bleak reflections were interrupted by the ratcheting sound of the far access door being unlocked, and the door swinging open and closed. The corridor light did not turn on, allowing the newcomer to advance in the semi dark. A pair of soft soled shoes tread quietly down the hallway toward his cell. He detected no hurry in the approach nor did the person pause in front of any of the other cells. Elliot was quite sure that his own cell was the man's destination so he swung his legs off the bunk and peered down the darkened hallway to see who came.

It was impossible to distinguish enough detail in the advancing figure to know who it might be, but based on the size of the silhouette, he presumed it was a guard. The man stopped a few feet from the bars of the cell, his face still in the shadow. As Elliot suspected, it was a guard. He stood motionless for a moment and then brought his hand up to the cross bar on the cell gate and Elliot saw something in the hand. Elliot stood up and moved to the back of the cell, as far away from the shadowed stranger as space would allow. Memories of the drug theft flashed through his mind. He had stolen from a powerful bike gang, and set them up to commit murder so they would be caught for it. He knew that bike gangs as powerful as the Henchmen had a long reach, and that even getting to someone in jail was not beyond their abilities.

"Forsman," the guard said in a hushed voice that, despite the low volume, still carried weight. "I have something for you." The guard then turned away and went back the way he came. Elliot waited until he heard the access door click shut before he was able to exhale. He advanced to the front of the cell where the guard had stood and, lying on the cross bar was a folded piece of paper. He picked it up, opened it, and turned his back to the cell door to let the weak corridor light wash across the note.

*"Elliot, The DNA results came back. There was no DNA match found in the CODIS database so we are unable to identify the killer. The killer is not Jack Chalwell. The DNA from the hair is that of a female.*

*Jacques Bessette, MD.*

The words slammed into him and he held the bars with both hands as he closed his eyes and processed the note. *How is that possible?* He asked himself. His mind peeled back through the facts of the case. He examined all the scraps of information he had gathered, and in particular, those related to Mamelon. He felt his chest tighten and his hands go cold. *"What have I done?"* he asked himself.

He thought about all the murders attributed to Mamelon. He thought about the detached manner that a killer of that ilk would need to be successful. And he thought about how unlikely it would be that a hot-headed dullard like Jack Chalwell would be able to murder for so long without being caught.

"Mamelon," he snorted when he whispered the name. The nipple, the teat. It was so obvious now. Of course Mamelon was female.

He thought back to Margie's profile of the killer, she said he would be *'the type of psychopath that walks among us undetected, chooses his victims as part of a larger plan, and executes them in a manner that ensures he won't be caught.'* She called him *a Chameleon Killer.*

He thought about the personal nature of Rebecca Boyle's murder; *classic betrayal* is how Margie referred to it. Betrayal of what? Jack Chalwell hardly knew her, she said so herself. He rebuked himself silently for assuming that Rebecca had betrayed Chalwell. The girl's relationship with Theresa Chalwell was another matter. Theresa called Rebecca her prodigy. They were close, and Theresa was witness to Rebecca helping JFK bring down the drug empire. His initial instincts about Jack Chalwell had been correct. Jack Chalwell wasn't smart enough to run the drug operation, but his wife Theresa was. She resurrected a failing senior's home on her own. She had the cool demeanor, and the confident swagger, of someone who knew she was the smartest person in the room.

He considered the photograph he had pulled down off the carwash wall. The photo showed two tourists in the foreground. The tourists he now knew were Labrosse and Anderson. Standing behind them was Chalwell, the skipper of their fishing charter. The photograph would have been taken at the very beginning, when the idea of creating a drug operation was being hatched. The photo contained the 3 principals. Jack Chalwell, Joseph Labrosse, and Joel Anderson. The 3 J's in J3T Industries.

He had never given the photographer in that photo more than a second thought. He recalled the shadow of a slender arm of the photographer extended as if telling the tourists to look at the hand, not the camera. He remembered the look of adoration on Chalwell's face, not looking at the outstretched hand, but into the photographer's face. No, it was more than adoration, it was love. The "T" in J3T was not Telecom as he originally thought, but Theresa. The fourth principal in the drug operation, the brains

behind the operation, Theresa Chalwell is the one
they call Mamelon.

His eyes snapped open as the truth hit home.

"Guard," he yelled through the iron bars. "Guard,
there's been a mistake. Guard!"

No guard came. Guards come in the morning.

# Chapter 72

"Can I get you a glass of wine?" asked the flight attendant.

"Please, Pinot Grigio if you have it," she replied, as always, gracious and understanding.

"Certainly."

Theresa Gregoire watched out the window as the last of the Canadian coastline slipped away beneath.

Her thoughts drifted back to the events of the past week, as they had many times over the past few days.

*She had to admit, the PI was good, and she took comfort in the fact that she had not underestimated him. He was getting too close and, despite the intel they received from Ogrodnik, he would have eventually cracked the case and exposed the drug operation. When they intercepted the PI's phone call about the drugs hidden in the long term storage garage, she immediately sensed a trap. The decision was easy. She would sacrifice Jack and Joel and allow them to take the fall. It turned out even better than she hoped when she found out the Henchmen were waiting for them. Let the truth be told, she had tired of Jack years ago. He had given them what they needed to start up the operation, a resident presence in the Caribbean where banks were less vigilant about the source of their funds. He was expendable, like all the rest of them. She smiled to herself as she thought about how events had unfolded. Gone, was her old identity, along with the only people who could identify her. Kept, was the fortune they had amassed over the years. Her only regret was leaving the senior's residence behind.*

She pondered the manner in which fate had brought herself and Forsman together again after all those years. It was so many years since she first saw him, she'd almost forgotten about him, almost. She looked up to see the freckled face of a young child peering over the seat in front of her.

"What's your name?" the child asked.

"My name is Theresa, what's your name?"

"My name is Abby. I like gravy."

"Hello Abby," she laughed. "I like gravy too," she smiled broadly in a manner that made people want to know her better.

"What's that?"

"That's a tattoo."

"What is it?"

"Dice," she replied, "tumbling dice," as she pulled her sweater sleeve down to cover the tattoo. The mother hauled the child back to face the front and apologized for the interruption.

"So sorry. She gets a bit restless."

"No worries I'm used to being around kids, I love them to death."

Theresa turned her thoughts back to her future. She would stay in Paris for a few weeks before moving on to parts unknown. She had time, and she had money.

**The End**

*Coming in the Fall of 2018*
*The third installment of the Elliot Forsman mysteries.*

**Passage into Darkness**

An elderly philanthropist hires JFK to look into an unidentified body of a young Asian female that washed up on the shores of the St. Lawrence River. While Elliot is busy investigating, the bodies of a number of other young Asian women are found in a burned out house. The Montréal Chief of Police, Manon Petit, thinks that the bodies in the house may be connected to the dead girl Elliot is investigating. Working against her moral compass, she is forced to enlist Elliot and JFK Investigations in her efforts to contain the issue before it explodes. Elliot Forsman is asked to use whatever methods he can to stop the murders, methods that aren't necessarily sanctioned by officers of the law.

Elliot soon finds himself embroiled in the middle of a human trafficking ring that proves to be too much for him and JFK, and he realizes that in order to bring the traffickers to justice, more people will die.

Made in the USA
Middletown, DE
18 July 2021

44404993R00219